Praise for Sue Grafton and *"I" Is for Innocent*

"[An] exciting mystery . . . wry, action-packed."
—*The Washington Post Book World*

"Compelling . . . Kinsey is as candid, observant, funny, loyal, and determined as ever. . . . Grafton has moved the private eye story closer to real life than did either Hammett or Chandler . . . allowing fictional creations of every gender, nationality, sexual preference or political agenda to continue to sleuth down mean streets in the pursuit of crime."
—*Los Angeles Times Book Review*

"Kinsey Millhone is back, as outwardly tough and secretly vulnerable as ever. It's her hard shell that allows her to work so successfully as a private investigator, but it's the soft, squishy part in the middle that makes her such an appealing character. . . . Kinsey Millhone is one of us and not some superwoman. We like her better that way. As Grafton presents her, she may not be the best private eye around, but she is certainly one of the most human."
—*Chicago Tribune*

"Grafton structures 'I' like a courtroom drama. . . . It's a refreshing change, one that strengthens the already excellent series. . . . Grafton is setting a standard that's going to prove difficult for others in her crowded field to match, let alone surpass."

—*People*

"I" Is for

Innocent

By Sue Grafton

Kinsey Millhone mysteries:

"A" Is for Alibi
"B" Is for Burglar
"C" Is for Corpse
"D" Is for Deadbeat
"E" Is for Evidence
"F" Is for Fugitive
"G" Is for Gumshoe
"H" Is for Homicide
"I" Is for Innocent
"J" Is for Judgment
"K" Is for Killer
"L" Is for Lawless
"M" Is for Malice
"N" Is for Noose
"O" Is for Outlaw
"P" Is for Peril
"Q" Is for Quarry

Keziah Dane
The Lolly Madonna War

"I" Is for
Innocent

sue
grafton

A Kinsey Millhone Mystery

Fawcett Books • New York

A Fawcett Book
Published by The Random House Ballantine Publishing Group
Copyright © 1992 by Sue Grafton

www.ballantinebooks.com

Library of Congress Catalog Card Number: 97-90200

ISBN: 0-449-00064-8

This edition published by arrangement with Henry Holt and Company.

Manufactured in the United States of America

First Ballantine Books Mass Market Edition: May 1993
First Ballantine Books Trade Edition: May 1997

10 9 8 7 6 5 43 2

For my granddaughter, Erin,
with a heart full of love.

Acknowledgments

The author wishes to acknowledge the invaluable assistance of the following people: Steven Humphrey; Sam Eaton, Attorney-at-Law; B. J. Seebol, J.D.; John Mackall, Attorney-at-Law; Debra Young, Attorney-at-Law; Joe Driscoll, Joe Driscoll & Associates Investigations; Lieutenant Terry Bristol and Sergeant Carol Hesson, Santa Barbara County Sheriff's Department; Detective Lawrence Gillespie, Coroner's Bureau, Santa Barbara Sheriff's Department; Eric S. H. Ching; Debby Davison, KEYT-TV; Richard Dodge, Far West Gun & Supply; Charles Sunderlin, Premier Products Manager, Heckler & Koch; George E. Rush; Florence Michel; David Elder; and Carter Blackmar.

"I" Is for

Innocent

1

I feel compelled to report that at the moment of death, my entire life did not pass before my eyes in a flash. There was no beckoning white light at the end of a tunnel, no warm fuzzy feeling that my long-departed loved ones were waiting on The Other Side. What I experienced was a little voice piping up in an outraged tone, "Oh, come on. You're not serious. This is really *it*?" Mostly, I regretted I hadn't tidied my chest of drawers the night before as I'd planned. It's painful to realize that those who mourn your untimely demise will also carry with them the indelible image of all your tatty underpants. You might question the validity of the observation since it's obvious I didn't die when I thought I would, but let's face it, life is trivial, and my guess is that dying imparts very little wisdom to those in process.

My name is Kinsey Millhone. I'm a licensed private investigator operating out of Santa Teresa, which is ninety-five miles north of Los Angeles. For the past seven years, I'd been running my own small agency adjacent to the home offices of California Fidelity Insurance. My agreement with the company entitled me to the use of an attractive corner suite in exchange for the investigation of arson and wrongful death claims on an "as needed" basis. In early November, that arrangement was abruptly terminated when a hotshot efficiency expert was transferred to Santa Teresa from the CF branch office in Palm Springs.

I hadn't thought I'd be affected by the change in company management since I was operating as an independent contractor instead of a bona fide California Fidelity employee. However, at our first (and only) meeting, this man and I took an instant dislike to each other. In the fifteen minutes that constituted our entire relationship, I was rude, pugnacious, and uncooperative. The next thing I knew I was out on the street with my client files packed up in assorted cardboard boxes. Let's not even mention the fact that my association with CF had culminated in the wholesale bust-up of a multimillion-dollar auto insurance scam. All *that* netted me was a surreptitious handshake from Mac Voorhies, the company vice-president and avowed chickenheart, who assured me he was just as appalled by this guy as I was. While I appreciated the support, it didn't solve my problem. I needed work. I needed an office in which to do the work. Aside from the fact that my apartment was too small to serve the purpose, it felt unprofessional. Some of my clients are unsavory characters and I didn't want those bozos to know where I lived. I had troubles enough. With the recent sharp rise in property taxes, my landlord had been forced to double my rent. He'd been more upset about the hike than I had, but according to his accountant, he'd had no choice. The rent was still very reasonable and I had no complaints, but the increase couldn't have come at a more awkward time. I had used my savings to pay for my "new" car, a 1974 VW—this one pale blue, with only one minor ding in the left rear fender. My living expenses were modest, but I still didn't have a sou left at the end of the month.

I've heard that no one gets fired without secretly hoping for the liberation, but that sounds like the kind of pronouncement you make before you've been given the boot. Being fired is the pits, ranking right up there with infidelity in its brutalizing effect. The ego recoils and one's self-image is punctured like a tire by a nail. In the weeks since I'd been terminated, I'd gone through all the stages one suffers at the diagnosis of a soon-to-be-fatal disease: anger, denial, bargaining, drunkenness, foul language, head colds, rude hand gestures, anxiety, and eating disorders of sudden onset. I'd also entertained a steady stream of loathsome thoughts about the man responsible. Lately, however, I'd begun to wonder if it wasn't true, this notion of a repressed desire to be unceremoniously shit-canned. Maybe I was bored with CF. Maybe I was burned out. Maybe I was simply longing for a change of scene. Whatever the truth, I'd begun to adjust and I could feel the optimism rising through my veins like maple syrup. It was more than a matter of survival. One way or another, I knew I'd *prevail*.

For the time being, I was renting a spare room in the law offices of Kingman and Ives. Lonnie Kingman is in his early forties, five foot four, 205 pounds, a weight-lifting fanatic, perpetually pumped up on steroids, testosterone, vitamin B_{12}, and caffeine. He's got a shaggy head of dark hair, like a pony in the process of shedding a winter coat. His nose looks like it's been busted about as often as mine has. I know, from the various degrees framed and hung on his wall, that he received a B.A. from Harvard and an M.B.A. from Columbia, and then graduated *summa cum laude* from Stanford Law School.

His partner, John Ives, while equally credentialed, prefers the quiet, nonglamorous aspects of the practice. His forte is appellate civil work, where he enjoys a reputation as an attorney of uncommon imagination, solid research, and exceptional writing skills. Since Lonnie and John established the firm some six years ago, the support staff has expanded to include a receptionist, two secretaries, and a paralegal who doubles as a runner. Martin Cheltenham, the third attorney in the firm, while not a formal partner, is Lonnie's best friend, leasing office space from him in the same way I do.

In Santa Teresa, all the flashy cases seem to go to Lonnie Kingman. He's best known for his criminal defense work, but his passion is complex trials in any case involving accidental injury or wrongful death, which is how our paths crossed in the first place. I'd done some work for Lonnie in the past and, aside from the fact that I'm occasionally in need of his services myself, I figured he'd be good for the referrals. From his point of view, it didn't hurt to have an investigator on the premises. As with California Fidelity, I was not an employee. I worked as an independent contractor, providing professional services and billing accordingly. To celebrate the new arrangement, I went out and bought myself a handsome tweed blazer to wear with my usual jeans and turtleneck. I thought I looked pretty snappy in the outfit.

It was a Monday early in December when I first got involved in the Isabelle Barney murder case. I'd driven down to Cottonwood twice that day, two ten-mile round-trips, trying to serve a subpoena on a witness in a battery case. The first time, he wasn't home. The second time, I caught him just as he pulled into his driveway from work. I handed him the papers, disregarding his annoyance, and took off again with my car radio thundering to mask his parting remarks, which were rude. He used a couple of words I hadn't heard in years. On my way into town, I did a detour past the office.

The Kingman building is a three-story stucco structure, with parking tucked in at ground level and two floors of offices above. Across the facade, there are six pairs of floor-to-ceiling French doors that open inward for ventilation, each flanked by tall wooden shutters painted the soft verdigris of a greening copper roof. A shallow wrought-iron bracket is secured across the lower half of each set of doors. The effect is largely decorative, but in a pinch might prevent a suicidal dog or a client's sulky child from flinging itself out the window in a fit of pique. The building straddles the property and has a driveway that passes through an arch on the right, opening up into a tiny parking lot in the rear. The one drawback is the parsimonious assignment of parking spaces. There are six permanent tenants and twelve parking spots. Since Lonnie owns the building, his law firm had been allotted four: one for John, one for Martin, one for Lonnie, and one for Lonnie's secretary, Ida Ruth. The remaining eight places were parceled out according to the individual leases. The rest of us had a choice of street parking or one of the public lots three blocks away. The local rates are absurdly cheap, given big-city standards, but on my limited budget the tab mounts up. Street parking downtown isn't metered, but it's restricted to ninety minutes and the meter maids are quick to ticket you if you cheat by so much as a minute. As a consequence, I spent a lot of time either moving my car or cruising the area trying to ferret out a spot that was both close by and free. Happily, this exasperating situation only extends until 6:00 P.M.

It was then 6:15 and the third-floor windows along the front were dark, suggesting that everyone had already gone home for the day. When I drove through the arch, I saw Lonnie's car was still in its slot. Ida Ruth's Toyota was gone so I eased my car into her space, next to his Mercedes. An unfamiliar pale blue Jaguar sedan was parked in John's slot. I hung my head out the car window and craned my neck. Lonnie's office lights were on, two oblongs of pale yellow against the slanting shadows from the roof. He was probably with a client.

The days were getting steadily shorter, and a gloom settled over the town at that hour. Something in the air generated a longing for a wood fire, companionship, and the kind of cocktail that looks elegant in the print ads and tastes like liniment. I told myself I had work to do, but in truth it was just a way to postpone going home.

I locked my car and headed for the stairwell, which was tucked into a hollow core that extended up the center of the building like a chimney flue. The stairs were inky, and I had to use my little keychain flashlight to break up the darkness. The third-floor corridor was in shadow, but I could see lights in the reception area through the frosted glass in the front door. By day, the whole third-floor complex was cheerful and well lighted, with white walls, burnt orange carpeting, a forest of greenhouse plants, Scandinavian furniture, and original artwork in bright crayon tones. The office I was renting had served as a combination conference room and kitchen, and was outfitted now with my desk and swivel chair, file cabinets, a small flop-out couch that could double as a bed in an emergency, a telephone, and my answering machine. I was still listed in the yellow pages under Investigators, and people calling the old number were advised of the new. In the weeks since the move, while some business had trickled in, I'd been forced to resort to process serving to make ends meet. At twenty bucks a pop, I was never going to get rich, but on a good day I could sometimes pick up an extra hundred bucks. Not bad, if I could sandwich it in with other investigative work.

I let myself in quietly, not wanting to disturb Lonnie if he was in the middle of a conference. His office door was open and I glanced in automatically as I went past. He was chatting with a client, but when he caught sight of me, he raised his hand and beckoned. "Kinsey, could you spare a minute? There's someone here I want you to meet."

I backtracked to his doorway. Lonnie's client was seated in the black leather wing chair, with his back to me. As Lonnie stood up, his client stood, too, turning to look at me as we were introduced. His aura was dark, if you buy that kind of talk.

"Kenneth Voigt," Lonnie said. "This is Kinsey Millhone, the private investigator I was telling you about."

We shook hands, going through the usual litany of greetings while we checked each other out. He was in his early fifties with dark hair and dark brown eyes, his brows separated by deep indentations that had been set there by a scowl. His face was blunt, his wide forehead softened by a tongue of thinning hair that was brushed to one side. He smiled politely at me, but his face didn't brighten much. A pale sheen of perspiration seemed to glimmer on his forehead. While he was on his feet, he shed his sport coat and tossed it on the couch. The shirt he wore under it was dark gray, a short-sleeved Polo with a three-button placket open at the neck. Dark hair curled from his shirt collar and a mat of dark hair covered his arms. He was narrow through the shoulders and the muscles in his arms were stringy and undeveloped. He should have worked out at a gym, for his stress levels, if nothing else. He took out a handkerchief, dabbing at his forehead and his upper lip.

"I want her to hear this," Lonnie was saying to Voigt. "She can go through the files tonight and start first thing in the morning."

"Fine with me," Voigt said.

The two sat down again. I folded myself into one corner of the couch and pulled my legs up under me, considerably cheered by the prospects of a paycheck. One advantage in the work for Lonnie is he screens out all the deadbeats.

Lonnie offered me a word of explanation before the conversation continued. "The P.I. we were using just dropped dead of a heart attack. Morley Shine, you know him?"

"Of course," I said, startled. "*Morley* died? When was this?"

"Last night about eight. I was gone over the weekend and

didn't get back till after midnight so I didn't hear about it myself until this morning when Dorothy called me."

Morley Shine had been around ever since I could remember, not a close friend, but certainly a man I could count on if I found myself in a pinch. He and the fellow who'd trained me as a P.I. had been partners for years. At some point, they'd had a falling-out and each had gone into business for himself. Morley was in his late sixties, tall and slump-shouldered, probably eighty pounds overweight, with a round, dimpled face, wheezing laugh, and fingers yellowed from all the cigarettes he smoked. He had access to snitches and informants in every correctional facility in the state, plus contacts in all the relevant local information pools. I'd have to quiz Lonnie later about the circumstances of Morley's death. For the time being, I concentrated on Kenneth Voigt, who had backed up his narrative so he could get a running start.

He stared down at the floor, hands clasped loosely in his lap. "My ex-wife was murdered six years ago. Isabelle Barney. You remember the case?"

The name meant nothing. "I don't think so," I said.

"Someone unscrewed the fisheye in the middle of the front door. He knocked, and when she flipped on the porch light and peered out, he fired a thirty-eight through the spyhole. She died instantly."

My memory kicked in with a jolt. "That was her? I do remember that much. I can't believe it's been six years." I nearly added my only other recollection, that the guy alleged to have killed her was her estranged husband. Apparently not Kenneth Voigt, but who?

I made eye contact with Lonnie, who interjected a comment, picking up on my question as if with ESP. "The guy's name is David Barney. He was acquitted, in case you're curious."

Voigt changed positions in his chair as if the very name made him itch. "The bastard."

Lonnie said, "Go on with your story, Ken. I didn't mean

to interrupt. You might as well give her the background as long as she's here."

It seemed to take a few seconds for him to remember what he'd been saying. "We were married for four years . . . a second marriage for both. We have a ten-year-old daughter named Shelby who's off at boarding school. She was four when Iz was killed. Anyway, Isabelle and I had been having problems . . . nothing unusual as far as I knew. She got involved with Barney. She married him a month after our divorce became final. All he wanted was her money. Everybody knew that except poor, dumb Iz. And I don't mean any insult to her when I say that. I loved the woman, truly, but she was gullible as they come. She was bright and she was talented, but she had no sense of self-worth, which made her a sitting duck for anybody with a kind word. You probably know women like that. Emotionally dependent, no self-esteem to speak of. She was an artist, and while I had tremendous admiration for her ability, it was hard to watch her throw her life away. . . ."

I found myself tuning out his analysis of her character. His generalizations about women were obnoxious and he'd evidently told the same story so often his rendering of events was flat and passionless. The drama was not about her anymore, it was the tale of his reaction. My eye wandered over to the pile of fat manila folders on Lonnie's desk. I could see VOIGT/BARNEY written across the spine. Two cardboard boxes stacked against the wall contained additional files, judging by the labels affixed to one side. Everything Voigt was saying was going to be right there, a compilation of facts without all the editorials attached. It seemed weird to me—what he said might be true, but it wasn't necessarily believable. Some folks are like that. The simplest recollection just sounds false in the rendering. He went on for a bit, speaking in closely knit paragraphs that didn't yield the opportunity for interruption. I wondered how often Lonnie had served as his audience. I noticed he'd disconnected, too. While Kenneth

Voigt's mouth was moving, Lonnie picked up a pencil and began to turn it end over end, tapping on his legal pad first with the point and then with the eraser. I returned my attention to Ken Voigt.

"How'd the guy get off?" I asked as soon as he paused for breath.

Lonnie jumped in, apparently impatient to get down to the meat of the matter. "Dink Jordan prosecuted. What a yawn that was. Jesus. I mean, the man is competent but he's got no style. He thought he could win on the merits of the case." Lonnie snorted at the absurdity of the assumption. "So now we're suing the shit out of David Barney for wrongful death. I hate the guy. Just hate him. The minute he pled not guilty, I told Ken we should jump on the son of a bitch with hobnail boots. I couldn't talk him into it. We filed and got him served, but then Ken insisted we sit on it."

Voigt frowned uncomfortably. "You were right, Lon. I see it now, but you know how it is. My wife, Francesca, was opposed to our reopening the investigation. It's painful for everyone . . . me more than most. I simply couldn't handle it."

Lonnie crossed his eyes. He didn't have a lot of sympathy for what people could or couldn't handle. *His* job was to handle it. Voigt's job was to turn him loose. "Hey, okay. Skip that. It's water under the bridge. It took a year to get him tried and acquitted on the criminal charges. In the meantime, Ken here watches David Barney work his way through Isabelle's money. And believe me, there's plenty of it, most of which would have gone to his daughter, Shelby, if Barney'd been convicted. Finally, the family reaches a point where they can't stand it anymore, so Ken comes back to me and we get into gear. Meanwhile, Barney's attorney, guy named Foss, files a discretionary motion to dismiss for lack of prosecution. I whip into court and tap-dance my tiny heart out. The motion was denied, but the judge made it clear he wasn't happy with me.

10

"Now, of course, David Barney and this jerk who represents him are using every delay they can think of, and then some. They dicker around and dicker around. We're going through all the discovery, right? The guy's been acquitted in criminal court so what difference does it make what he says at this point? But he's tight-lipped. He's tense. That's because he's guilty as hell. Oh, and here. Check this. Ken here has a guy shows up . . . turns out he shared a cell with David Barney. This guy's been following the case. He sits in on the trial, just to see what's going on, and he's telling us Barney as good as admitted he killed her as he's walkin' out the courtroom *door*. The informant's been hard to nail down, which is why I want to get the sucker served first thing."

"What good's it going to do?" I asked. "David Barney can't be tried again on the murder one."

"Exactly. Which is why we kicked it over to the civil side. We've got a much better shot at him there, which he damn well knows. The guy's really dragging his feet, doing everything he can to hinder and obstruct. We file a motion. He's got thirty days to answer so his attorney—what a geek—waits until day twenty-nine and then files a demurrer. Anything to string it out. He's throwing up roadblocks left and right.

"We bring Barney in for a deposition and he pleads the Fifth. So we take him into court and force him to testify. The judge *orders* the guy to answer because he has no Fifth Amendment rights. There's no danger of prosecution because jeopardy has attached. Back we go on the depo. So now he takes the Fifth again. We take him in on the contempt, but in the meantime we're running up against the court statute—"

"Lonnie?" I said.

"We're humming and humming and it's not working for us. We're coming up to the five-year statute and we really need to make the case happen. We're on the master calendar and we've been given priority, and now *Morley* drops dead—"

"Looonnnnie," I sang. I raised my hand to get his attention.

He stopped.

"Just tell me what you need and I'll go out and get it for you."

Lonnie laughed and tossed his pencil at me. "This is why I like her. No bullshit," he said to Voigt. He reached over and pushed the stack of files in my direction. "This is everything we got, though it's a bit disorganized. There's an inventory on top—just make sure it's all in there somewhere before you start work. Once you're familiar with the basics, we can figure out where the gaps are. In the meantime, I want you two to get acquainted. You're going to be seeing a lot of each other in the next month."

Voigt and I smiled politely at Lonnie without looking at one another. He didn't seem to feel any more excited about the prospects than I did.

I ended up staying at the office until midnight. The accumulated files on Isabelle Barney spilled over the tops of the two cardboard cartons, each of which weighed over forty pounds. I nearly developed a hernia hauling the boxes from Lonnie's office to mine. There was no way I could get through all the data at one sitting so I figured I might as well take my time. Lonnie wasn't kidding when he said the files were disorganized. According to the inventory, the first box should have contained copies of police reports, transcripts from the murder trial, the complaint Lonnie'd filed in the civil action in the Santa Teresa County Superior Court, all the demurrers, answers, and cross-complaints. I

2

couldn't even be sure that the trial transcripts were complete. What files I could spot were lumped together in one of those annoying hodgepodges that make finding anything a chore.

The second box supposedly contained copies of all of Morley Shine's reports, affidavits, transcripts from the numerous depositions taken, and pages of supporting documentation. Fat chance. I could see the list of witnesses that Morley had talked to—he'd been billing Lonnie on a regular monthly basis since June 1—but not all of the corresponding written reports were in evidence. It looked like he'd served about half the subpoenas for the upcoming trial, but most of those seemed to be repeat witnesses from the criminal proceedings. Eight signed civil subpoenas, with instructions for service attached, were clipped together in a folder. I didn't see that he'd served any new witnesses . . . unless the yellow server's copies were filed somewhere else. From a scribbled note, I gathered that the informant's name was Curtis McIntyre, whose telephone number was a disconnect and whose last known address was no good. I made a note to myself to track him down first as per Lonnie's request.

I leafed through page after page of interrogatories and responses, making an occasional note to myself. As with a jigsaw puzzle, what I hoped to do was to familiarize myself with the picture on the box lid and then proceed to put the pieces together one section at a time. I knew I'd be repeating some of Morley Shine's investigation, but his approach tended to be a bit ham-fisted and I thought I'd do better if I started from scratch, at least in the sensitive areas. I wasn't sure what to do about the gaps in the files. I hadn't finished going through the boxes yet and I could tell I was going to have to empty everything out and repack the data so they would match the index. Certain avenues Morley'd pursued appeared to be dead ends and could probably be eliminated unless something new cropped up. He'd probably been keeping all the current files in his office or at home, which I did myself if I was still in the process of transcribing notes.

The bare bones of the story were much as Kenneth Voigt had indicated. Isabelle Barney died sometime between 1:00 and 2:00 A.M. on December 26 when a .38-caliber weapon was fired at point-blank range through the peephole in her front door. The ballistics expert called it "a near-contact shooting," with the hole in the door acting almost like an extension of the barrel and Isabelle's eye almost touching the door. The wood around the hole was blown out at right angles to the hole and toward Isabelle, with some fragments probably blown back toward the killer as well. In a dry parenthetical note, the ballistics expert suggested that the blast might well have forced "material" back into the barrel itself, perhaps jamming the gun, and thus making a second shot problematic, if not impossible. I skipped the rest of that paragraph.

The muzzle flash had singed the wood inside the hole, charring it slightly. The report noted powder residue on the outside of the door around the hole, inside the hole, and also around the hole on the inside of the door. Much of the area was splintered by the gas pressure. The bird shot and the remnants of blue plastic cap removed from the wound indicated that the bullet was a Glaser Safety Slug, a light, high-velocity round consisting of bird shot suspended in a viscous medium encased in a copper jacket with a plastic nose cap. When the slug hits a medium like flesh with a high water content, the plastic cap separates, the copper jacket peels back, and the bird shot spreads out rapidly, transferring all of the energy in the slug to the flesh. Because each piece is small and of low mass, it dumps its energy quickly and stays in the body, hence the name Safety Slug. Bystanders are not endangered by an overpenetrating bullet, and since the Safety Slug also disintegrates against hard surfaces (such as skulls . . .), ricochets are minimized as well. No getting around it, I thought, this killer was just too considerate.

According to the pathologist, the bullet, along with fragments of metal and wood, entered the victim's right eye. The autopsy report spelled out in highly technical detail the destruction to soft tissue left in its wake. Even with my sketchy knowledge of anatomy, it was clear death was instantaneous and therefore painless. The machinery of life had shut down long before the nervous system had a chance to register the agony such a wound would inflict.

It's hard to have faith in your fellow man when you're forced to look at some of his handiwork. I disconnected my emotional machinery while I studied the autopsy X rays and photographs. I work best when I'm armed with an unflinching view of reality, but the detachment is not without its dangers. Unplug yourself often and you risk losing touch with your feelings altogether. There were ten color photographs, each with a nightmarish quality of violated flesh. This is what death is, I reminded myself. This is what homicide really looks like in the raw. I've met killers—soft-spoken, pleasant, and courteous—whose psychological denial is so profound that their perpetration of a killing seems inconceivable. The dead are mute, but the living still have voice with which to protest their innocence. Often their objections are noisy and pious, impossible to refute since the one person who could condemn them has been silenced forever. The final testimony from Isabelle Barney was framed in the language of her fatal injury, a devastating portrait of waste and loss. I tucked the pictures back in the envelope and moved on to a copy of the case notes Dink Jordan had sent over to Lonnie.

Dink's real name was Dinsmore. He referred to himself as Dennis, but nobody else did. He was in his fifties, bland and gray, a man without energy, humor, or eloquence. As a public prosecutor he was competent, but he had no sense of theater. His delivery was so slow and so methodical it was like reading the entire Bible through a microscope. I'd once watched him lay out his closing arguments in a spectacular felony murder trial with two jurors nodding off and two more so bored they were nearly comatose.

David Barney's attorney was a man named Herb Foss,

whom I didn't know at all. Lonnie claimed he was a jerk, but you had to give him credit for getting David Barney off.

While there had been no witnesses to the shooting and the murder weapon was never found, evidence showed that Barney had purchased a .38-caliber revolver some eight months before the murder. He claimed the gun had been removed from his bed table at some point during the Labor Day weekend, when the couple had given a large dinner party in honor of some friends from Los Angeles, Don and Julie Seeger. When he was questioned about his reasons for not filing a police report, he maintained that he'd discussed it with Isabelle, who'd been reluctant to confront her guests with the alleged theft.

During the trial, Isabelle's sister testified that the couple had been talking for months about a separation. David Barney contended that the breach between them wasn't serious. However, the gun theft incident precipitated a quarrel, which culminated in Isabelle's ordering him to move out. There seemed to be much disagreement about the prognosis for the marriage. David Barney claimed the relationship was stable but stormy, that he and Isabelle had been in the process of negotiating their differences. Observers seemed to feel that the marriage was dead, but *that* might have been wishful thinking on their part.

Whatever the truth, the situation deteriorated rapidly. David Barney moved out on September 15 and then proceeded to do everything in his power to regain Isabelle's affections. He made frequent phone calls. He sent flowers. He sent gifts. When his attentions became annoying, instead of giving her the breathing space she requested, he redoubled his efforts. He left a single red rose on the hood of her car every morning. He left jewelry on her doorstep, sent her sentimental cards in the mail. The more she rejected him, the more obsessed he became. During October and November, he called her day and night, hanging up if she answered. When she had her number changed, he managed to acquire the new unlisted number and continued phoning her at all hours. She got an answering machine. He continued to call, leaving the line open until the message tape ran out. She told friends she felt she was under siege.

In the meantime, he leased a house in the same stylish section of Horton Ravine. If she left the house, he followed her. If she stayed home, he parked across the road and watched the house through binoculars, keeping track of visitors, repairmen, and the household help. Isabelle called the police. She filed complaints. Finally, her attorney had a restraining order issued, prohibiting phone calls, written communication, and his approach anywhere within two hundred yards of her person, her property, or her automobile. His determination seemed to subside, but by then the harassment had taken its toll. Isabelle was terrified.

By the time Christmas came, she was a nervous wreck, eating little, sleeping poorly, subject to anxiety, panic, and tremors. She was pale. She was haggard. She was drinking too much. She was agitated by company and frightened to be alone. She sent the four-year-old Shelby to live with her father. Ken Voigt had remarried, though some witnesses suggested that he'd never quite recovered from his divorce from her. Isabelle took tranquilizers to get through the day. At night, she popped down sleeping pills. Finally, the Seegers prevailed on her to pack her bags and accompany them on a trip to San Francisco. They were en route to Santa Teresa to pick her up when the electronic fuel injection on the car went out. They called and left a message to let her know they'd be late.

From midnight until approximately 12:45, Isabelle, feeling anxious and excited about the trip, had a lengthy telephone conversation with a former college roommate who lived in Seattle. Some time after that, she heard a rap at the door and went downstairs, assuming the Seegers had arrived. She was fully dressed, smoking a cigarette, her suitcases already lined up in the foyer. She flipped on the porch light and put her eye to the spyhole before opening the door. Instead of seeing visitors, she was staring down the bore of the .38 that killed her. The Seegers showed up at 2:20 and realized something was wrong. They alerted Isabelle's sister, who was living in a cottage on the property. She used her key to let them in through the rear. The alarm system was still armed at the perimeter. As soon as they spotted her, the Seegers called the police. By the time the medical examiner arrived at the scene, Isabelle's body temperature had dropped to 98.1. Using the Moritz formula and adjusting for the temperature in the foyer, her body weight, clothing, and the temperature and conductivity of the marble floor on which she lay, the medical examiner placed the time of death roughly between 1:00 A.M. and 2:00 A.M.

At noon the next day, David Barney was arrested and charged with first-degree murder, to which he entered a plea of not guilty. Even that early in the game, it was clear that the evidence against him was largely circumstantial. However, in the state of California, the two elements of a homicide—the death of the victim and the existence of "criminal agency"— may be proved circumstantially or inferentially. A finding of murder in the first degree can be sustained where no body is produced, where no direct evidence of death is produced, and where there is no confession. David Barney had signed a prenuptial agreement that limited his financial settlement if they divorced. At the same time, he was listed as the prime beneficiary on her life insurance policies, and as her widower he stood to inherit the community property portion of her business, which was estimated at two point six million bucks. David Barney had no real alibi for the time of her death. Dink Jordan felt he had more than enough evidence to convict.

As it happened, the trial lasted three weeks, and after six hours of closing arguments and two days of deliberations, the jury voted for acquittal. David Barney walked out of the courtroom not only a free man, but very rich. Interviewed later, some jurors admitted to a strong suspicion that he'd killed her, but they hadn't been persuaded beyond a reasonable doubt. What Lonnie Kingman was attempting, by filing the wrongful death suit, was to retry the case in civil court, where the burden of proof is based on a preponderance of evidence instead of the "reasonable doubt" formula of a criminal prosecution. As I understood matters, it would still be necessary for the plaintiff, Kenneth Voigt, to establish that David Barney killed Isabelle, and, further, that the killing was felonious and intentional. But the onus would be eased by the shift to proof by preponderance. What was at stake here was not Barney's freedom, but any profits he'd garnered from the crime itself. If he'd killed her for money, at least he'd be stripped of his gains.

I realized I was yawning for the third time in a row. My hands were filthy and I'd reached the point in my reading where my mind was wandering. Morley Shine's methodology had really been slipshod and I found myself irritated with the poor man in death. There's nothing quite as irksome as someone else's mess. I left the files where they were and locked my office door. I let myself out into the third-floor corridor and locked the door behind me.

Mine was the only car left in the parking lot. I pulled out of the driveway and turned right, heading toward town. When I reached State Street, I hung a left and headed home, cruising through the empty, well-lighted downtown area of Santa Teresa. Most of the buildings are only two stories high, the Spanish-style architecture of the ground-hugging variety due to frequent earthquakes. In the summer of 1968, for instance, there was a swarm of sixty-six tremors, ranging in severity from 1.5 to 5.2 on the Richter scale, the latter being strong enough to slop half the water out of a swimming pool.

I felt a surge of regret when I passed my old building at 903 State. By now, someone new had probably moved into the space. I ought to talk to Vera, the CF claims manager, to find out what had happened in the weeks since I'd been gone. I hadn't seen her since she and Neil got married on Halloween night. As a side effect of being fired, I was losing touch with a lot of people I knew—Darcy Pascoe, Mary Bellflower. The notion of Christmas in the new office setting seemed strange somehow.

I narrowly missed the light at the intersection of Anaconda and 101. I came to a stop and turned my engine off, waiting the four minutes for the light to turn green again. The highway was deserted, empty lanes of asphalt stretching out in both directions. The light finally changed and I zoomed across, turning right at Cabana, the boulevard paralleling the beach. I took another right onto Bay and a left onto my street, which was narrow and treelined, mostly single-family dwellings with an occasional condo. I found a parking spot two doors away from my apartment. I locked my car and scanned the darkened neighborhood by habit. I like to be out by myself at this hour, though I try to be vigilant and exercise appropriate caution. I let myself into the side yard, lifting the gate on its hinge to avoid the squeak.

My apartment was once a single-car garage attached to the main house by a breezeway, which had been converted to a sunroom. Both my apartment and the sunroom had been reconstructed after a bomb blast and I now had an additional loft sleeping space with a second bath built in. My outside light was on, compliments of my landlord, Henry Pitts, who never goes to bed without peering out his window to see if I'm safely home.

I locked the door behind me and went through my usual nighttime routine, securing all the doors and windows. I turned on my little black-and-white TV for company while I tidied my apartment. Since I'm usually gone during the day, I find myself doing personal chores at night. I've been known to vacuum at midnight and grocery shop at 2:00 A.M. Since I live alone, it isn't hard to keep the place picked up, but every three or four months I do a systematic cleaning, tackling one small section at a time on a rotating basis. That night, even taking time to scrub the kitchen, I was in bed by 1:00.

Tuesday, I woke at 6:00. I pulled on my sweats and tied the laces of my Nikes in a double spit knot. I brushed my teeth, splashed some water on my face, and ran wet fingers through my sleep-flattened hair. My run was perfunctory, more form than content, but at the end of it I was at least in touch with some energy. I used the time to tune into the day, a moving meditation meant to focus my mind as well as coordinate my limbs. I was dimly aware that I hadn't been taking very good care of myself of late . . . a combination of stress, irregular sleep, and too much junk food. Time to clean up my act.

I showered and dressed, ate a bowl of cereal with skim milk, and headed back to the office.

As I passed Ida Ruth's desk, I paused for a quick chat about her weekend, leisure she usually fills with backpacking, horse trails, and hair-raising rock climbs. She's thirty-five and unmarried, a robust vegetarian, with windswept blond hair and brows bleached by the sun. Her cheekbones are wide, her ruddy complexion unsoftened by makeup. While she's always dressed well, she looks like she'd prefer wearing flannel shirts, chinos, and hiking boots. "If you want to talk to Lonnie, you better scoot on in. He's got a court appearance coming up in ten minutes."

"Thanks. I'll do that."

I found him at his desk. He'd shed his coat and had his shirtsleeves rolled up. His tie was askew and his shaggy hair stood out around his head like wheat in need of threshing. Through the windows behind him, I could see clear blue skies with a scrim of mauve-and-gray mountains in the background. It was a gorgeous day. A thick tumble of vivid magenta bougainvillea camouflaged a white brick wall two buildings away.

"How's it going?" he asked.

"All right, I guess. I haven't finished going through the boxes yet, but it seems pretty disorganized."

"Yeah, well, filing was never Morley's strong suit."

"Girls just naturally do that so much better," I said dryly.

Lonnie smiled as he jotted a note to himself, presumably concerning the case he was working on. "We ought to talk fees. What's your hourly rate?"

"What was Morley charging?"

"The usual fifty," he said idly.

He had opened a drawer and was sorting through his files so he couldn't see my face. Morley was getting fifty? I couldn't believe it. Either men are outrageous or women are fools. Guess which, I thought. My standard fee has always been thirty bucks an hour plus mileage. I only missed half a beat. "Bump it up five bucks and I won't charge you mileage."

"Sure," he said.

"What about instructions?"

"That's up to you. Carte blanche."

"Are you serious?"

"Of course. You can do anything you want. As long as you keep your nose clean," he added in haste. "Barney's attorney would love nothing better than to catch us with our pants down, so no dirty tricks."

"That's no fun."

"But it allows you to testify without being thrown out of court and that's critical."

He glanced at his watch. "I gotta run." He grabbed his suit coat from a hanger and shrugged back into it. He straightened his tie and snapped his briefcase shut and was halfway out the door.

"Lonnie, wait a minute. Where do you want me to start?"

He smiled. "Find me a witness who can put the guy at the murder scene."

"Oh, right," I said to the empty room.

I sat down and read another five pounds of garbled information. Maybe I could sweet-talk Ida Ruth into helping me reconstruct the files. The first box seemed immaculate by comparison to the second. My first chore was going to be to stop by Morley Shine's house to see what files he had there. Before I left the office, I made a few preliminary calls. I had a pretty good sense of who I wanted to talk to and it was then a matter of setting up some appointments. I got through to Isabelle's sister, Simone, who agreed to talk to me around noon at her place. I also had a quick chat with a woman named Yolanda Weidmann, who was married to Isabelle's former boss. He was tied up in his home office and would be until three, so she suggested I stop by later in the afternoon. The third call I placed was to Isabelle's longtime best friend. Rhe Parsons wasn't in, but I left a message on her machine, giving her my name and telephone number, indicating that I'd try again.

3

Since the police station was only a block away, I decided to start with Lieutenant Dolan in Homicide. He was out with the flu, but Sergeant Cordero was there. I spotted Lieutenant Becker in the corner deep in conversation with someone I took to be a suspect, a white guy in his twenties, looking sullen and uncooperative. I knew Becker better than Cordero, but if I waited until he was free, he'd end up quizzing me about my relationship with Jonah Robb in Missing Persons. I hadn't seen Jonah in six or eight months and I didn't want to generate any contact at this point.

Sheri Cordero was an oddity in the department. Being a female and Hispanic, she managed to fill two minority slots simultaneously. She was twenty-nine, short, buxom, smart, tough, somewhat abrasive in ways that I could never quite define. She never said anything offensive, but the guys in the department were not entirely at ease with her. I understood what she was up against. The Santa Teresa Police Department is better than most, but it's never easy being a woman and a cop. If Sheri erred on the side of being humorless, it was no surprise. She was in the middle of a phone conversation, which she converted to Spanish the minute I arrived. I sat down in the Leatherette-and-metal chair beside her desk. She held up a finger, indicating she'd be with me momentarily. She had a little artificial Christmas tree on her desk. It was decorated with candy canes and I helped myself to one. The nice thing about being in the presence of someone on the telephone is that you can study the person at your leisure without being thought rude. I unwrapped the candy cane and tossed the cellophane in the trash. She was clearly engaged in the subject at hand, gesturing vigorously to make her point. She had a good face, rather plain, and she wore little makeup. One of her two front teeth had a corner clipped off and it added a whimsical note to an otherwise stern expression. While I watched, she began to doodle on a legal pad—a cowboy stabbed in the chest with a cartoon knife.

She finished her conversation and turned her attention to me without any visible transition. "Yes?"

"I was looking for Lieutenant Dolan, but Emerald tells me he's out sick."

"He's got that bug that's been going around. Have you had that thing? I was out for a week. It's the pits."

"So far I've been spared," I said. "How long's he been out?"

"Just two days. He'll come dragging back in looking like death. Is there something I can help you with?"

"Probably. I've been hired by Lonnie Kingman in a wrongful death suit. The defendant is David Barney. I was curious about the scuttlebutt. Were you here back then?"

"I was still a dispatcher, but I've heard 'em talk. Man, they were pissed when he walked. He looked good for the shooting, but the jury wasn't buying. Talk about frustrated. Lieutenant Dolan was mad enough to bite through nails."

"From what I hear, David Barney's former cellmate claims he as good as confessed once the verdict came down."

"You're talking about Curtis McIntyre. Guy's in the county jail, and if you want him, you better make it quick. He gets out this week after doing ninety days on a battery," she said. "Did you hear about Morley Shine?"

"Lonnie mentioned that last night, but I didn't hear the details. How'd it happen?"

"What I heard he just keeled over dead. He'd been in bed with the same damn flu, but I guess he was feeling better. He was having dinner Sunday night? You know Morley. He hated to miss a meal. Got up from the table and dropped in his tracks."

"He had heart trouble?"

"For years, but he never took it serious. I mean, he was under doctor's care, but it never seemed to faze him. He was always joking about his ticker."

"That's too bad," I said. "I'm really sorry to see him go."

"Me, too. I can't believe how terrible I feel. Roll call somebody told me Morley Shine died? I busted out crying. I swear to God, I surprised myself. It's not like we were close. We used to talk over at the courthouse if I was waiting to testify on a case. He was always hanging around there, chain-smoking Camels, munching Fritos or something from the vending machine. It bums me out all those old guys are dropping dead. How come they didn't take better care of themselves?"

Her phone rang and she was quickly caught up in another matter. I gave her a quick wave and moved away from her desk. In essence, she'd told me what I'd wanted to know. The cops were convinced David Barney was guilty. That didn't make it true, but it was another precinct heard from.

I stopped off in Records and asked Emerald if I could borrow the phone. I called Ida Ruth and had a quick chat with her, asking her to set up an interview for me with Curtis McIntyre at the jail later in the morning. Visiting hours are ordinarily limited to Saturday afternoons, 1:00 to 3:00, but since I was working as Lonnie Kingman's representative, I could talk to him at my convenience. Oh, the joys of the legitimate endeavor. I'd spent so many years skulking through the bushes, I could hardly get used to it.

With that taken care of, I asked her for Morley Shine's home address. Morley had lived in Colgate, the township bordering Santa Teresa on the north. Colgate consists largely of "lite" industry and tract housing with assorted businesses lined up along the main street. Where the area was once farmland and citrus groves, the uninhabited countryside has now given way to service stations, bowling alleys, funeral homes, drive-in theaters, motels, fast-food restaurants, carpet outlets, and supermarkets, with no visible attention paid to aesthetics or architectural unity.

Morley and his wife, Dorothy, owned a modest three-bedroom home off South Peterson in one of the older housing developments between the highway and the mountains. My guess was the house had gone up in the fifties before the builders really got clever about differentiating exteriors. Here, the Swiss-chalet-style trim was painted either dirt brown or blue, the two-car garages designed so they stuck out in front, overpowering the entrances. Wooden shutters matched the wooden flower boxes planted with drooping pansies, which on closer inspection turned out to be entirely fake. The whole neighborhood seemed dispirited, from the patchy lawns to the cracked concrete driveways where every second house had a car up on blocks. Somehow the Christmas decorations only made things worse. Most of the houses were trimmed now in multicolored lights. One of Morley's neighbors seemed to be in competition with the house across the street. Both had covered every available stretch of yard with seasonal items, ranging from plastic Santas to plastic wise men.

This was now Tuesday morning. Morley had died on Sunday night, and while I was uneasy about intruding, it seemed important to retrieve what I could of the paperwork before some well-meaning relative went through and trashed everything he had. I knocked at the front door and waited. Morley had never cared much for detail and I noticed his house had the same slapdash quality. The blue paint on the porch rail, uneven to begin with, had begun to peel with age. I had the depressing sensation of having been here before. I could picture the shoddy interior: cracked tile on the kitchen counters, buckling vinyl tile on the floors, wall-to-wall carpeting trampled into traffic patterns that could never be cleaned of soil. The aluminum window frames would be warped, the bathroom fixtures corroded. A battered green four-door Mercury had been pulled off onto the side grass. I pegged it as Morley's, though I wasn't sure why. It was just the sort of clunker that he'd have found appealing. He had probably purchased it new in the year oughty-ought and would have driven it resolutely until the engine died. A new red Ford compact was parked in the driveway, the frame on the license plate advertising a local car rental company; probably someone from out of town. . . .

"Yes?" The woman was small, in her midsixties, looking energetic and competent. She wore a pink floral-print blouse with long sleeves, a tweed skirt, hose, and penny loafers. Her gray hair was honest and her makeup was light. She was in the process of drying her hands on a dish towel, her expression inquiring.

"Hi. My name is Kinsey Millhone. Are you Mrs. Shine?"

"I'm Dorothy's sister, Louise Mendelberg. Mr. Shine just passed away."

"That's what I heard and I'm sorry to disturb you. He was in the middle of some work for an attorney named Lonnie Kingman. I've been asked to take over his caseload. Did I come at a bad time?"

"There's never going to be a good time when someone's

just died," she replied tartly. This was a woman who didn't take death seriously. In its aftermath, she'd come along to do the dishes and tidy up the living room, but she probably wouldn't devote a lot of time to the hymn selection for the funeral service.

"I don't want to be more of a bother than I have to. I was sorry to hear about Morley. He was a nice man and I liked him."

She shook her head. "I've known Morley since he and Dorothy met in college back in the Depression. We all adored him, of course, but he was such a fool. The cigarettes and his weight and all the drinking he did. You can get away with a certain amount of that when you're young, but at his age? No, ma'am. We warned him and warned him, but would he listen? Of course not. You should have seen him on Sunday. His color was awful. The doctor thinks the heart attack was aggravated by the flu he had. His electrolyte balance or something of the sort." She shook her head again, breaking off.

"How's she doing?"

"Not that well, to tell you the truth, which is why I came down from Fresno in the first place. My intention was to help out for a couple of weeks just to give him some relief. You know she's been sick for months."

"I didn't know that," I said.

"Oh, my, yes. She's a mess. She was diagnosed with stomach cancer this last June. She had extensive surgery and she's been taking chemotherapy off and on ever since. She's just skin and bone and can't keep a thing down. It's all Morley talked about and here he up and went first."

"Will they do an autopsy?"

"I don't know what she's decided about that. He just saw the doctor a week ago. Dorothy wanted him on a diet and he finally agreed. An autopsy's not required under the circumstances, but you know how they are. Doctors like to get in there and poke and pry. I feel so sorry for her."

I made some sympathetic sounds.

She gestured briskly. "Anyway, enough said. I suppose you came to take a look at his study. Why don't you step on in here and let me show you where it is. You just take what you want, and if you need to come back, you can help yourself."

"Thanks. I can leave you a list of any files I take."

She waved off the suggestion. "No need to do that. We've known Mr. Kingman for years."

I moved into the foyer. She proceeded down a short hallway with me following. There was no sign of Christmas. With Mrs. Shine's illness and now Morley's death, there might have been a sense of relief that no such effort would be required this year. The house smelled of chicken soup. "Does Morley still have an office here in Colgate?" I asked.

"Yes, but with Dorothy so sick, he did most of his work here. I believe he still went in most mornings to pick up his mail. Did you want to look there as well?" She opened a door to what had clearly once been a bedroom, converted now to office space by the addition of a desk and file cabinets. The walls were painted beige and the beige shag carpeting was just as shabby as I'd imagined it.

"That's what I was thinking. If I can't find the files here, it probably just means he had them out at the office. Is there some way I could get a key?"

"I'm not sure where he kept them, but I'll check with Dorothy. My goodness," she said then as she looked around. "No wonder Morley didn't want anyone in here."

The room was faintly chilly, the disorder that of a man who operates his affairs according to no known system. If he'd realized he was going to drop dead, would he have straightened up his desk? Unlikely, I thought. "I'll Xerox what I need and bring the files back as soon as possible. Will someone be here in the morning?"

"What's tomorrow, Wednesday? As far as I know. And if not, just go around to the back and set them on the dryer in the service porch. We usually leave that door open for the cleaning woman and the visiting nurse. I'm going to find you a key to Morley's office. Dorothy probably knows where it is."

"Thanks."

While I waited for the woman to return, I did one circuit of the room, trying to get a feel for Morley's methods of paper management. He must have tried to get himself under control at intervals because he'd made up files labeled "Action," "Pending," and "Current." There were two marked "To Do," one marked "Urgent," and an accordion folder he'd designated as his "Tickler" file. The paperwork in each seemed outdated, mismatched, as disorderly as the room itself.

Louise stepped back into the study from the hall with a ring of keys in hand. "You better take this whole batch," she said. "Lord only knows which is which."

"You won't need these?"

"I can't think why we would. You can drop them off tomorrow if you'd be so kind. Oh. And I brought you a grocery bag in case you need to load things up."

"Will there be a service?"

"The funeral's Friday morning at the Wynington-Blake here in Colgate. I don't know if Dorothy will be able to manage it or not. We held off on it because Morley's brother is flying in from South Korea. He's a project engineer with the Army Corps of Engineers at Camp Casey. He can't get to Santa Teresa until late Thursday. We scheduled the service on Friday for ten o'clock. I know Frank will be jet-lagged, but we just couldn't delay it any longer than that."

"I'd like to be there," I said.

"That would be lovely," she said. "I know he'd appreciate that. You can let yourself out when you're done. I have to give Dorothy her shot."

I repeated my thanks, but she was already moving on to the next chore. She smiled at me pleasantly and closed the door behind her.

I spent the next thirty minutes unearthing every file that seemed relevant to Isabelle's murder and the subsequent civil suit. Lonnie would have had a fit if he'd known how haphazardly Morley went about his work. In some ways, the measure of a good investigation is the attention to the paperwork. Without meticulous documentation, you can end up looking like a fool on the witness stand. The opposing attorney loves nothing better than discovering that an investigator hasn't kept proper records.

I packed item after item in the grocery bag—his calendar, his appointment book. I checked his desk drawers and his "in" and "out" boxes, making sure there wasn't a stray file stashed somewhere behind the furniture. When I was confident I'd lifted every pertinent folder, I put his key ring in my shoulder bag and closed the study door behind me. At the far end of the hall, I could hear the murmur of voices, Louise and Dorothy conversing.

As I returned to the front door, I passed the archway to the living room. I made an unauthorized detour to what had to be Morley's easy chair, upholstered in ancient cracked leather, the cushions conforming to his portly shape. There was an ashtray that had been emptied of cigarette butts. The end table still bore the sticky circles where his whiskey tumblers had sat. Snoop that I am, I checked the end-table drawer and felt down in the crevices of the chair. There was nothing to find, of course, but I felt better for it.

Next stop was Morley's office, located on a little side street in "downtown" Colgate. This whole residential section had been converted into small businesses: plumbers' shops, auto detailing services, doctors' offices, and real estate brokerages. The former single-family dwellings were identical frame bungalows. The living room in each now served as the front office for an insurance company or, in Morley's case, a beauty salon from which he rented a room with a bath at the rear. I went around to the outside entrance. Two steps led up to a small concrete porch with a small overhanging roof. The office door had a big pane of frosted glass in the upper half, so I couldn't see in. Morley's name was engraved on a narrow plaque to the right of the door, the kind of plate I could imagine his wife having made for him the day he went into business. I tried key after key, but none of them fit. I tried the door again. The place was locked up tighter than a jail. Without even thinking about it, I walked around to the rear and tried the window back there. Then I remembered I was playing by the rules. What a bummer, I thought. I'd been hired to do this. I was entitled to see the files, but not allowed to pick the lock. That didn't seem right somehow. What were all the years of breaking and entering for?

I went back around to the front and entered the beauty salon like a law-abiding citizen. The windows had been painted with mock snowdrifts, two of Santa's elves holding a painted banner reading MERRY X-MAS across the glass. There was a big decorated Christmas tree in the corner with a few wrapped boxes under it. There were four stations altogether, but only three were occupied. In one, a plastic-caped woman in her forties was having her hair permed. The beautician had divided the damp strands into sections, inserting small white plastic rollers as dainty as chicken bones. The permanent wave solution filled the air with the scent of spoiled eggs. In the second station, the woman in the chair had her head secured in a perforated bathing cap while the beautician pulled tiny strands through the rubber with what looked like a crochet hook. Tears were rolling down the woman's cheeks, but she and the beautician were chatting away as if this were an everyday occurrence. To my right, a manicurist worked on a client, who was having her fingernails painted a bubblegum pink.

On the back wall, I spotted a paneled door that was probably connected to Morley's office. There was a woman in the rear folding towels into tidy stacks. When she saw my hesitation, she moved up to the front. Her name tag said: Betty. Given her occupation, I was surprised she didn't have a better cut. She'd apparently fallen into the hands of one of those cruel stylists (usually male) who delight in mismanaging the hair of women over fifty. The particular cut that had been inflicted on this woman consisted of a shaved backside and a frizzy pouf along the front that made her neck look wide and her facial expression fearful. She fanned the air, her nose wrinkling. "Pee-yew! If they're smart enough to get a man on the moon, why can't they make a perm lotion that don't stink?" She picked up a plastic cape from the nearest chair and assessed me with a practiced eye. "Boy oh boy. You sure do have a hair emergency. Take a seat."

I looked around to see who she was talking to. "Who, me?"

"Aren't you the one who just called?"

"No, I'm here on some business for Morley Shine, but his office is locked up."

"Oh. Well, I hate to be the one to tell you, honey, but Morley passed away this week."

"I'm aware of that. Sorry. I guess I should have introduced myself." I took out my identification and held it out to her.

She studied it for a moment and then frowned, pointing to my name. "How do you pronounce that?"

"Kinsey," I said.

"No, the last name. Does that rhyme with *baloney?*"

"No, it doesn't rhyme with *baloney*. It's *Mill*-hone."

"Oh. *Mill*-hone," she said, mimicking me dutifully. "I thought it was Mill-*hony*, like the lunch meat." She looked back at the photocopy of my private investigator's license. "Are you from Los Angeles, by any chance?"

"No, I'm a local."

She looked up at my hair. "I thought maybe that was one of those new mod cuts like they do down on Melrose. Asymmetrical, they call it, with a geometrical ellipse. Something like that. Usually looks like it's been whacked off with a ceiling fan." She laughed at herself, giving her chest a pat.

I leaned back to catch a glimpse of myself in the nearest mirror. It did look kind of weird. I'd been growing my hair for several months now and it was definitely longer on one side than it was on the other. It also seemed to have a few ragged places and a stick-up part near the crown. I experienced a moment of uncertainty. "You think I need a cut?"

She hooted out a laugh. "Well, I should hope to shout. It looks like some lunatic hacked your hair off with a pair of nail clippers!"

I didn't think the analogy was quite as funny as she did. "Maybe some other time," I said. I decided to get down to business before she talked me into a haircut I would later regret. "I'm working for an attorney by the name of Lonnie Kingman."

"Sure. I know Lonnie. His wife used to go to my church. What's he got to do with it?"

"Morley was doing some work for him and I'm taking over the case. I'd like to get into his office."

"Poor guy," she said. "With his wife sick and all that. He moped around here for months, doing nothing as far as I could tell."

"I think he did a lot of work from his home," I said. "Uh, can I get into his office through here? I saw the door back there. Does that connect to his suite?"

"Morley used to use it when he had a bill collector on his doorstep." She began to walk me toward the back, which I took as cooperation.

"Was that often?" I asked. It was hard for me to mind my own business when I had someone else's business within range of me.

"It was lately."

"Would you mind if I stepped in and picked up the files I need?"

"Well, I don't see why not. There's nothing in there worth stealing. Go ahead and help yourself. It's just a thumb-lock on this side."

"Thanks."

I let myself in through the connecting door. There was one room, the back bedroom in the days when the bungalow was used as a residence. The air smelled musty. The carpeting was a mud brown, a color probably chosen because it wouldn't show dirt. What showed up instead was all the lint and dust. There was a small walk-in closet that Morley used for storage, a small bathroom with a brown vinyl tile floor, a commode with a wooden seat, a small Pullman sink, and a fiberglass shower stall. For one depressing moment, I wondered if this was how I'd end up: a small-town detective in a dreary nine-by-twelve room that smelled of mold and dust mites. I sat down in his swivel chair, listening to the creak as I rocked back. I snagged his Month at a Glance. I checked his drawers one by one. Pencils, old gum wrappers, a stapler empty of staples. He'd been sneaking fatty foods on the sly. A flat white bakery box had been folded in half and shoved down in the wastebasket. A large grease stain had spread across the cardboard and the remains of some kind of pastry had been tossed in on top. He probably came into the office every morning to sneak doughnuts and sweet rolls.

I got up and crossed to the file cabinets on the far wall. Under "V" as in VOIGT/BARNEY, I found several manila file folders stuffed with miscellaneous papers. I removed the folders and began to stack them on the desk. Behind me the door banged open and I felt myself jump.

It was Betty, from the beauty shop. "You find everything you need?"

"Yes. This is fine. Turns out he kept most of his files at home."

She made a face, tuning in to the musty odor in the room. She went over to the desk and picked up the wastebasket. "Let me get this out of here. The trash isn't picked up until Friday, but I don't want to risk the ants. Morley used to order his pizzas here where his wife couldn't check on him. I know he was supposed to diet, but I'd see him in here with cartons of take-out Chinese, bags from McDonald's. I tell you, the man could eat. Of course, it wasn't my place to make a fuss, but I wished he'd taken a little bit better care of himself."

"You're the second person who's said that today. I guess you have to let people do what they're going to do." I picked up the files and the calendar. "Thanks for letting me in. I imagine someone will come over in a week or so and clean the place out."

"You're not looking for office space yourself?"

"Not this kind," I said without hesitation. It occurred to me later she might have taken offense, but the words just popped out. The last I saw of her, she was opening his front door so she could stick the wastebasket out on the porchlet.

I returned to my car, dumped the stack of files in the backseat, and backtracked into town, where I turned into the parking garage adjacent to the public library. I grabbed a clipboard from the backseat, locked my car, and headed for the library. Once inside, I went down to the periodicals room, where I asked the guy at the counter for the six-year-old editions of the *Santa Teresa Dispatch*. In particular, I wanted to look at the news for December 25, 26, and 27 of the year Isabelle Barney was murdered. I took the reel of tape to one of the microfilm readers and threaded it through the viewer, patiently cranking my way back through time until I reached the period that interested me. I made notes about the few significant events of that weekend. Christmas had fallen on a Sunday. Isabelle had died very early on Monday. Maybe it'd be helpful to jog people's memories with a few peripheral facts. A storm had dumped heavy rain over most of California, resulting in a major pileup on the northbound 101 just south of town. There'd been a minor crime wave that included the hit-and-run fatality of an elderly man, who'd been struck by a pickup out on upper State Street. There was also a market robbery, two household burglaries, and a suspected-arson fire, which destroyed a photographer's studio in the early-morning hours of December 26. I also jotted down a reference to an incident in which a two-and-a-half-year-old boy suffered minor injuries when he fired a .44-caliber revolver left in the car with him. As I read the news accounts, I could feel my own memory ignite briefly. I'd forgotten all about the fire, which I'd actually caught sight of as I drove home at the close of a stakeout. The harsh glow of the blaze had been like a torch against the lowering night sky. The rain had contributed a surreal misty counterpoint and I'd been startled when James Taylor's rendition of "Fire and Rain" suddenly came on my car radio. The fragment of memory terminated as abruptly as a light going out.

I combed the rest of the reel, but nothing much stood out. I went back to the beginning and made copies of everything except the print ads and the classifieds. I rewound the film and tucked the reel of tape back in the box. I paid for the copies at the main desk on my way out, thinking about the people whose whereabouts I'd have to question for those couple of days. How much would I remember if someone quizzed me about the night Isabelle was killed? One fragment had been restored, but the rest was a blank.

4

I retrieved my car from the public lot and drove out to the Santa Teresa County Sheriff's Department Detention and Corrections Facility. Morley's interview with Curtis McIntyre was one of the documents I'd found in the proper file, though the subpoena had never been served. He'd apparently spoken to Curtis mid-September and no one had talked to him since. According to Morley's notes, McIntyre had been in a holding cell with Barney his first night in the can. He claimed they'd established a friendship of sorts, more on his part than Barney's. He'd found himself intrigued because Barney was a man who seemed to have everything. Curtis, accustomed to doing jail time with losers, had followed the case in the papers. When the trial came up, he'd made a point of being in attendance. He and Barney hadn't talked much until the day he was acquitted. As David Barney left the courtroom, Curtis McIntyre had stepped forward to offer his congratulations. At that point, according to the informant, David Barney made the remark that implied he'd just gotten away with murder. I couldn't tell if Curtis had elaborated on that or not.

I parked out in front of the jail, across the lot from the Santa Teresa County Sheriff's Department with its fleet of black-and-whites. I moved up the walk and pushed through the front door into the small reception area, approaching the L-shaped counter with the glass partition along the top. I'd done an overnight at the jail nearly six weeks before and I was glad to be returning in a legitimate guise. It felt much better walking in the front door than it had going in the back in the company of an arresting officer.

I signed in at the desk and filled out a jail visitation pass. The woman at the counter took the information and disappeared from the window. I waited in the lobby, perusing the bulletin board while she called down for someone to bring Curtis up to the interview room. On the wall near the pay phone, all the better bail bondsmen were listed, along with the Santa Teresa taxicab companies. Getting yourself arrested is usually an unexpected piece of misery. Once your bail's been posted, if your car's been impounded, you find yourself stuck out in the boonies—an added element of distress after a night of humiliations.

The woman behind the counter caught my attention. "Your client's coming up in a minute. Booth two."

"Thanks."

I traversed the short hallway and passed through the door leading to the visitors' booths. There were only three in that section, set up so that inmates could confer in private with their attorneys, probation officers, or anyone else they had a legitimate reason to consult. I let myself into the second "room," which was maybe four feet wide, furnished with a glass window, a four-foot length of counter, and a footrail of the sort you'd find in a bar. I hied myself up to the counter and put my foot up, leaning on my elbows. Beyond the glass was a roomette that mirrored the one I was in, with a door in the back wall through which the inmates were brought. Within minutes, the door opened and Curtis McIntyre was ushered in. He seemed puzzled at the unscheduled visit, perplexed at the sight of me when he'd probably expected his attorney.

He was twenty-eight, lean and long-waisted with hips so narrow they hardly held his pants up. He looked good in jail blues. His shirt was short-sleeved, showing long, smooth arms, the perfect epidermal canvas for a dragon tattoo. My guess was that somebody'd once told Curtis he had soulful eyes because he seemed determined to make deep, meaningful eye contact with me. He was clean-shaven, with an innocent-looking face (for a convicted felon). His hair was ill cut, which was no big surprise as the man had been in jail for months. I didn't picture his having a regular salon cut and blow-dry in the best of circumstances.

I introduced myself, explaining my purpose, which was to get his written statement. "From Mr. Shine's notes, I gather you met David Barney in a holding cell the first night after his arrest."

"You single?"

I checked behind me. "Who, me?"

He smiled the kind of smile you'd have to practice in the mirror, eyes boring into mine. "You heard me."

"What's that got to do with it?"

His voice softened to the coaxing tone reserved for stray dogs and women. "Come on. Just tell me. I'm a nice guy."

I said, "I'm sure you're very nice, but it's none of your business."

This amused him. "How come you're afraid to answer? Are you attracted to me? Because I'm attracted to you."

"Well, you're very forthcoming and I appreciate that, Curtis. Uh, now, could you tell me about the time you spent with David Barney?"

He smiled faintly. "All business. I like that. You take yourself serious."

"That's right. And I hope you'll take me serious, too."

He cleared his throat, sobering, clearly trying to make a good impression. "Him and me were in a cell together. He was arrested on a Tuesday and we didn't go before the judge until Wednesday afternoon. Seemed like a nice guy. By the time his trial come up, I'se out, so I figured I'd sit in on it and see what all the fuss was about."

"Did the two of you talk about the murder at the time of his arrest?"

"Naw, not really. He was upset, which I could understand. Lady got shot in the eye, that's ugly. I don't know what kind of person'd do a thing like that," he said. "Turns out it was him, I guess."

"What did you talk about?"

"I don't know. Nothin' much. He was asking what all I was in for and stuff like that, what judge I thought we'd pull for the arraignment the next day. I give him a rundown on which ones are tough, which is most of 'em. Well, that one guy's a pussy, but the rest is mean."

"What else?"

"That's about it."

"And on the basis of that, you sat through the whole trial?"

"Not the whole trial. You ever sit through a whole trial? It's boring, idn't it? I'se glad I never went to law school."

"I'll bet." I checked through my notes. "I've read the deposition Mr. Kingman took—"

"You single?"

"You asked me that before."

"I bet you are. You know how I know?" He tapped himself on the temple. "I'm psychic."

"Well, then, you can probably tell me what I'm going to ask you next."

He flushed happily. "Not really. I don't know you that well, but I'd like to."

"Maybe you'll be able to intuit the answers to some questions I have."

"I'll try. Absolutely. Go ahead. I'm all ears." He lowered his head and his expression became serious.

"Tell me again what he said to you once the acquittal came down."

"Said . . . let's see now. He goes, something like . . . 'Hey, dude. How you doin'? How about that? Now you see what a high-priced attorney buys?' And I'm like, 'Way to go, man. That's great. I never thought you done her.' He just got this big shi—pardon me—this big grin. He kind of leaned over close and said, 'Ha ha ha, I guess the joke's on them.'"

This seemed like an improbable conversation to me. I'd never met David Barney, but I couldn't believe he'd talk like that. I watched Curtis's face. "And from that, you concluded what?"

"I concluded he done her. You have a boyfriend?"

"He's a cop."

"Bullshiiiit. I don't believe you. What's his name?"

"Lieutenant Dolan."

"What's he do?"

"Homicide. STPD."

"Don't you never date anybody else?"

"He's too jealous for that. He'd rip your head right off your neck if he found out you were hustling me. Did you talk to David Barney any other time?"

"Besides jail and court? I don't think so. Just them two occasions."

"It seems odd that he'd say that."

"How come? Let's discuss that." He put his chin on his fist, ready to engage me in protracted discourse.

"The man hardly knows you, Curtis. Why would he confide something so significant? And right there in court. . . ." I cupped a hand to my ear. "With the sound of the judge's gavel still ringing in the air."

44

Curtis frowned thoughtfully. "You'd have to ask him that, but if you're asking me, I'd say he knows I'm a jailbird. He might have felt more comfortable with me than all his high-tone friends. Anyhow, why not? Trial was over. What's anybody going to do? Even if they heard him there's no way they can touch him on account of double jeopardy."

"Where were you when this conversation was taking place?"

"Outside the door. It was Department Six. He come out and I clapped him on the shoulder, shook his hand—"

"What about reporters? Wasn't he being mobbed at that point?"

"Oh, God, yes. They was everyplace. Yelling his name, stickin' microphones in his face, asking how he felt."

I could feel the skepticism rise. "And in the middle of it he stopped and made that remark?"

"Well, yeah. He leaned over and spoke in my ear just like I said. You're a private detective? Is that really what you do?"

I shrugged to myself and began to print his account of events. "That's really what I do," I said.

"So like when I get out, if I have a problem, I can look you up in the phone book?"

I wasn't paying much attention to him since I was in the process of converting his version into a written statement. "I guess so." If you can read.

"How much do you charge for a service like that? What's that cost?"

"Depends on what you want."

"But about what?"

"Three hundred bucks an hour," I said, lying automatically. At fifty bucks an hour he might possibly afford me.

"Go onnn. I don't believe it."

"Plus expenses."

"Goddamn, I can't believe it. Are you shittin' me or what? Three hundred an *hour*. Every hour you work?"

"It's the truth."

"You sure make a lot of money. For a girl? Lord," he said.

"How about if you lend me some? Fifty dollars, or a hundred. Just till I'm out and then I can pay you back."

"I don't think men should borrow money from women."

"Who else you gonna borrow from? I mean, I don't know dudes with dough. Unless they're drug kings, something like that. Santa Teresa, we don't even get the kings. We get more like the jacks." He snorted out a laugh. "You have a gun?"

"Sure I do," I said.

He rose halfway off his seat and peered down through the glass like I might have a six-shooter strapped to one hip. "Hey, come on. Let me see."

"I don't have it with me."

"Where's it at?"

"My office. I keep it down there in case somebody should refuse to pay a bill. Could you read this and see if it accurately reflects your recollection of your conversation with Mr. Barney?" I passed it under the glass partition, along with a pen.

He barely glanced at it. "Close enough. Hey, you print pretty good."

"I was a whiz in grade school," I said. "Could I ask you to sign it?"

"How come?"

"So we'll have a record of your testimony. That way if you forget, we can refresh your memory in court."

He scribbled a signature and passed the statement back. "Ask me something else," he said. "I'll tell you anything."

"This is fine. Thanks a lot. If I have any other questions, I'll be in touch."

After I left Curtis, I sat out in the parking lot watching cop cars come and go. This was too good to be true. Here's Curtis McIntyre driving nails into David Barney's coffin and it just didn't sound right. David Barney refused to talk now, nearly five years after the fact, two years since his acquittal. From what Lonnie'd said, extracting the most benign information from the man had been like pulling teeth. Why would he blab a makeshift confession to a dimwit like Curtis? Oh, well. It's hard to reconcile the inconsistencies in human nature. I started the car and pulled out of the parking lot.

According to the files, Isabelle Barney's sister, Simone Orr, was still living on the Barney property in Horton Ravine, one of two exclusive neighborhoods favored by the Santa Teresa well-to-do. Promotional materials from the Chamber of Commerce refer to Horton Ravine as a "sparkling jewel in a park-like setting," which should give you some idea how puffed up these pamphlets can get. To the north, the Santa Ynez Mountains dominate the sky. To the south lies the Pacific Ocean. The views are always described as "breathtaking," "stunning," or "spectacular."

In the real estate ads describing the area words like *serenity* and *tranquillity* abound. Every noun has an adjective attached to give it the proper tone and substance. The "lush, well-manicured" lots are large, maybe five acres on average, and zoned for horses. The "elegant, spacious" homes are set well away from the roads, which wind through hills "dotted" with bay, sycamore, live oak, and cypress. Lots of *dotted*s and *amid*s.

I found myself rhapsodizing in salespeak as I drove up the long, circular drive to the stately, secluded entrance to this classic Mediterranean home with its sweeping, panoramic views of serene mountains and sparkling ocean. I drove into the splendid flagstone courtyard and parked my used VW amid a Lincoln and a Beamer. I got out and entered a walled garden, passing along the handsome paved gallery. The entire four-acre parcel was dotted with seasonal perennials, lush ferns, and imported palms. Also, two gardeners trailing four hundred yards of hose between them.

I'd put a call through to Simone in advance of my arrival and she'd instructed me carefully how to reach her little cottage, which was situated on the lower terrace amid lush lawns and assorted outbuildings, like the poolhouse and the tool-shed. I rounded the eastern wing of the house, which I'd been told was designed by a well-known Santa Teresa architect whose name I'd never heard. I crossed the Spanish tiled entertainment terrace, complete with custom-built, black-bottom swimming pool, lava rock waterfall, spa, wading pool, and koi pond surrounded by short, perfectly trimmed hedges of lantana and yew. I descended a flight of stairs and followed a flagstone path to a wooden bungalow tucked up against the hillside.

The house was tiny, built of board and batten, with a steeply pitched shingle roof and wooden decking on three sides. The exterior was Shaker blue, the trim painted white. Wood frame windows formed the upper portion of the walls on all sides. The top half of the Dutch door stood open. December in Santa Teresa can be like spring in other parts of the country—gray days, a bit of rain, but with a lot of blue sky shining through.

I stopped in my tracks, completely smitten with the sight. I have a special weakness for small, enclosed spaces, a barely disguised longing to return to the womb. After the death of my parents, when I first went to live with my maiden aunt, I established a separate residence in an oversize cardboard box. I had just turned five and I can still remember the absolute absorption with which I furnished this small corrugated refuge. The floor was covered with bed pillows. I had a blanket and a lamp with a fat blue ceramic base and a sixty-watt bulb that heated the interior to a tropical pitch. I would lie on my back, reading endless picture books. My favorite was about a girl who discovered a tiny elf named Twig who lived in an overturned tomato-juice can. Fantasies within fantasies. I don't remember crying. For four months, I hummed and I read my library books, a little closed-circuit system designed to deal with grief. I ate cheese-and-pickle sandwiches like the ones my mother made. I fixed them myself because they had to be just right. Some days I substituted peanut butter for the cheese and that was good. My aunt went about her business, leaving me to work through my feelings without intrusion. My parents died Memorial Day. That fall, I started school. . . .

"Are you Kinsey?"

I turned to look at the woman as if waking from a sleep. "That's right. And you're Simone?"

"Yes. Nice to meet you." She carried a pair of gardening scissors and a shallow wicker basket piled with cut flowers, which she set down. Her smile was brief as she held out her hand for me to shake. I judged her to be in her late thirties or very early forties. She was slightly shorter than I with wide shoulders and a stocky build, which she managed to minimize by the clothes she wore. Her hair was a reddish-blond, a fine flyaway shade much darker at the roots, cut shoulder length and crinkled from a perm. Her face was square, her mouth wide. Her eyes were an unremarkable shade of blue with mascara-darkened lashes and fine reddish brows. The outfit she wore was a black-and-white geometric print, a washable silk jacket over a long black tunic top, her long loose skirt brushing the tops of black suede boots. Her fingers were blunt and there was clear polish on her nails. She wore no jewelry and very little makeup. Belatedly, I noticed that she used a cane. I watched while she transferred it from her left hand to her right. She adjusted her stance and shifted some of her weight to the cane as she leaned down and picked up the basket at her feet.

"I have to get these in water. Come on in." She opened the bottom portion of the Dutch door and I followed her in.

I said, "Sorry to have to trouble you again on this. I know you talked to Morley Shine several months ago. I suppose you heard about his death."

"I spotted his obituary in this morning's paper. I called Lonnie's office first thing and he said you'd be in touch." She moved over to the small tiled kitchen peninsula that served as both a work surface and a breakfast bar, with two wooden stools tucked under it. She hooked the cane over the edge of the counter and took out a clear glass pitcher, which she filled with tap water. She bunched the flowers nicely and stuck them in the makeshift vase, then set the arrangement on the windowsill and dried her hands on a towel.

"Have a seat," she said. She pulled out one stool and perched on it while I took the other.

"I'll try not to take too much of your time," I said.

"Listen, if it helps convict the shitheel, you can take all the time you want."

"Isn't it a bit awkward, your living on the property just a hundred yards away from him?"

"I hope so," she said. The depth of bitterness in her voice seemed to affect its very pitch. She looked up in the direction of the big house. "If it's awkward for me, think how it must feel to him. I know it galls him that I refuse to be driven off. He'd love nothing better than to force me out."

"Can he do that?"

"Not as long as I have anything to say about it. Izzy left me the cottage. It was part of her will. She and Kenneth bought the property many years ago. They paid a small fortune for it. When that marriage folded, she got it as part of the financial settlement. She had it listed as her sole and separate property when she and David got married. She also made him sign prenups."

"Sounds very businesslike. Did she do that with the others?"

"She didn't have to. The first two had money. Kenneth was number two. With David, it was different. Everybody told her he was after her money. I guess she thought the prenups would prove he wasn't. What a joke."

"So he'll never get title to this place?"

Simone shook her head. "She rewrote her will, leaving him a life interest. When he dies—which I hope is real soon, I might add—it goes to her daughter, Shelby. The little house is mine—as long as I'm alive, of course. When I die, it reverts."

"And you're not afraid?"

"Of David? Absolutely not. He got away with murder once, but the man's not a fool. All he has to do is sit tight. If he wins this civil suit, it's all his, isn't it?"

"It looks like it."

"He could come out of the whole deal smelling like a rose. So why in the world would he jeopardize that? Something happened to me, he's the first place they'd look."

"What if he loses?"

"My guess is he'd head straight for Switzerland. He's probably salting away money in a secret bank account. He's too clever to kill again. What would be the point?"

"But why did Isabelle set it up like that? Why tempt the Fates? As I understand it, between the prenuptial agreement and the terms of the will, she might as well have gone ahead and stuck her head in the noose."

"She was in love with the guy. She wanted to do right by him. She was also a realist. He was husband number three and she didn't want to get ripped off. Look at it from her perspective. You marry some guy, you don't think he's going to *kill* you. If you really thought that, you wouldn't marry him in the first place." Her eyes strayed to her watch. "Jesus, it's nearly one. I don't know about you, but I'm starving. Have you had lunch?"

"You go ahead," I said. "I shouldn't be too much longer. I'll grab a bite on the way back to the office."

"It's no problem. Please join me. I'm just making sandwiches. I'd like the company."

The invitation seemed genuine and I smiled in response. "All right. That'd be nice."

5

She moved into the tiny kitchen area and began to take items from the tiny fridge.

"Can I do anything to help?"

"No, thanks. There isn't really room enough for two of us to work. Guys love it, unless it turns out they have a passion for cooking. Then they take over here and I sit out there where you are."

I half turned on the stool, checking out the room behind me. "Great house," I remarked.

She flushed with pleasure. "You like it? Isabelle designed it . . . the start of her career."

"She was an architect? I didn't know that."

"Well, she wasn't really, but she passed for one in some respects. Look around if you like. It's only three hundred square feet."

"Is that all? It seems bigger." I stepped out onto the front porch, curious to see how the general layout related to the interior. Since the windows were cranked open, I could talk to her easily as I rounded the structure. The cottage felt as if it had been miniaturized, scaled down from human-size dimensions to a little playhouse for grown-ups. Every comfort seemed attended to, without flourish or wasted space. There was even a small chimney. I stuck my head in the window so I could peer at the compact fireplace. Many interior surfaces, including the hearth, sills, and countertops, were covered with hand-painted blue-and-white tiles in a flower motif. "This is wonderful."

Simone flashed me a smile.

I withdrew from the window and circled the perimeter. Herbs had been planted in every sunny spot. I could smell rosemary and thyme when the breeze whiffled through. The house was situated on an apron of grass that spread out in a half-moon. Below, the hillside fell away steeply into a tangle of live oak and chaparral. The view was to the mountains across the town of Santa Teresa. I reentered the only door, which opened into the kitchen. "You'll have to see my place sometime. It has a similar feel to it. A perfect little hideaway."

I continued my survey while she cut several slices from a loaf of wheat bread. The place was so small I could tour without moving far. The furnishings were antique: a crude pine table, two cane-bottom chairs, a corner cabinet with wavy, blue-tinted glass panes, a brass bed with a patchwork quilt, white on white. The bathroom was small, the only portion of the house that was fully enclosed. The rest was essentially one large room, with areas defined according to function. Everything was open, airy, tidy, full of light. Every detail was perfect, like a series of illustrations for a glossy household magazine. There were views from the front and side windows, but none from the back, where the slope rose again sharply to the main house above.

I pulled a stool up to the counter and watched her make sandwiches. She'd assembled plates, cutlery, and blue-and-white cloth napkins, which she passed to me. I set two places at the table. "If she wasn't an architect, how'd she do this?"

"She was like an unpaid apprentice to a local architect. Don't ask me how she managed it or why he agreed. She sort of went in when it suited her and did what she pleased."

"Not a bad deal," I said.

"That's where she met David. He came to work for the same firm. Her boss's name was Peter Weidmann. Have you talked to him yet?"

"No, but I intend to, as soon as I leave here."

"Oh, good. He and Yolanda live close by. About a mile from here. He's a nice man, retired now. He really taught Isabelle a lot. She was an artist by nature, but she didn't have the discipline. She could do anything she wanted, but she was always such a dilettante—full of great ideas, but lousy at development. She lost interest in most things—until she started doing this."

"This, meaning what?"

"She designed tiny houses. Mine was the first. Somehow *Santa Teresa Magazine* heard about it and did a big photo spread. The response was incredible. Everybody wanted one."

"For guests?"

"Or for teens, in-laws, art studios, meditation retreats. The beauty is you can tuck one into any corner of your property . . . once you get past the zoning sharks. She and David pulled out of Peter's firm when this whole thing took off. The two of them went into business and made a fortune overnight. She was written up everywhere, from the snooty publications to the mundane. *Architectural Digest, House & Garden, Parade*. Plus, she won all these design awards. It was astonishing."

"What about David? How did he fit in?"

"Oh, she had to have him. She was such an airhead about

business. She originated the designs, did preliminary sketches, and roughed out the floor plans. David had a degree and he was AIA, so he was responsible for drafting, all the blueprints and specs, things of that sort. He also did the marketing, advertising . . . the grunt work, in effect. Hasn't anybody told you this?"

"Not a bit," I said. "I met Ken Voigt last night and he talked about Isabelle briefly. As I said on the phone, I've read all the files, but this is the first time I've heard the particulars. How did Barney feel about her getting all the glory?"

"He probably resented it, but what could he do? His career had gone nowhere. The same was true of Peter Weidmann."

Simone moved to the table with a pitcher of iced tea and a plate of sandwiches. We sat down to eat. The coarse-textured bread was thinly sliced and lightly buttered. Leaves hung out of the sandwich like the trimmings from a garden.

"Watercress," she said when she caught my expression.

"My favorite," I murmured, but it turned out to be good—very peppery and fresh. "You have a picture of her?"

"Oh sure. Hang on and I'll get it."

"No hurry. This is fine," I said with my mouth full, but she was up and moving over to the bed table, returning seconds later with a photograph in an ornate silver frame.

She passed me the picture and sat down again. "She and I were twins. Fraternal, not identical. She was twenty-nine when that was taken."

I studied the picture. It was the first glimpse I'd had of Isabelle Barney. She was prettier than Simone. She had a softly rounded face with glossy dark hair that fell gracefully to her shoulders, silky strands forming a frame for her wide cheekbones. Her eyes were a clear brown. She had a strong short nose, a wide mouth, muted makeup, if any. She seemed to be wearing some kind of scoop-necked T-shirt, dark brown like her hair. I found myself nodding. "I can see the resemblance. What's your family background?"

I passed the picture back and she propped it up at one end of the table. Isabelle watched us gravely as the conversation continued. "Both our parents were artists and a bit eccentric. Mother had family money so she and Daddy never really did much. They went to Europe one summer on a six-week tour and ended up staying ten years."

"Doing what?"

She took a bite of sandwich, chewing some before she answered. "Just bumming around. I don't know. They traveled and painted and lived like Bohemians. I guess they hung out on the fringes of polite society. Expatriates, like Hemingway. They came back to the States when World War Two broke out and somehow ended up in Santa Teresa. I think they read about it in a book and thought it sounded neat. Meanwhile, money was getting tight and Daddy decided he'd better pay more attention to their investments. He turned out to be a whiz. By the time we were born, they were rolling in it again."

"Who was the oldest, you or Isabelle?"

She took a sip of her iced tea and dabbed her mouth with a napkin. "I was, by thirty minutes. Mother was forty-four when she had us and nobody had a clue she was carrying twins. She'd never been pregnant so she assumed she was in menopause when she first stopped having periods. She was a Christian Scientist and refused to see a doctor until the last possible minute. She'd been in labor fifteen hours when she finally agreed to have Daddy take her to the nearest hospital. They barely got her upstairs when I arrived. She was all set to hop off the table and go home again. She figured that was the end of it and the doctor did, too. He was expecting the placenta when Isabelle slid out."

"Your parents still living?"

She shook her head. "Both died within a month of each other. We were nineteen at the time. Isabelle got married for the first time that year."

"Are you married?"

"Not me. I feel like I've been married, watching her go through hers."

"Voigt was the second?"

"Right. Number one was killed in a boating accident."

"What was it like being twins? Were the two of you alike?"

"Unh-unh. No way. God, we couldn't have been more different. She inherited the family talent and all the vices that went with it. Artwise, she excelled, but it all came so easily she didn't take it seriously. The minute she mastered a skill, she lost interest. Drawing, painting. She did a little bit of everything. She made jewelry, she sculpted. She got into textiles and did incredible work, but then she got restless. She wasn't satisfied. She always wanted to do something else. In a way, the tiny houses saved her, though she might have gotten bored if she'd lived long enough."

"I gather, from what Ken says, she had a problem with low self-esteem."

"Among other things. She had all the inclinations of an addict. She smoked. She drank. She took pills any chance she got. She toked two or three joints a day. For a while, she dropped acid."

"How'd she get any work done? I'd be a basket case."

"It didn't affect her in the least. Besides, she could afford all that stuff, which is too bad in a way. She never really had to work because we inherited money. Fortunately, she never got into cocaine or she'd have gone through every cent."

"Wasn't that hard on you, her being out of control?"

"It was hard on all of us. I was always the heavy—parental, responsible. Especially since we were so young when our parents died. Isabelle got married, but I still felt like her mother. I admired her tremendously, but she was difficult. She couldn't sustain a relationship. She had nothing to give on a day-to-day basis. She was very self-involved. It was 'me, me, me.' "

"Narcissistic," I supplied.

"Yes, but I don't want to give the wrong impression. She

had some wonderful qualities. She was warm and witty and she was terribly bright. She was fun. She had a good time. She really knew how to play. She taught me a lot about how to lighten up."

"Tell me about David Barney."

"David. That's a tough one," she said and then paused to consider. "I'll try to be fair. I'd say he's handsome. Charming. Trivial. He and his wife moved up here from Los Angeles when he joined Peter's firm."

"He was married?"

"Not for long."

"What happened to his ex?"

"Laura? She's still around someplace. After David dumped her, she was forced to go to work, like every other ex-wife in town. God, women are getting screwed in divorces these days. For every guy who claims he's been 'taken' by some babe, I can show you six, eight, ten women who've been 'had' financially. Anyway, I'm sure she's in the book."

"Go on."

"Yes, well, David was a snob. He didn't want to work for a living any more than Isabelle did, except she was loving every minute of the work, not surprisingly. I mean, she had this sudden celebrity status and she ate it up. He was pushing her to sell the business while it was hot, before it peaked. He had some cockamamie scheme about prefabs and franchises. I'm not really sure what his idea was, but she hated it. By then, she was disenchanted with the marriage anyway, feeling bullied and suffocated. She wanted out from under."

"If they'd divorced, the business would have been considered community property, wouldn't it?"

"Sure. It would have been divided in half and he'd have lost really big. What'd she need him for? She could find half a dozen guys to fill his slot, but that wasn't true for him. Without her, he had zip. On the other hand, if she *died*, the business came to him intact . . . more or less. Her portion would go to Shelby, but he didn't have to worry about a four-year-old. At that point, Isabelle had already come up with so many preliminary sketches he could afford to coast and survive on the proceeds. Plus, with her dead, he must have counted on collecting the insurance. Again, some would go to Shelby, but he's still going to rake in a bunch."

"*If* he wins," I said. "Where's the house he leased when they separated?"

She flapped her hand toward the ocean. "As you leave the drive you turn left and it's down half a mile. A big white monstrosity, one of those contemporary houses made out of glass and concrete. It's so ugly, you can't miss it."

"Within easy walking distance?"

"He could have crawled it's so close."

"Were you here at the cottage the night she was killed?"

"Well, yes, but I didn't hear the shot. She'd phoned down here earlier to tell me the Seegers would be arriving late. They'd called about the car trouble and she didn't want me to worry if I saw lights on in the house. We chatted for a while and she sounded great. She'd been such a mess."

"Because of his harassment?"

"And the quarrels and the threats. Her life was a nightmare, but she was excited about San Francisco, looking forward to a little shopping, the theater, and the restaurants."

"What time did you talk to her?"

"About nine, I guess. It wasn't late. Isabelle was a night owl, but she knew I was usually in bed by ten. The first time I realized there was something wrong was when Don Seeger came down. He said they were worried because they couldn't get Isabelle to answer the door. They could see the fisheye was missing from the door and the hole looked burned. I grabbed a robe, got my key, and went up to the main house with him. We went in through the back door and found her in the foyer. I felt like a zombie. I was absolutely numb. So cold. It was awful, the worst night of my life." I could see tears for the first time and her face was suffused with pain.

She fumbled in her pocket for a Kleenex and blew her nose. "Sorry," she murmured.

I studied her for a moment. "And you really think he killed her?"

"There's not a doubt in my mind. I just don't know how you're going to prove it."

"Me neither," I replied.

It was 2:34 when I left Simone and returned to my car. A heavy marine layer had begun to settle in, obscuring the view. The afternoon light already had the gray feel of twilight and the air was chilly. There was something distinctly unpleasant about having to pass the main house. I glanced quickly at the windows that looked out over the courtyard. There were lights burning in the living room, though the rooms upstairs were dark. No one seemed to be aware of my passing. The BMW was still parked where it had been when I arrived. The Lincoln was gone. I unlocked my car and slid under the steering wheel. I tucked the key in the ignition and paused to scan the house again.

On this side, a loggia ran along the second story, the red tile roof supported by a series of white columns. A vine had grown up the pillars and trailed now along the overhang, lacy green with a white blossom, probably fragrant if you got close enough. The front door was bisected by a shadow from the balcony overhead, the view further eclipsed by the branches of the live oaks that crowded the walled garden. Because the driveway was long and curved up at such an angle, the house wasn't visible from the road below. A passerby might have caught sight of someone, approaching or departing, but at 1:30 in the morning, who'd be up and about? Teenagers, perhaps, getting home from a date. I wondered if there'd been a concert or a play that night, some charitable event that might have kept the area residents out after midnight. I'd have to check back through the papers and find out what was going on, if anything. Isabelle had been killed in the early morning hours on the day after

Christmas, which didn't sound promising. The fact that no one had ever stepped forward with information made the possibility of a witness seem even more remote.

I started the car and shifted into reverse, backing around to my left so I could head down the driveway. David Barney had claimed he was out for a night jog when Isabelle was shot. Night jogging, right, in a neighborhood dark as pitch. Much of Horton Ravine had a rural feel to it—wooded stretches without streetlights and no sidewalks at all. While no one could corroborate his story, there was no one to contradict it either. It didn't help matters that the cops had never come up with a single piece of evidence tying Barney to the scene. No witnesses, no weapon, no fingerprints. How was Lonnie going to nail the sucker if he had no ammunition?

I eased the VW down the driveway and hung a left at the bottom. I kept one eye on the odometer and the other on the road, cruising past several houses until I spotted the one that I was looking for—the place David Barney leased when he left Isabelle's. The house in question was the architectural equivalent of a circus tent: white poured concrete, with a roof line broken into wedges that fanned out from a center pole. Each triangular section was supported by three gaily painted metal pipes. Most of the windows were irregularly shaped, angled to catch some aspect of the ocean view. My guess was that inside the floors would be aggregate concrete, with the plumbing and furnace ducts plainly visible and raw. Add some corrugated plastic panels and an atrium done up in wall-to-wall Astroturf and you'd have the kind of house *Metropolitan Home* might refer to as "assured," "unsparing," or "brilliantly iconoclastic." "Unremittingly tacky" would also cover it. Pay enough for anything and it passes for taste.

I parked my car on the berm and hiked back along the road. I reached Isabelle's driveway in exactly seven minutes. Walking up the drive might take another five at best. If you made the trip at night and didn't want to be seen, you'd have to step off into the bushes if a car went past. At that hour, you weren't likely to find anyone else out on foot. Returning to my car, I timed myself again. Eight minutes this round, but I wasn't really pushing it. I made a note of the numbers on the mailboxes by the road. The neighbors might know something that would be of help. I'd have to do a door-to-door canvass to satisfy myself on that point.

I'd scheduled my appointment with the Weidmanns for 3:30, which gave me twenty minutes to spare. In most investigations I'm hired for, the object of the exercise is to flush out culprits: burglars, deadbeats, embezzlers, con artists, perpetrators of insurance fraud. Occasionally, I take on a missing-persons search, but the process is much the same—like picking at a piece of knitting until you find a loose thread. Pull at the right point and the whole garment comes unraveled. This one was different. Here, the quarry was known. The question wasn't who, but how to bring him down. Morley Shine had already done a thorough (though poorly organized) investigation and he'd come up with zilch. Now it was my turn, but what was left? I made some doodles on the page, hoping something would occur to me. Most of my doodles looked like great big goose eggs.

It's been my observation that the rich like to subdivide into the haves and the have-mores. What's the point in achieving status if you can't still be compared favorably with someone else in your peer group? Just because the wealthy band together doesn't mean they've relinquished their desire to be judged superior. The circle is simply more select and the criteria more exotic. The assessment of personal real estate is a case in point. Mansions, while easily distinguished from middle-income tract houses, can be further classified according to a few easily remembered yardsticks. The size and location of the property should be given first consideration. Additionally, the longer the

6

driveway, the more points will be accorded. The presence of a private security guard or a pack of attack-trained dogs would naturally be counted more discerning than mere electronic equipment, unless of an extremely sophisticated sort. Beyond that, one must factor in such matters as guesthouses, spiked gates, reflecting pools, topiary, and excessive outdoor lighting. Obviously the fine points will vary from community to community, but none of these categories should be overlooked in assessing individual worth.

The Weidmanns lived on Lower Road, one of Horton Ravine's less prestigious addresses. Despite the pricey tone of the neighborhood, half the homes were nondescript. Theirs was unremarkable, a one-story pale green stucco, adorned with wrought-iron porch supports and topped with a flat rock-composite roof. The lot was large and nicely landscaped, but the house was too close to the road to count for much. Given the fact that Peter Weidmann was an architect, I'd expected a lavish layout, an entertainment pavilion or an indoor pool, embellishments that would reflect the full range of his design talents. Or maybe this one did that.

I parked on a concrete apron to one side of the house. Once on the porch, I rang the bell, and waited. I half expected a maid, but Mrs. Weidmann came to the front door herself. She must have been in her seventies, smartly turned out in a two-piece black velour sweatsuit and a pair of Rockport walking shoes.

"Mrs. Weidmann? I'm Kinsey Millhone," I said, holding out my hand politely.

She seemed disconcerted by the move and there was one of those embarrassing delays until we actually shook hands. There was something in the hesitation—distaste or prudery—that caused me to bristle inwardly. Her hair was a stiff cap of platinum blond, parted down the middle, the strands separating into two tense curls, like rams' horns in the center. She had bags under her eyes and her upper lids had begun to droop, reducing the visible portion of her irises to mere hints of blue. Her skin was a peachy color, her cheeks tinted a hot pink. She looked like she'd just flunked a stress test, but a closer examination showed she was simply wearing foundation and blusher in a shade far too vivid for her coloring.

She stared at me, as if waiting for a little door-to-door salesmanship. "What was this regarding? I'm afraid it's slipped my mind."

"I work for Lonnie Kingman, Kenneth Voigt's attorney in his suit against David Barney—"

"Oh! Yes, yes, yes. Of course. You wanted to speak to Peter about the murder. Terrible. I believe you said the other fellow died. What was his name, that investigator. . . ." She tapped her fingers on her forehead as if to stimulate thought.

"Morley Shine," I said.

"That's the one." She lowered her voice. "I thought he was dreadful. I didn't like him."

"Really," I said, feeling instantly defensive. I'd always thought Morley was a good investigator and a nice man besides.

She wrinkled her nose and the corners of her mouth turned up. "He smelled so peculiar. I'm sure the man drank." Her expression was one of perpetual pained smiles superimposed on profound disapproval. Age plays cruel tricks on the human face; all our repressed feelings become visible on the surface, where they harden like a mask. "He was here several times, asking all these silly questions. I hope you don't intend to do that."

"I will have to ask some, but I hope not to be a bother. May I come in?"

"Of course. Please excuse my bad manners. Peter's in the garden. We can chat out there. I was going out for my walk when you knocked, but I can do that in a bit. Do you exercise?"

"I jog."

"Jogging's very bad. All that pounding is much too hard

on the knees," she said. "Walking's the thing. My doctor is Julian Clifford . . . do you know him?"

I shook my head.

"He's a top orthopedic surgeon. He's also a neighbor and a very dear friend. I can't tell you how often he's warned me about the harm people do in their determination to jog. It's absurd."

"Really," I said faintly.

She went on in this vein, her tone argumentative though I offered no resistance. I had no intention of altering my regimen for a woman who thought Morley smelled bad. Her shoes made no sound as we crossed the marble-tiled foyer and moved down a hallway to the rear of the house. While the exterior was strictly fifties ranch style, the interior was furnished in an Oriental motif: Persian carpets, matching silk-paneled screens, ornate mirrors, a black lacquer chest inlaid with mother-of-pearl. She had two matching cloisonné vases the size of umbrella stands. Many items seemed to come in pairs, one placed on either side of something grotesque.

I followed her through the kitchen and out the back door, where a concrete patio ran across the rear of the house. Four low steps led down to a brick walk that extended into a small formal garden. Toward the rear of the property, I could see a woody area peppered with toadstools, some growing singly, some in fairy rings. The air smelled damply of dead leaves and mosses. A few forlorn birds were still perched in the treetops, their singing disconsolate as winter crept closer.

The patio furniture was wrought iron and canvas, the seat cushions fading from exposure to the weather. Peter Weidmann was napping, a thick hardback book lying open in his lap. I'd glanced at a copy in a bookstore recently: Part One of some celebrity's boring autobiography "as told to" some writer who'd been hired to render it intelligent. It looked as if he'd read all the way to page five. A sprinkling of cigarette butts surrounded his chair. He was probably not allowed to smoke in the house.

He looked like a man who'd lived all his life in a business suit. Now retired, he wore dark, stiff jeans and a new plaid flannel shirt, packing creases still showing, two buttons open to expose a portion of his white undershirt. Why does a man like that look so vulnerable in leisure clothes? He was narrow through the face, with black unruly eyebrows and short-cropped white hair. He and Yolanda had reached that stage in their fifty-year marriage where she looked more like his mother than his wife.

"This is called active retirement," she said with a laugh. "I wish I could retire, but of course, I never had a job." Her tone of voice was jocular, though her comment was bitter. The pretended humor barely served to mask the bite underneath. She nudged his shoulder, relishing the excuse to disturb his peace and quiet. "Someone to see you, Peter."

"I can come back a little later. There's no need to wake him."

"He won't mind a bit. It's not as if he's done any hard work today." She leaned close and said, "Peter."

He roused himself with a start, disoriented by the depths of his sleep and the sudden voice in his ear.

"We have company. It's about Isabelle and David. This young woman is Mr. Kingman's secretary." She turned to me with a sudden worry. "I hope that's right. You're not an attorney yourself, are you?"

"I'm a private investigator."

"I didn't think you looked like an attorney. Your name again is what—?"

Mr. Weidmann set his book aside and rose to his feet. He extended his hand. "Peter Weidmann."

We shook hands. "I'm Kinsey Millhone. Sorry to disturb you."

"That's quite all right. Would you like some coffee or a cup of tea?"

"Thanks, but I'm fine."

Yolanda said to him, "Well, it's much too chilly to be out on the porch." And then to me, "He's had the flu twice this winter and I'm not about to go through that again. I was exhausted from all the fetching and carrying. Men are such babies when it comes to being sick." The complaint was accompanied by a wink to me. She'd claim she was teasing if Peter took offense.

"I'm afraid I don't make a very good patient," he said.

"It's not something you'd want to be good at," I replied.

He made a gesture toward the house. "We can talk in the den."

We formed a little three-person procession into the house, which seemed nearly stuffy after the damp air outside. The den was small and the furniture had the same shabby feel as the porch chairs. I suspected the house was divided into "his" and "hers." "Her" portion was well appointed—expensive, overdecorated, filled with objects probably collected from various trips to foreign ports. She'd co-opted the living room, the formal dining room, the kitchen, the breakfast room, and most probably all the bathrooms, the guest bedroom, and the master suite. He'd been accorded the back porch and the den, where he'd carefully hoarded all the household items she was threatening to throw out.

As soon as we entered the paneled den, she began to wave her hands in the air, making a face about the smell of cigarette smoke. "For heaven's sake, Peter, this is dreadful. I don't see how you can stand it." She moved over and cranked a window open, fanning the air with a magazine she'd picked up.

I'm not all that fond of cigarette smoke myself, but with her making such a scene, I found myself coming to his defense. "Don't worry about it. It doesn't bother me," I said.

She picked up a filled ashtray and made a face. "Well, it might not bother you, but it's disgusting," she said. "Just let me fetch the Airwick." She moved out of the room taking the offending ashtray with her. The tension level dropped a notch. I turned my attention to the wall above the fireplace, which was hung with framed "celebrity" photographs. I moved closer to have a look. "These are you?"

"In the main," he said.

There were pictures of Peter Weidmann with the mayor at a groundbreaking ceremony, Isabelle Barney in the background; Peter at a banquet receiving some kind of placard; Peter at a construction site, posed with the contractor. The latter photo had apparently been run in the local newspaper because someone had clipped it, framed it, and hung it beside the original. The caption identified the occasion as the dedication of a new recreational facility. From the various cars visible in the background, I judged the majority of the pictures had been taken in the early seventies. Along with the commercial projects, there were photographs of residential sites. Two photographs featured minor-level "movie stars" whose homes he'd apparently designed and built. I took a moment to view the whole gallery, as interested in seeing Isabelle as I was in seeing him. I like to watch people at work. Our occupations bring out aspects of our personalities no one would ever dream of if they met us in "civilian" settings.

In his hard hat and coveralls, Peter looked young, very sure of himself. It wasn't simply that the pictures had been taken years ago when he was, in fact, younger. This must have been the apex of his career, with everything going right. He had had big projects in the works. He must have had recognition, influence, money, friends. He looked happy. I glanced over at the man beside me, so lusterless by comparison.

I caught him watching my reaction. "This is great," I said.

He smiled. "I've been very fortunate." He pointed to one of the photos. "Sam Eaton, the state senator," he said. "I did a house for him and his wife, Mary Lee. This is Harris Angel, the Hollywood film producer. You've probably heard of him."

I said, "The name sounds familiar," though it didn't at all.

Yolanda returned with the Airwick. "Maria put this in the refrigerator of all places," she said. She set the bottle on the table and exposed the wick. The scent that wafted out, a cross between Raid and shoe polish, made me long for the smell of cigarette smoke instead.

I took in the rest of the room at a glance. There was a stack of newspapers on the floor beside Peter's leather wing chair, a smaller pile of papers on the ottoman, magazines on the end table, and evidence of lunch dishes. There was a library table arranged under the windows that overlooked the back-yard. On it was an old portable typewriter, a stack of books, and a second ashtray filled with cigarette butts. An old din-ing-room chair was pulled up to the table, with a second chair nearby piled high with paperbacks. The wastebasket was full.

She caught my eye. "He's working on a history of Santa Teresa architecture." I realized in a flash that in spite of her hostility, she was also proud of him.

"Sounds interesting."

"It's just something I'm fooling around with," he put in.

She had to laugh again. "I've got plenty for him to do if he gets tired of that. Have a seat if you can find a place. I hope you can stand the mess. I won't even let the cleaning woman in here. It's too far gone. She can do the whole house in the time it takes her to get this one room straightened up."

He smiled uncomfortably. "Now, Yolanda. Be fair. I clean the place myself . . . sometimes as often as twice a year."

"But not this year," she said, topping him.

He let the subject matter drop. He cleared his leather wing chair for her and pulled over a dining-room chair for me. I pushed some files aside, making room to sit.

"Just put those files on the floor," she said.

"This is fine." I was already tired of the game they played

—her put-downs, his collusion, my *pro forma* reassurances. "Did you want to get your walk in? I didn't mean to hold you up."

Her expression shifted. Being brittle herself, she was easily injured. "I can certainly do that if you think I'm in the way."

"Now, now, now. You stay right where you are," he said. "I'm sure she's here to talk to both of us."

"I suppose we could have some sherry," she said hesitantly.

He waved her into the chair. "I'll do that. You just have a seat."

"Please don't go to any trouble. I have to be somewhere else shortly." This was not entirely true, but I wasn't sure how much more I could endure. I took my notebook out of my handbag and leafed through the pages. "Let me ask a couple of questions and then I can get out of here. I don't want to take any more of your time than I have to."

Peter sank into a chair. "Exactly what is it you're doing?"

Yolanda adjusted one of the rings she wore, making sure the square-cut diamond was properly centered on her finger. "You'll have to pardon Peter. I only explained it to him twice."

"This is a follow-up to Morley Shine's investigation," I said, ignoring her. "Frankly, we're hoping to strengthen the plaintiff's case. Did you have contact with David or Isabelle on the day she died?"

He said, "I don't remember anything specific, but it seems unlikely."

"Well, of course it's unlikely. You were in the hospital, don't you remember? Your heart attack was December fifteenth that year. You were at St. Terry's until January second. I was afraid to tell you about Isabelle because I didn't want you upset."

His look was blank. "I suppose that's right. I'd forgotten that it all happened in that same period," he said to her. And then to me, "They'd pulled out of the firm by then and set up offices of their own."

"Taking any client they could," she inserted with acid.

"Was there bad blood about that?"

She fiddled primly with her ring. "Not to hear him tell it, but of course there was."

"Now, Yolanda, that's not true. I wished her all the best."

"Peter hates to make a fuss. He won't confront anyone, least of all someone like her. After all he'd done."

"As I understand it, Isabelle came up with the idea for tiny houses while she was working for you."

"That's right."

"What about . . . what's it called . . . proprietary rights? Wouldn't the idea actually belong to you?"

Peter started to answer, but Yolanda broke in. "Of course. He never even asked her to sign the form. The woman walked out with everything. He wouldn't even press the point, though I begged him to. In effect, Isabelle stole millions from him—literally millions. . . ."

I formed my next question with care. I could already tell Peter was much too circumspect to be of any use in my investigation. Yolanda, the spite queen, was going to serve me well if I could set her up right. "You must have been furious."

"And why wouldn't I be? She was a self-indulgent, degenerate—" She bit off the sentence.

"Go on," I said.

"Yolanda," Peter said with a warning look.

She amended her stance. "I wouldn't want to speak ill."

"It won't hurt her at this point. I understand she was excessive—"

"Excessive doesn't *begin* to cover it. She was downright dishonest!"

Peter leaned toward his wife. "I don't think we should present a totally biased view. You may not have been fond of her, but she *was* talented."

"Yes, she was," Yolanda said, coloring. "And I suppose—to be fair about it—her problems were not all her fault. Sometimes I almost felt sorry for her. She was neurotic and high-strung. The woman had everything but happiness. David latched onto her like a parasite and he sucked her dry."

I waited for more, but she seemed to have run down. I looked at Peter. "Is that your analysis?"

"It's not my place to judge."

"I'm not asking you to judge her. I'd like your point of view. It might help me understand the situation."

He thought about that one briefly and apparently decided it made sense. "She was unfortunate. I don't know what else to say."

"How long did she work for you?"

"A little over four years. An informal apprenticeship."

"Simone told me she didn't actually have an architectural degree," I said.

"That's correct. Isabelle had no formal design training. She had wonderful ideas. She bubbled over with enthusiasm. It was almost as if the same reservoir fed both her creativity and her destruction."

"Was she a manic-depressive?"

"She seemed to live with very high levels of anxiety, which is why she drank," he said.

"She drank because she was an alcoholic," Yolanda put in.

"We don't know that," he said.

She had to laugh at that, patting herself on the chest to curb her merriment. "You'll never get a man to admit a beautiful woman is flawed."

I could feel the tension collecting again at the back of my neck. "What sort of man is David Barney? I gather he's an architect. Is he talented?"

Yolanda said, "He's a carpenter with pretensions."

Peter brushed her response aside. "He's a very good technician," Peter said.

"Technician?"

"That's not meant as criticism."

"He's the defendant. You can criticize all you like."

"I'm reluctant to do that. After all, we're in the same profession even though I'm retired. It's a small town. I don't feel it's my place to comment on his qualifications."

"What about the man himself?"

"I never cared for him personally."

"Oh, for God's sake, Peter. Why don't you tell her the truth? You can't stand the man. Nobody can abide him. He's sly and dishonest. He manipulates left and right—"

"Yolanda—"

"Don't you 'Yolanda' me! She's asked for an opinion and I'm giving her mine. You're so busy being nice you forget how to tell the truth. David Barney is a spider. Peter thought we should all socialize, and we did, over my protest. I felt it was going too far. When the two of them were in Peter's firm, I tried to be pleasant. I didn't care for David, but I did what was expected. Isabelle had brought in a great deal of business and we were appreciative of that. Once she got involved with David . . . he was not a good influence."

I refocused my attention. She'd be great on the witness stand if she could keep from losing it. "How'd she manage to bring in so much business?"

"She had a lot of money and she traveled in the right circles. People looked up to her because it was clear she had exquisite taste. She was very stylish. Whatever she took up, everyone else followed suit."

"When she and David left, they took a lot of clients with them?"

"That's not unusual," Peter said hastily. "It's unfortunate, of course, but it happens in every business."

"It was a disaster," Yolanda said. "Peter retired shortly afterwards. The last time we saw them was the dinner party they gave Labor Day weekend."

"When the gun disappeared?"

The two exchanged a look. Peter cleared his throat again. "We heard about that later."

"We heard about it at the time. There was a frightful quarrel upstairs in the master bedroom. Of course, we didn't know the subject, but that's certainly what it was."

"What's your theory about who might have taken it?"

"Well, *he* did, of course," Yolanda said without the slightest hesitation.

7

I stopped by the office briefly and typed up my notes. The light on my answering machine was blinking merrily. I punched the Replay button and listened to the message. It was Isabelle's friend Rhe Parsons, sounding harried and dutiful, the kind of person who returns a phone call just to get it over with. I tried her number, letting the phone ring while I leafed through one of the files sitting on my desk. Where was I going to find a witness who could put David Barney at the murder scene? Lonnie's suggestion was facetious, but what a coup that would be. Four rings . . . five. I was just about to hang up when someone answered abruptly on the other end. "Yes?"

"Oh, hi. This is Kinsey Millhone. May I speak to Rhe Parsons?"

"You're doing it. Who's this?"

"Kinsey Millhone. I left a message—"

"Oh, right, right," she cut in. "About Isabelle. I don't understand what you want."

"Look, I know you talked to Morley Shine a couple of months ago."

"Who?"

"The investigator who was handling this. Unfortunately, he had a heart at—"

"I never talked to anyone about Isabelle."

"You didn't talk to Morley? He was working for an attorney in the lawsuit filed by Kenneth Voigt."

"I don't know about any of this stuff."

"Sorry. Maybe I was misinformed. Why don't I tell you what's going on," I said. I went through a brief explanation of the lawsuit and the job I'd been hired to do. "I promise I won't take any more of your time than I have to, but I would like to have a quick chat."

"I'm swamped. You couldn't have called at a worse time," she said. "I'm a sculptor with a show coming up in two days. Every minute I've got is devoted to that."

"What about coffee or a glass of wine later this afternoon? It doesn't have to be nine to five. I can come at your convenience."

"But it has to be today, right? Can't it wait a week?"

"We have a court date coming up." We're all busy, I thought.

"Look, I don't mean to sound bitchy, but she's been gone for six years. Whatever happens to David Barney, it won't bring her back to life. So what's the point, you know?"

I said, "There's no point to anything if you get right down to it. We could all blow our brains out, but we don't. Sure, she's gone, but her death doesn't have to be senseless."

There was a silence. I knew she didn't want to do it and I hated to press, but this was serious.

She shifted her position, still annoyed, but willing to bend a bit. "Jesus. I teach drawing at Adult Ed from seven to ten o'clock tonight. If you stop by, we can talk while the students work. That's the best I can do."

"Great. That's perfect. I appreciate your help."

She gave me directions. "Room ten, at the back."

"I'll see you there."

I arrived home at 5:35 and saw that Henry's kitchen light was on. I walked from my back door to his, peering in through the screen. He was sitting in his rocker with his daily glass of Jack Daniel's, reading the paper while his supper cooked. Through the screen, I was assailed by the heady scent of frying onions and sausage. Henry set his paper aside. "Come on in."

I opened the screen door and stepped into the kitchen. A big pot of water was just coming to a boil and I could see tomato sauce simmering on the back burner. "Hi, babe, how are you? Whatever you're cooking, it smells divine."

He'd be handsome at any age, but at eighty-three he was elegant—tall, lean, with snowy white hair and blue eyes that seemed to burn in his tanned face. "I'm putting together a lasagna for later. William gets in tonight." Henry's older brother William, who was eighty-five to his eighty-three, had suffered a heart attack in August and hadn't been doing well since. Henry had debated a trip back to Michigan to see him, but had decided to postpone the visit until William's health improved. Apparently he was better because Henry'd received a call to say he was coming here.

"That's right. I forgot. Well, that should be an adventure. How long will he stay?"

"I agreed to two weeks, longer if I can stand him. It'll be a pain in the ass. Physically, he's recovered, but he's been depressed for months. Really down in the dumps. Lewis says he's totally self-obsessed. I'm sure Lewis is sending him out here to get even with me."

"What did you do to him?"

"Oh, who knows? He won't say. You know how parental Lewis gets. He likes to have me think about my sins in case there's one I haven't told him about. I stole a girl from him once back in 1926. I think this is to retaliate for her, but maybe not. He's got a long memory and not a shred of beneficence." Henry's brother Lewis was eighty-six. His brother Charlie was ninety-one, and his only sister would be ninety-four on the thirty-first of December. "Actually, I'll bet it wasn't his idea at all. Nell's probably throwing William out. She never liked him that much and now she says all he does is talk about death. She doesn't want to hear it with a birthday coming up. Says it's bumming her out."

"What time's his plane get in?"

"Eight-fifteen, if it doesn't crash, of course. I thought I'd bring him back here for salad and lasagna, maybe go up to Rosie's for a beer after that. You want to join us for supper? I made a cherry pie for dessert. Well, actually, I made six. The other five go to Rosie to pay off my bar tab." Rosie's is the local tavern, run by a Hungarian woman with an unpronounceable last name. Since Henry's retirement from commercial baking, he's begun to barter his wares. He also caters tea parties in the neighborhood, where he's much in demand.

"Can't do it," I said. "I've got an appointment at seven and it may run late. I thought I'd grab a quick bite up at Rosie's before I head out."

"Maybe you can catch us tomorrow. I don't know how we'll spend the day. Depressed people never do much. I'll probably sit around and watch him take his Elavil."

The building that houses Rosie's looks as if it might once have been a grocer's. The exterior is plain and narrow, the plate-glass windows obscured by peeling beer ads and buzzing neon signs. The tavern is sandwiched between an appliance repair shop and an ill-lighted Laundromat whose patrons wander into Rosie's to wait out their washing cycles, chugging beer and smoking cigarettes. The floors are wooden. The walls are plywood, stained a dark mahogany. The booths that line the perimeter are crudely built, destined to give you splinters if you slide too fast across the seat. There are eight to ten tables with black Formica tops, usually one leg out of four slightly shorter than the rest. Mealtime at Rosie's is often spent trying to right the wobble, with the endless intervention of stacked paper matchbooks and folded napkins. The lighting is the sort that makes you look like you've been abusing your Tan-in-a-Bottle.

Dinner was uneventful once I knuckled under and ordered what Rosie told me. She's a formidable presence: in her sixties, Hungarian, short, top-heavy, a merciless enforcer for the food Mafia. The special that night was called *gulyashus,* which had to translate to "beef stew."

"I was thinking of a salad. I need to clean up my act after too much junk food."

"Salad is for after. The *gulyashus* comes first. I make very authentic. You're gonna love it," she said. She was already penciling the order in the little notebook she'd begun to carry. I wondered if she kept a running account of all the meals I'd eaten there. I tried to peek at the page once and she rapped me with her pencil.

"Rosie, I don't even know what *gulyashus* is."

"Just hush and I'm telling you."

"Tell me then. I can't wait."

She had to get herself all settled for the recital, like a concert violinist with her feet placed properly. She makes a point of speaking lumpy English which she apparently thinks contributes to her authority. "In Hungarian, the word *gulyás* means 'herdsman.' Like a shepherd. This dish originate in ninth century. His very good. The shepherd cook up these cubes of meat with ongion, very little moisture. No paprika then so I don't use myself. When all the liquid is boil out, the meat is dried in the sun and then stored in this bag made of the sheep's . . . how you say . . ."

"Balls?"

"Estomach."

"Previously digested. Very tasty. I'll take it. I don't want to hear the rest."

"Good choice," she said complacently.

The dish she brought was actually what my aunt used to call "galoshes," cubes of beef simmered with onion and thickened with sour cream. It really was wonderful and the tart salad afterward was the perfect contrast. Rosie allowed me to have a glass of mediocre red wine, some rolls and butter, and a cheese tray for dessert. The dinner cost only nine dollars so I couldn't complain. Dimly I wondered if, for total obedience, I'd sold out too cheap.

While I drank my coffee, she stood by my table and complained. Her busboy, Miguel, a sullen lad of forty-five, was threatening to quit if she didn't give him a raise. "Is ridiculous. Why should he get more? Just because he learned to wash a dish like I teach him? He should pay me."

"Rosie!" I said. "The man started washing dishes when Ralph quit six months ago. Now he's doing two jobs and he ought to be paid. Besides, it's nearly Christmas."

"Is easy work," she remarked, undismayed by the notions of fair play, justice, or seasonal generosity.

"It's been two years since his last raise. He told me that himself."

"You taking his side, I see."

"Well, of course I am. He's been a good employee. Without him, you'd be lost."

Her look was stubborn. "I don't like men who pout."

The Adult Education facility where Rhe Parsons was teaching was located on Bay Street, on the far side of the freeway about two blocks from St. Terry's Hospital. Once an elementary school, the complex consisted of some offices, a small auditorium, and countless portable classrooms. Room ten was at the rear of the parking lot, an oversize art studio with a door on either end. Light poured out onto the walkway. I have a natural aversion to educational institutions, but drawing seemed benign—unlike math or chemistry. I peered in.

The interior was unfurnished except for easels and a few straight-backed wooden chairs. In the center of the room there was a low platform where a woman in a bathrobe, presumably the model, was perched on a tall wooden stool, reading a magazine. Students milled about, their ages ranging from late thirties into the seventies. In Santa Teresa, most adult education courses are offered free of charge. In a lab class like this there might be a two-dollar fee for materials, but most enrollment is open and costs the students nothing. I stood in the back of the studio. Behind me, cars were still pulling into the parking lot. It was 6:52 and people were still arriving, chatting as they entered the classroom. I watched as several women dragged additional easels from a small supply room. A coffee urn had been set up and I could see a big pink bakery box, probably filled with cookies to have with coffee during the break. A tape of Kitaro's *Silk Road* was playing, the sound low, infiltrating the room with a seductive tone. I could smell oil paint and chalk dust and the first bubbling evidence of strong coffee perking.

I spotted the woman I assumed to be Rhe Parsons emerging from a small supply closet with a roll of newsprint and a box of pencils; jeans, a denim work shirt with the sleeves rolled up, a pack of cigarettes visible in her left breast pocket. No makeup, no bra. She wore heavy leather sandals and a hand-tooled leather belt. Her hair was dark, pulled back in a French braid that extended halfway down her back. I placed her in her late thirties and wondered if she'd been at Woodstock once upon a time. I'd seen clips of the concert and I could picture her cavorting barefoot through the mud, stark naked, with a joint, her hair down to her waist and daisies painted on her cheek. Growing up had made her crabby, which happens to the best of us. She set the pencils on the counter and carried the newsprint to a big worktable where she began to cut off uniform sheets, using an industrial-size paper cutter. Several students without sketch pads formed a ragged line, waiting for her to finish. She must have sensed my scrutiny. She looked up, catching sight of me, and then went on about her business. I crossed the room and introduced myself. She couldn't have been more pleasant. Perhaps, like many habitually cranky people, her irritation passed in the moment, to be replaced by something sunnier.

"Sorry if I seemed short with you on the telephone. Let me get these guys going and we can talk out in the breezeway." She checked her watch, which she wore on the inner aspect of her wrist. It was seven straight up. She clapped her hands once. "Okay, people. Settle down. We're paying Linda by the hour. We're going to start with quick sketches, one minute each. This is to loosen up so don't worry about the small stuff. Think big. Fill the paper. I don't want any tight-ass tiny images. Betsy's going to be the timekeeper. When the bell rings, grab the next sheet of newsprint and start again. Any questions? Okay, then. Let's have some fun with this."

There was a bit of a scramble while the late students found empty easels. The model hopped off the stool, dropped her robe, and struck a pose, leaning forward with her hands on the wooden stool, a graceful curve to her back. It was comforting to see that she looked like an ordinary mortal—round and misproportioned, her torso softened by motherhood. The woman working next to me studied the model briefly and began to draw. Fascinated, I watched her capture the line of the model's shoulder, the arch of her spine. The quiet in the room was intense against the lyrical meandering of the music.

Rhe was watching me. Her eyes were a khaki green, her brows ragged. She moved toward the rear exit and I followed. The night air was fifteen degrees cooler than the room itself. She reached for a cigarette and lit it, leaning against one of the supports. "You ever draw? You seemed interested."

"Can you really teach people how to do that?"

"Of course. You want to learn?"

I laughed. "I don't know. It makes me nervous. I've never done anything remotely artistic."

"You ought to try it. I bet you'd like it. I teach the basics fall semester. This is life drawing, for people with a little drawing experience. Do what I tell you, you could pick it up in no time." Her gaze strayed out across the parking lot.

"Are you expecting someone?"

She looked back at me. "My daughter's stopping by. She wants to borrow my car. Hang around long enough and I may bum a ride home."

"Sure, I could do that."

She went back to the subject, maybe hoping to postpone any talk of Isabelle. "I've been drawing since I was twelve. I can remember when it happened. Sixth grade. We were out on a field trip in a little park with a pond. Everybody else drew the fountain with these flat stick people at the edge. I drew the spaces between the chicken wire in the fence. My drawing looked real. Everybody else's looked like sixth graders on a field trip. It was like an optical illusion . . . something shifted. I felt my brain do a sudden quickstep and it made me laugh. After that, I was like this art prodigy . . . the star of my class. I could draw anything."

"I envy you that. I always thought it'd be neat. Can I ask about Isabelle? You said your time was in short supply."

She looked away from me then, her voice dropping somewhat. "You might as well. Why not? I talked to Simone this afternoon and she filled me in."

"Sorry about the confusion over Morley Shine. According

to the files, he'd already talked to you. I was just going to fill in the blanks."

She shrugged. "I never heard a word from him, which is just as well. I'd have *really* been annoyed if I had to have the same conversation twice. Anyway, what is it you want to know?"

"How'd you meet?"

"Out at UCST. We took a printmaking class. I was eighteen, unmarried, with a kid on my hands. Tippy was two. I knew who the father was. He's always pitched in with her and helped me out with the money, but he's not the kind of guy I'd ever marry. . . ."

I pictured a dope dealer with his nose pierced, a tiny ruby sitting on his nostril like a semiprecious booger, long, unwashed hair tumbling halfway down his back.

". . . Isabelle had just turned nineteen and she was engaged to the guy who was later killed in a boat. We were both way too young for the shit that was coming down, but it bonded us like cement. We were friends for fourteen years. I really miss her."

"Are you close to Simone?"

"In some ways I am, but it's not like Isabelle. For sisters, they were very different . . . remarkably so. Iz was special. She really was. Very gifted." She paused to take the last drag from her cigarette, which she flipped into the parking lot. "Tip adored Isabelle, who was like a second mother to her. She told Iz the secrets she didn't have the nerve to tell me. Which is just as well, in my opinion. There are things I'm not sure any mother needs to know about her kid." She interrupted herself by holding an index finger up. "Let me take a break here and see how the class is doing."

She moved to the doorway and looked in on the class. I saw one of the students, a man in his sixties, turn a befuddled face toward her. He put a tentative hand up. "Hang on a sec," she said, "I better earn my paycheck."

The man who'd summoned her launched into a long-winded question. Rhe used hand gestures as she made her response, almost like American Sign Language for the deaf. Whatever her point, he didn't seem to get it at first. The model had changed her pose and was perched again on the stool, one bare foot resting on the second rung. I could see the angle of her hip and the line where her buttock was flattened out by the wood. Rhe had moved on. I waited while she completed the circuit, making her way from one easel to the next.

I heard footsteps behind me and I turned, glancing back. A young woman was approaching in tight jeans and high-heeled cowboy boots. She wore a Western-cut shirt and a big leather bag slung across her shoulder like a mail pouch. Her face was a clumsier version of Rhe's, though I suspected the maturation process would refine her features somewhat. At the moment, she looked like a rough pencil sketch for a portrait in oil. Her face was wide, her cheeks still rounded with the last vestiges of baby fat, but she had the same green eyes, the same long, dark hair pulled up in a braid. I placed her in her late teens or very early twenties. Bright-looking, good energy. She flashed me a smile.

"Is my mother in there?"

"She'll be out in a minute. Are you Tippy?"

"Yes," she said, surprised. "Do I know you?"

"I was just talking to your mom and she said you'd be stopping by. My name is Kinsey."

"You teach here, too?"

I shook my head. "I'm a private investigator."

She half smiled, getting ready for the punch line. "For real?"

"Yep."

"Cool. Investigating what?"

"I'm working for an attorney on a case going into court."

Her smile faded. "Is this about my aunt Isabelle?"

"Yes."

"I thought that already went to court and the guy got away with it."

"We're trying again. A different angle this time. We may nail him if we're lucky."

Tippy's expression seemed to darken. "I never liked him. What a creep."

"What do you remember?"

She made a face . . . reluctance, resistance, a touch of regret perhaps. "Nothing much, except we all cried a bunch. Like for weeks. It was awful. I was sixteen when she died. She wasn't my real aunt, but we were really close."

Rhe emerged from the classroom with her key ring in her hand. "Hi, baby. I thought that was you out here. I see you met Miss Millhone."

Tippy gave her mother's cheek a kiss. "We were just waiting for you. You look tired."

"I'm okay. How was work?"

"Work was fine. Corey says I might get a raise, but it's only like three percent."

"Don't knock it. Way to go," Rhe said. "What time are you picking Karen up?"

"Fifteen minutes ago. I'm already late."

Tippy and I watched while Rhe slipped the car key from the ring and then pointed toward the parking lot. "It's in the third row, to the left. I want the car back by midnight."

"We're not even out until quarter of!" Tippy yelped in protest.

"As soon as possible after that. And don't run me out of gas the way you did last time."

"It was empty when you gave it to me!"

"Would you just do what I say?"

"Why, you have a date?" Tippy asked impishly.

"Tippy . . ."

"I'm just teasing," she said. She plucked the key from her mother's hand and started off across the parking lot, bootheels clacking.

" 'Gee, Mom, I hope this isn't inconvenient,' " Rhe called toward her departing form. " 'Thank you, darling mother.' "

"You're welcome," Tippy called back.

Rhe shook her head with the kind of mock disgust that only a totally smitten parent indulges in. "Twenty years they're totally self-involved, then they turn around and get married."

"I know people must say this to you all the time, but you really don't look old enough to be her mother."

Rhe smiled. "I was sixteen when she was born."

"She seems like a neat kid."

"Well, she is, thanks to AA, which she joined when she was sixteen."

"Alcoholics Anonymous? Are you serious?"

"The drinking started when she was ten. I was working to support us and the baby-sitter was a lush. Tip would go there after school and guzzle beer every chance she got. I never had a clue! Here I am thinking it's neat because my child is so docile and obedient. She never once complained. She never whined if I was late or had to leave her overnight. I had other friends who were single moms like me. They had a bitch of a time. Their kids ran away, or caused trouble. Not my little Tippy. She was so easy to get along with. She didn't do well in school and she had the 'flu' a lot, but otherwise she seemed fine. I guess I was in denial, because I know now she was drunk or hung over half the time."

"You're lucky she straightened out."

"Part of that was Izzy's death. It did us in. It made us closer. We lost the best friend we ever had, but at least it brought us back together."

"How'd you find out about her drinking?"

"She reached a point where she was drinking so much I couldn't miss it. By the time she reached high school, she was really out of control. Popping pills. She smoked dope. She'd had her driver's license six months and she'd already had two wrecks. Plus, she stole anything that wasn't nailed down. This was actually the autumn before Isabelle's murder at Christmastime. She'd started her junior year, cutting classes, flunking tests. I couldn't handle it. I kicked her out, so she

went to live with her father. When Iz died, she came back."
She stopped to light another cigarette. "Jesus. Why'm I telling you this stuff? Look, I gotta get back to class. Do you
mind hanging out? I really do need a ride home if you can
do me that."

"Sure. I'd be happy to."

8

I drove her home at 10:30 after class had
ended. Most of the students were gone by five
after ten, cars spilling out of the darkened parking lot with the sweep of headlights, engines
thrumming. I offered to help her tidy up, but
she said it'd be quicker if she did it herself. I
wandered around the room, doing an idle survey while she emptied the coffee urn and rinsed
it out, put away the drawing supplies, and then
flipped out the lights. She locked the doors behind us and we headed for my VW, which was
the only car left in the parking lot.

As we drove through the gated driveway, she
said, "I live in Montebello. I hope that's not too
far out of your way."

"Don't worry about it. I'm on Albanil, near the beach. I can come back along Cabana and it's no big deal."

I turned right onto Bay, and then right again on Missile, picking up the freeway about two blocks down. She gave me directions to her place and for two miles we chatted idly, while I tried to decide what I could learn from her. "How'd you first hear about Isabelle's death?"

"The cops called about two-thirty and told me what had happened. They asked if I'd come over there and just sit with Simone. I threw some clothes on, hopped in the car, and barreled over there right away. I was just in shock. The whole time I was driving, I kept talking to myself like some kind of nut. I didn't cry till I got there and saw the look on Simone's face. The Seegers were a mess. They kept telling the same story over and over again. I don't know which of us was in worse shape. Actually, I think I was. Simone was numb and out of it until David showed up. Then she lost it completely. She really came unglued."

"Oh, that's right. He claimed he was jogging in the middle of the night. Did you believe him?"

"God, I don't know. I did and I didn't. He'd been doing night runs for years. He said he liked it because it was quiet and he didn't have to worry about all the traffic and exhaust fumes. I guess he suffered from insomnia and roamed the house at all hours."

"So he used the jogging to wind down when he couldn't sleep?"

"Well, yeah, but on the other hand, the night of the murder, it seemed awfully contrived." She twisted a finger in an imaginary dimple in her cheek like a ditzy blonde. " 'What a coincidence. I was just passing by on my two A.M. run.' "

"Simone tells me he was living down the road at that point."

She made a face. "In that awful house. He told the cops he was just getting back from a run when he saw the lights up at Isabelle's and stopped to see what was going on."

"Did he seem upset?"

"Well, I wouldn't say that, but then nothing seemed to move him. It was one of her big complaints. He was an emotional robot."

"You mentioned Simone going nuts. What'd you mean by that?"

"She got hysterical when he showed up, convinced he'd killed Isabelle. She always maintained the story about the stolen gun was pure bullshit. We'd all been in the house on countless other occasions. Why would any one of us suddenly sneak upstairs and steal David's thirty-eight, for God's sake? She figured it was part of a setup. I guess I'd have to agree."

"So, you were at the dinner party Labor Day weekend when the gun disappeared?"

"Sure, I was there and so was everybody else. Peter and Yolanda Weidmann, the Seegers, the Voigts."

"Kenneth was there? Her ex-husband and his wife?"

"Hey, current etiquette. One big happy family, except of course for Francesca. That's Kenneth's wife, the long-suffering. What a martyr she was. Sometimes I think Isabelle just invited them to bug her. All Francesca had to do was refuse to go."

"What was her problem?"

"She knew Ken was still hung up on Isabelle. After all, Iz was the one who gave Kenneth the boot. He married Francesca on the rebound."

"Sounds like a soap opera."

"It gets worse," Rhe said. "Francesca's beautiful. Have you met her?" I shook my head and she went on. "She's like a model, perfect features and a body to die for, but she's insecure, always choosing men who withhold. You know what I mean? Ken was ideal because she knew she'd never really have his full attention."

I said, "Let me ask you this. I heard his version last night and he claims Isabelle was the one who was insecure. Is that true?"

"Not from my point of view, but she may have shown a different side of herself to men," she said. She pointed to a series of driveways coming up on the left. "It's this first one," she said.

We were in the section of Montebello known as the slums, where the houses only cost $280,000 each. I pulled up in front of a small stucco cottage painted white. She opened the car door on her side, getting out. "I'd ask you in for some wine, but I really do have to get to work. I'll be up half the night."

"Don't worry about it. That's fine. I'm bushed. I appreciate your time," I said. "By the way, where's the show?"

"The Axminster Gallery. There's a champagne reception Friday evening at seven. Stop by and see it if you can."

"I'll do that."

"And thanks for the ride. If you think of any other questions, you can let me know."

Henry's house was dark by the time I got home. There were no messages on my machine. As a way of unwinding, I tidied up the living room and scrubbed the downstairs bath. Cleaning house is therapeutic—all those right-brain activities, dusting and vacuuming, washing dishes, changing sheets. I've come up with many a personal insight with a toilet brush in hand, watching the Comet swirl around in the bowl. Tomorrow night I'd dust my way up the spiral staircase, then tackle the loft and the upstairs bathroom.

I slept well, got up at 6:00 A.M., and did my usual run, whizzing through my morning routine on automatic pilot. On my way into the office, I stopped off at the bakery and bought a huge Styrofoam container of *caffé latte* with a lid. I had to park my car two blocks away, and by the time I got to my desk the coffee was the perfect drinking temperature. While I sipped, I sat and stared at the file folders strewn across every available surface. I was going to have to straighten things up just to figure out what was what. I drained half the coffee and set the cup aside.

I pushed my sleeves up and went to work, getting organized. I emptied both boxes, plus the brown grocery bag full of files I'd picked up at Morley's house, adding in the few additional files from his office. I rearranged the piles alphabetically and then painstakingly reconstructed the sequence of reports, using Morley's invoices as a master index. In some instances (Rhe Parsons being a case in point), I had a name itemized on his bill without a file to match. For "Francesca V.," whom I took to be the current Mrs. Voigt, I found a file folder neatly labeled, but there was no report in it. The same was also true of a Laura Barney, who I assumed was David's ex-wife. Had Morley talked to them or not? The former Mrs. Barney apparently worked at the Santa Teresa Medical Clinic in some capacity. Morley'd noted a telephone number, but there was no way to tell if he'd gotten through to her. He'd been paid for sixty hours' worth of interviews, in some cases with accompanying travel receipts, but the corresponding paperwork didn't add up to much. I made a penciled notation of any name without attendant notes or a written report.

By 10:30, I had a list of seventeen names. Just as a spot check, I tried two. First, I placed a call to Francesca, who answered after one ring, sounding cool and distant.

I identified myself and verified, first of all, that she was married to Kenneth Voigt. "I'm reorganizing some files and I wondered if you remember what date you talked to Morley Shine."

"I never talked to him."

"Not at all?"

"I'm afraid not. He called and left a message about three weeks ago. I returned his call and we agreed to meet, but then he canceled for some reason. As a matter of fact, I asked Kenneth about it just last night. It seemed odd somehow. Since I testified at the first trial, I assumed I'd be called the second time around."

I glanced down at Morley's memo, which seemed to indicate they'd had a meeting. "We better set up an appointment as soon as possible."

"Hang on a minute and I'll get my book." She put the phone down on her end and I heard the tap of heels across hardwood. She returned to the telephone with a rustle of paper. "I'm busy this afternoon. What's this evening look like for you?"

"That sounds fine to me. What time?"

"Could we make it seven? Kenneth usually doesn't get home until nine, but I'm assuming you don't need him to sit in."

"Actually, I'd prefer to have the time alone."

"Good. Then I'll see you at seven."

I tried the clinic next and found myself connected with what I guessed was the reception desk. The person who answered was female and sounded young.

"Santa Teresa Medical Clinic, this is Ursa. May I help you?"

I said, "Can you tell me if you have a Laura Barney working at the clinic?"

"Mrs. Barney? Sure. Hang on and I'll get her."

I was placed on hold briefly.

"This is Mrs. Barney."

I introduced myself, explaining, as I had with Francesca, who I was and why I was calling. "Can you tell me if you talked to Morley Shine in the last couple of weeks?"

"As a matter of fact, I had an appointment with him last Saturday, but he never showed up. I was very annoyed because I'd canceled some plans in order to make time for him."

"Did he give you any indication what he meant to ask?"

"Not really, but I assumed it was in conjunction with this lawsuit coming up. I was married to the man acquitted of criminal charges."

"David Barney."

"That's right. We were married for three years."

"I'd like to talk to you. Can we set up a time this week?" In the background, I could hear another line begin to ring insistently.

"I'm usually here until five. If you stop by tomorrow I can probably make some time."

"Four-thirty or five?"

"Either one is fine."

"Good. I'll stop by as close to four-thirty as I can make it. I'll let you pick up your other call."

She said thanks and clicked off.

I went back to my list and called nine other names at random. Not one of them had ever heard from Morley Shine. This was not looking good. I buzzed Ida Ruth in the outer office. "Is Lonnie still in court?"

"As far as I know."

"What time's he get back?"

"Lunchtime, he said, but he sometimes skips lunch and heads for the law library instead. Why, what's up? You want to get a message to him?"

A low-level dread had begun to churn in my chest. "I better go over there and have a chat with him myself. Which courtroom, did he say?"

"Judge Whitty, Department Five. What's going on, Kinsey? You sound very strange."

"I'll tell you later. I don't want to commit myself quite yet."

I walked over to the courthouse, which was only two blocks away. The day was sunny and clear, with a mild breeze ruffling the grass on the courthouse lawn. The architecture of the building itself is Mediterranean, complete with towers, turrets, sandstone arches, and open-air galleries. The exterior landscaping is a bright mix of magenta bougainvillea, red bottlebrush, junipers, and imported palms. A low growing fringe of ground cover along the sidewalk threw out a heady perfume.

I went up the wide concrete steps, through ornate wooden doors. The corridor was empty. The floor was paved with glossy irregular stone tiles the color of old blood. The lofty ceilings were hand-stenciled and crisscrossed with dark beams. The lighting fixtures were wrought-iron replicas of Spanish lanterns, the windows secured by sturdy grillwork. The place might have been a monastery once; all cold surfaces, stripped of ornament. As I passed, the door to the jury assembly room opened and prospective jurors poured out into the hallway, filling the air with the tap-tapping of footsteps and the murmur of voices. Soon I could hear the incessant squeaking of stall doors in the rest rooms across the hall. Department 5 was located another two doors down the hall on the right, the lighted sign above the door indicating that court was still in session. I eased the door open and slipped into a seat in the rear.

Lonnie and opposing counsel were involved in a case management conference, their voices droning on the warm air like big fat bumblebees. The judge was in the process of referring the case to judicial arbitration, setting the dates for both the completion of the arbitration and a future case management conference. As usual, I wondered how individual fates could be decided through a process that sounded, on the face of it, so dull. When the judge broke for lunch, I waited by the door, catching Lonnie's eye as he turned and headed through the little swinging gate that separated the spectators' "pews" from the court. He took one look at my face and said, "What's the matter?"

"Let's go outside where it's private. You're not going to like this."

We walked side by side without a word, footsteps clattering, down the corridor, down the concrete steps, out the front entrance to the sidewalk. We struck off across the grass just far enough to ensure that we wouldn't be overheard. He turned and looked at me and I plunged in.

"I don't know a nice way to say this so I'll get right to the point. It turns out Morley's files are more than disorganized. Half the reports are missing and what he's got there is suspect."

"Meaning what?"

I took a deep breath. "I think he was billing you for work he never did."

Lonnie's face went blank as the news sank in. "You're shittin' me."

"Lonnie, he had a heart condition and his wife is very sick. From what I gather, he was hard up for money, but he didn't have the time or the energy to do much."

"How'd he think he could get away with that? I got a court date in less than a month. Did he think I wouldn't *notice?*" he asked. "Hell, what's the matter with me? I *didn't* notice, did I?"

I shrugged. "In the past, from what I've heard, his work was always great." Small comfort to an attorney who could end up in court with nothing in his hand but his dick.

Lonnie seemed to pale, apparently conjuring up the same image of himself. "Jesus, what was he thinking of?"

"Who knows what he was thinking? Maybe he was hoping he could get caught up."

"How bad is it?"

"Well, you still have the witnesses from the criminal trial. It looks like most of them have been subpoenaed, so you're cool on that score. I'm guessing maybe half the witnesses on the new list never heard from him. I could be wrong. All I did was a spot check. I'm really judging by the number of reports I can't find."

Lonnie closed his eyes and wiped his face with one hand. "I don't want to hear this. . . ."

"Look, we still have some time. I can go back and fill in, but if we run into a snag, we're up shit creek. Some of these people may not even be available."

"Jesus, this is my fault. I've been tied up with this other matter and it never occurred to me to question his paperwork. What I saw looked okay. I knew he was backlogged, but what he gave me seemed fine."

"Yeah, what's there *is* fine. It's what's not there that worries me."

"How long will it take?"

"Two weeks at the very least. I just wanted you to be aware of what you're up against. With the holidays coming up, a lot of people are going to be tied up or out of town."

"Do what you can. At two, I'm taking off for Santa Maria for a two-day trial. I get back late on Friday, but I won't come into the office until Monday morning. We can talk about it then."

"Will you be staying up there?"

"Probably. I could come home at night if I had to, but I hate losing the hour drive time each way. After a full day in court, I just want to grab a quick bite somewhere and then hit the sack. Ida Ruth will have the motel number if there's an emergency. In the meantime, do what you can, okay?"

"Sure."

I went back to the office. As I passed Lonnie's office door I spotted Ida Ruth talking on the telephone. She caught sight of me and waved frantically, motioning me back. She put the party on hold and then put her hand across the receiver, as if to further muffle her side of the conversation in progress. "I don't know who this guy is, but he's asking for you."

"What's he want?"

"He just read Morley's obituary. He says it's urgent he talk to whoever's taking over for him."

"Let me get back to my desk and I'll pick it up in there. Maybe he's got some information for us. What line's he on?"

She held up two fingers.

I trotted down the hall, closed the office door behind me, dumped my handbag, and reached across my desk, punching line two, which was blinking steadily. "This is Kinsey Millhone. Is there something I can help you with?"

"I read in the paper Morley Shine died. What happened?" The voice was well modulated, the tone cautious.

"He had a heart attack. Who is this?"

There was a pause. "I'm not sure that's relevant."

"It is if you want to talk to me," I said.

Another pause. "My name is David Barney."

My heart did one of those sudden hard bangs. "Excuse me. I'm the wrong person to ask about Morley Shine—"

He cut in, saying, "Listen to me. Now, just listen. There's something screwy going on. I talked to him last Wednesday—"

"Morley called you?"

"No, ma'am. I called him. I heard some ex-con named Curtis McIntyre is set to testify against me. He claims I told him that I killed my wife, but that's bullshit and I can prove it."

"I think we should stop this conversation right here."

"But I'm telling you—"

"Tell it to your attorney. You have no business calling me."

"I've told my attorney. I told Morley Shine, too, and look how he ended up."

I was silent for half a second. "What's that supposed to mean?"

"Maybe the guy was getting too close to the truth."

I rolled my eyes. "Are you implying he was murdered?"

"It's possible."

"So is life on Mars, but it's not likely. Why would anybody want to murder Morley Shine?"

"Maybe he'd found something that exonerated me."

"Oh, yeah, really. Such as what?"

"McIntyre claims he talked to me outside the courtroom the day I was acquitted, right?"

I said nothing.

"Right?" he asked again. I hate guys who insist on a line-by-line response.

"Make your point," I said.

"The fucker was in jail then. It was May twenty-first. Check his rap sheet for that year. You'll see it plain as day. I told Morley Shine the same thing Wednesday morning and he said he'd look into it."

"Mr. Barney, I don't think it's a good idea for us to talk

like this. I work for the opposition. I'm the enemy, you got that?"

"All I want to do is tell you my side of it."

I held the phone out and squinted at the receiver in disbelief. "Does your attorney know you're doing this?"

"To hell with that. To hell with him. I've had it up to here with attorneys, my own included. We could have settled this years ago if anybody'd had the decency to listen." This from a man who shot his wife in the eye.

"Hey, you have the legal system if you want someone to listen. That's what it's all about. You say one thing. Kenneth Voigt says something else. The judge will hear both sides and so will the jury."

"But you won't."

"No, I won't listen because it's not my place," I said irritably.

"Even if I'm telling the truth?"

"That's for the court to decide. That isn't my job. My job is to gather information. Lonnie Kingman's job is to put the facts before the court. What good is it going to do to tell me anything? This is stupid."

"Jesus Christ! Someone has to help me." His voice broke with emotion. I could hear mine getting colder.

"Talk to your attorney. He got you off a *murder* rap . . . so far, at any rate. I wouldn't mess with success if I were you."

"Could you meet with me . . . just briefly?"

"No, I can't meet with you!"

"Lady, I'm begging you. Five minutes is all I ask."

"I'm going to hang up, Mr. Barney. This is inappropriate."

"I need help."

"Then hire some. My services are taken."

I put the phone down and jerked my hand back. Was the man nuts? I'd never heard of a defendant trying to enlist the sympathies of the opposition. Suppose, in desperation, the guy came after me? I snatched up the phone again and buzzed Ida Ruth.

"Yessum?"

"The guy who just called. Did you give him my name?"

"Of course not. I'd never do such a thing," she said.

"Oh, shit. I just remembered. I gave it to him myself."

I picked up the phone again and placed a call to Sergeant Cordero in Homicide. She was out, but Lieutenant Becker picked up. "Hi, this is Kinsey. I need some information and I was hoping Sheri could help."

"She won't be back until after three, but maybe I can help. What's the scoop?"

"I was going to ask her to call the county jail and have someone check the jail release forms for a fellow named Curtis McIntyre."

"Wait a minute. Let me grab a pencil. That was McIntyre?"

"Right. He's an informant set to testify on a case for Lonnie Kingman. I need to know if he was incarcerated on May twenty-first, five years ago, which is when he claims he talked to the defendant. I can get the information by subpoena, but it's probably just a wild-goose chase and I hate to go to all the trouble."

"Shouldn't be hard to check. I'll call you back when I've got it, but it may take a while. I hope you're not in any crashing hurry."

"The sooner the better."

"Ain't that always the way?" Lieutenant Becker said.

Once I hung up the phone, I sat and thought about the situation, wondering if there was a quicker means of verifying the information. I could certainly wait until midafternoon, but it would prey on my mind. David Barney's call had left me feeling restless and out of sorts. I was reluctant to waste time checking out what was probably pure fabrication on his part. On the other hand, Lonnie was counting on Curtis McIntyre's testimony. If Curtis McIntyre was lying, we were sunk, especially with Morley's investigation coming unraveled at the same time. This was my first job for Lonnie. I could hardly afford to get fired again.

In my head, I reran the conversation I'd had with Curtis at the jail. In his account, he'd intercepted David Barney in the corridor just outside the courtroom on the day he was acquitted. I didn't think I could count on Barney's attorney, Herb Foss, to corroborate Curtis's claim, but could there have been another witness to their encounter? Just the countless reporters with their Minicams and mikes.

I grabbed my jacket and my shoulder bag. I left the office and dogtrotted the two blocks to the side street where I'd finally managed to squeeze my car into a bare stretch of curb. I took Capilla Boulevard across town, through the heart of the commercial district, and headed up the big hill on the far side of the freeway.

KEST-TV was located just this side of the summit. From the bluff where the station sat, there was a 180-degree living mural of the city of Santa Teresa: mountains on one side, the Pacific Ocean on the other. There was parking for about fifty cars and I pulled into a spot designated for visitors. I got out of the car and paused for a moment to take in the view. The wind was buffeting the dry grasses along the hill. In the distance, the pale ocean stretched to the horizon, looking flat and oddly shallow.

I remembered the story I'd once heard from a marine archaeologist. He told me there was evidence of primitive offshore villages, underwater now, located at the mouths of ancient sloughs or arroyos. Over the years, the sea had offered up broken vessels, mortars, abalone spangles, and other artifacts, probably eroding from former cemeteries and middens along the now-submerged beach. In legend, the Chumash Indians recount a time when the sea subsided and remained that way for hours. A house was exposed at the far reaches of the low tide . . . a mile out, or two miles . . . this miraculous shanty. People gathered on the beaches, murmuring with amazement. The waters receded further and a second house appeared, but the witnesses were too frightened to approach. Gradually the waters returned and the two structures vanished, covered by the slow swell of the incoming tide.

There was something eerie about the tale, Holocene ghosts offering up this momentary vision of a tribal site lost from view. Sometimes I wondered if I'd have dared venture out across that stretch of exposed channel. Perhaps half a mile out, it plunged downward like the sides of a mountain, underwater cliffs tumbling ever deeper to the canyon below. I pictured the sediment on the ocean bottom, glistening, dead gray from the lack of light, cobbled and pockmarked with all its blunt and stony treasures. Time covers the truth, leaving scarcely a ripple on the surface to suggest all the plains and valleys that lie below. Even now, dealing with a six-year-old murder, much was hidden, much submerged. I was left to gather artifacts washed up like rubble on the shores of the present, uneasy about the treasures, undiscovered, lying just out of reach.

I turned and went into the station. The building itself was a one-story stucco structure, painted a plain sand color, bristling with assorted antennae. I went into the lobby with its pale blue carpeting, furnished with the kind of "Danish Modern" furniture an affluent college student might rent for a semester. Christmas decorations were just going up: an artificial tree in one corner, boxes of ornaments stacked in a chair. On the wall to my right, numerous broadcast awards were mounted like bowling trophies. A color television was tuned to a morning game show, the gist of which seemed to be identifying a series of celebrities whose first names were Andy.

The receptionist was a pretty girl with long dark hair and vivid makeup. The name on the placard read Tanya Alvarez. "Rooney!" she called, her eyes pinned to the set. I turned and looked at the picture. "Andy Rooney" was correct and the audience was applauding. The next clue came up and she said, "Oh, shoot, who is that? What's-his-face? Andy Warhol!" Right again, and she flushed with pleasure. She looked over at me. "I could make a fortune on that show, except probably the day I got on it'd be some category I never heard of. Blowfish, or exotic plants. Can I help you?"

"I'm not sure. I'd like to look at some five-year-old news footage, if you have it."

"Something we taped?"

"That's what I'm assuming. This was the verdict on a local murder trial and I'm pretty sure you'd have covered it."

"Hang on a minute and I'll see if somebody back there can help you." She rang through to "somebody" in the bowels of the building, briefly describing the nature of my quest. "Leland'll be out in five minutes," she said.

I thanked her and spent the mandatory waiting period wandering from the front entrance, which looked out onto the parking lot, to the sliding glass doors on the far side of the reception area, which looked out onto a wide concrete patio furnished with molded white plastic chairs. A three-dimensional view of the city wrapped around the patio like a screen. I could imagine the station employees having lunch out in the hot sun—women with cotton skirts discreetly pulled up, men without shirts. A big dish antenna dominated the view. The air looked hazy from up here. . . .

"I'm Leland. What can I do for you?"

The fellow who'd appeared through the doorway behind me was in his late twenties and had to be a hundred pounds overweight. He had a mop of curly brown hair surrounding a baby face, with wire-rimmed glasses, clear blue eyes, flushed cheeks, and no facial hair. With a name like Leland, he was doomed. He looked like the kind of kid who'd been tormented by his schoolmates since the first day of school, too bright and too big to avoid the involuntary cruelties of other middle-class children.

I introduced myself and we shook hands. I explained the situation as succinctly as possible. "What occurred to me was that with local reporters present on the day Barney was acquitted, there were probably Minicams rolling as he emerged from the courtroom."

"Okay," he said.

" 'Okay' wasn't really the response I was looking for, Leland. I was hoping you had a way to go back and check the old news tapes."

Leland gave me a blank look. I wish a P.I.'s job were half as easy as they make it look on television. I've never opened a dead bolt with a pass of my credit card. I can't even force mine into a doorjamb without breaking it off. And what's it supposed to do once you slide it in there? Most of the latch bolts I've seen, the slanted angle is on the *inside* so it's not as though you could slip a credit card along the face of it and force the latch to move back. And where the angle faces the outside, the strike plate resists the insertion of even the most flexible object. Leland seemed to be taking the same implacable position.

"What's the matter? Don't you keep that stuff?"

"It's not that. I'm sure there's a copy of the footage you're looking for. The master tapes are catalogued by subject matter and date, cross-referenced and cross-filed on three-by-five index cards."

"You don't have it on computer?"

He shook his head, with just a hint of satisfaction. "The logistics of the system don't really matter much because I can't let you see the master tape without a properly executed subpoena."

"I'm working for an attorney. I can get a subpoena. This is no big deal."

"Go ahead then. I can wait."

"Yeah, well, I can't. I need the information as soon as possible."

"In that case, you got a problem. I can't let you see the master tape unless you have a subpoena."

"But if I could get it eventually, what difference does it make? I'm entitled to the information. That's the bottom line, isn't it?"

"No tickee, no washee. That's the bottom line," he said.

I was beginning to see why his imaginary classmates liked to torture him. "Could we try this?" I pulled out a mug shot of Curtis McIntyre. "Why don't you look at the tape and tell me if he's on it. That's all I want to know."

He stared at me with that blank look all petty bureaucrats assume while they calculate the probabilities of getting fired if they say yes. "Why do you want to know? I really wasn't listening before."

"This fellow claims he had a conversation with the defendant in a murder trial shortly after he was acquitted. He says the cameras were rolling as the guy left the courtroom, so if what he says is true, he ought to be clearly visible on the tape, right?"

"Yeeess," he said slowly. I could tell he thought there was some kind of trick to it.

"This isn't a violation of anybody's civil rights," I said reasonably. "Could you just look?"

He held his hand out. I gave him Curtis's mug shot. He continued to hold his hand out.

I stared for a moment. "Oh," I said. I opened my handbag and took out my wallet. I peeled off a twenty and put it in his palm. His expression didn't actually change, but I knew he was insulted. I'm sure it's the same look you'd get from a New York taxi driver if you tipped him a dime.

I peeled off another twenty. No reaction. I said, "I really hate corruption in someone so young."

"It's disgusting, isn't it?" he replied.

I added a third.

His hand closed. "Come with me."

He turned and headed back through the doorway and into a narrow corridor. I followed without a word. Offices opened up on either side of us. Occasionally, we passed other station employees wearing jeans and Reeboks, but no one was doing much. The spaces seemed cramped and irregular, with too much knotty pine veneer paneling and too many cheaply framed photographs and certificates. The whole interior of the building had been done up with the sort of do-it-yourself home improvements that later make a house impossible to sell.

At the rear, we passed into a tiny concrete cul-de-sac with a wood-and-metal stairway leading up to an attic. Just to the right was an old-fashioned wooden file cabinet, with a smaller wooden file sitting on top. He opened the drawer for the year we wanted and began to sort through the index cards, starting with the name Barney. "We won't have the actual field tapes," he remarked while he looked.

"What's a field tape?"

"That would be like the whole twenty minutes of tape the guy shot. We keep the ninety seconds to two minutes of edited footage that actually goes on the air."

"Oh. Well, even that would help."

"Unless the guy you're looking for stepped up and spoke to your suspect after the cameras finished rolling."

"True enough," I said.

"Nope. Nothing," he said. "Well, let's see here. What else could it be under?" He tried "Murder," "Trials," and "Courtroom Cases," but there was no reference to Isabelle Barney.

"Try 'Homicides,' " I suggested.

"Oh, good one." He shifted to the *H*'s. There it was, with a numerical designation that apparently referred to the number of the tape on file. We went up the narrow stairs and through a door so low we were forced to duck our heads. Inside, there was a warren of tiny rooms with six-foot ceilings, lined with videocassette containers, neatly labeled and filed upright. Leland located and retrieved the cassette we were looking for and then led me downstairs again and around to the right where there were four stations set up with monitoring equipment. He flipped on the first machine and inserted the tape. The first segment appeared on the screen in front of us. He pressed Fast Forward. I watched the news for that year whiz by like the history of civilization in two minutes flat, everybody very animated and jerky. I spotted a still of Isabelle Barney. "There she is," I yelped.

Leland backed the tape up and began to run it at normal speed. An anchorperson I hadn't seen for years was suddenly doing the voice-over commentary as snippets of the case, neatly spliced together, spelled out the highlights of Isabelle's death, David Barney's arrest, and the subsequent trial. The acquittal, in condensed form, had the speedy air of instant justice, well edited, swiftly rendered, with liberty for all. David Barney emerged from the courtroom looking slightly dazed.

"Hold it. Let me look at him."

Leland stopped the tape and let me study the image. He was in his forties with light brown wavy hair combed away from his face. His forehead was lined and there were lines radiating from the corners of his eyes. He had a straight nose and a tense grin over artificially even teeth. His chin was strong and I could see that he had strong hands with blunt-cut nails. He was slightly taller than medium height. His attorney looked very tall and gray and somber by comparison.

"Thanks," I said. I realized belatedly that I'd been holding my breath. Leland pushed Play and the coverage quickly switched to another subject altogether. He handed me Curtis McIntyre's mug shot. "No sign of him."

For the money I'd given him, he could have feigned disappointment. "Could it be the camera angle?" I asked.

"We got a wide and a close. You saw 'em come through the door alone. Nobody approached in the footage we caught. Like I said, the guy might have stepped up and spoken once the press conference was over."

"Well. Thanks," I said. "I guess I'll have to rely on my other source."

I went back to my car, not sure what to do next. If I got verification of Curtis McIntyre's incarceration, I intended to confront him, but I couldn't do that yet. In theory, I had numerous interviews to conduct, but David Barney's phone call had thrown me. I didn't want to spend time shoring up David Barney's alibi, but if what he said was true, we'd end up looking like a bunch of idiots.

I took the winding road down the backside of the hill and turned right on Promontory Drive, following the road along the ocean and through the back entrance to Horton Ravine. I used the next hour and a half canvassing the old neighborhood to see if anybody had been out and about on the night Isabelle was murdered. It didn't thrill me to be in range of David Barney, but I couldn't see a way around it and still get the information I wanted. A canvass by telephone is the same as not doing it. It's too easy for people to hang up, tell fibs, or shine you on.

One neighbor had moved and another had died. A woman on the adjacent property thought she'd heard a shot, but she hadn't paid much attention to the time and she'd later wondered if it hadn't been something else. Like what, I thought. I wasn't sure if it was my paranoia or not, but any time I heard what sounded like a gunshot, I checked the clock to see what time it was.

Of the eight remaining homeowners variously peppered along that stretch of road, none had been out that night and none had seen a thing. I got the impression that it had all happened far too long ago to bear worrying about at this point. A six-year-old murder doesn't engage the imagination. They'd already told their versions of the story one too many times.

I went home for lunch, stopping off at my apartment just long enough to check for messages. My machine was clear. I went next door to Henry's. I was looking forward to meeting William.

I found Henry standing in his kitchen, this time up to his elbows in whole wheat flour, kneading bread. Pellets of dough clung to his fingers like wood putty. Usually, Henry's kneading has a meditative quality, methodical, practiced, soothing to the observer. Today, his manner seemed faintly manic and the look in his eyes was haunted. Beside him, at the counter, stood a man who looked enough like him to be a twin; tall and slim, with the same snowy white hair and blue eyes, the same aristocratic face. I took in the similarities in that first glance. The differences were profound and took longer to assimilate.

Henry wore a Hawaiian shirt, white shorts, and thongs, his long limbs sinewy and tanned as a runner's. William wore a three-piece pin-striped suit, a starched white shirt, and a tie. His bearing was erect, nearly stiff, as if to compensate for the underlying feebleness I'd never known Henry to exhibit. William held a pamphlet in a slightly shaking hand and he pointed with a fork to a drawing of the heart. He paused for introductions and we went through the proper litany of inaugural sentiments. "Now where was I?" he asked.

Henry gave me a bland look. "William's been detailing some of the medical procedures associated with his heart attack."

"Quite right. You'll be interested in this," William said to me. "I'm assuming your knowledge of anatomy is as rudimentary as his."

"I couldn't pass a test," I said.

"Nor could I," William replied, "until this episode. Now Henry, you'll want to pay attention to this."

"I doubt that," Henry said.

"You see, the right side of the heart receives blood from the body and pumps it through the lungs, where carbon dioxide and other waste products are exchanged for oxygen. The left side receives the blood full of oxygen from the lungs and pumps it out into the body through the aorta. . . ." The diagram he was using looked like the road map of a park with lots of one-way roads marked with black-and-white arrows. "Block these arteries and that's where you have a problem." William tapped on the diagram emphatically with the fork. "It's just like a rockslide coming down across a road. All the traffic begins to pile up in a nasty snarl." He turned a page in the pamphlet, which he held open against his chest like a kindergarten teacher reading aloud to a class. The next diagram showed a cross section of a coronary artery that looked like a vacuum cleaner hose filled with fluffies.

Henry interrupted. "Have you had lunch?"

"That's why I came home."

"There's some tuna in the refrigerator. You can make us some sandwiches. Do you eat tuna, William?"

"I've had to give it up. It's a very fatty fish to begin with and when you add mayonnaise . . ." He shook his head. "Not for me, thanks. I'll open one of the cans of low-sodium soup I brought with me. You two go ahead."

"Turns out William can't eat lasagna," Henry said to me.

"Much to my regret. Fortunately, Henry had some fresh vegetables I was able to steam. I don't want to be a bother and I said as much to him. There's nothing worse than being a burden to your loved ones. A heart condition doesn't have to be a death sentence. Moderation is the key. Light exercise, proper nutrition, sufficient rest . . . there's no reason to believe I couldn't go on into my nineties."

"Everyone in our family lives into their nineties," Henry said tartly. He was slapping loaves into shape, plunking one after another into a row of greased pans.

I heard a dainty ping.

William removed his pocket watch and flipped the case open. "Time for my pills," he said. "I believe I'll take my medication and then have a brief rest in my room to offset the stress of jet lag. I hope you'll excuse me, Miss Millhone. It's been a pleasure meeting you."

"Nice to meet you, too, William."

We shook hands again. He seemed somewhat invigorated by his lecture on the hazards of fatty foods.

While I put the sandwiches together, Henry put six loaves of bread in the oven. We didn't dare say a word because we could hear William in the bathroom filling his water glass, then returning to his room. We sat down to lunch.

"I think it's safe to say this is going to be a very long two weeks," Henry murmured.

I moved over to the refrigerator and took out two Diet Pepsis, which I brought back to the table. Henry popped both tops and passed one back to me. While we ate, I filled him in on the investigation, in part because he likes hearing about the work I do, and in part because I find it clarifies my thinking when I hear what I have to say.

"What's your feeling about this Barney fellow?" he asked.

I shrugged. "The man's a creep, but then I don't think much of Kenneth Voigt, either. Talk about grim. Fortunately for them, the judicial system doesn't seem to hinge on my personal opinions."

"You think the informant is telling the truth?"

"I'll know a lot more when I find out where he was on May twenty-first," I said.

"Why would he lie? Especially when it's so easy to check? From what you've said, if he was actually in jail, all you have to do is go back and look at his paperwork."

114

"But why would David Barney lie about it when the same possibility applies? Apparently, nobody's thought to verify the date so far—"

"Unless Morley Shine checked it out before he died." Henry imitated the "significant moment" music on a radio drama: "Duh-duh-duh."

I smiled, mouth too full of sandwich to articulate a reply. "Oh, great. That's all I need," I said when I could. "I do my job right and I die, too." I wiped my mouth on a paper napkin and took a sip of Pepsi.

Henry gestured dismissively. "Barney's probably generating some kind of smoke screen."

"I hope that's what it is. If some of this shit checks out, I don't know what I'm going to do."

Famous last words. Before I left, I put in a call to Lieutenant Becker to see if he'd heard from Inmate Records.

"I just got off the phone with them. The guy was right. Curtis McIntyre was being arraigned that day on a burglary charge. He might have passed Barney in the hall on his way to see the magistrate, but he'd have been shackled to the other prisoners. There's no way they could have talked."

"I better find out what's going on here," I said.

"You better do it quick. McIntyre got out of jail this morning at six."

10 I headed back to the office and called Sergeant Hixon, a friend of mine out at the jail. She checked Curtis McIntyre's records and gave me the address he'd provided his last parole officer. Curtis seemed to spend a portion of each year taking advantage of the rent-free accommodations provided by the Santa Teresa County Sheriff's Department, which he probably considered the equivalent of a Hawaiian condominium vacation time-share. When he wasn't enjoying the free meals and volleyball at the local correctional facility, he apparently occupied a room at the Thrifty Motel ("Daily, Weekly, Monthly . . . Kitchens") on upper State Street.

I parked my VW across the road from this establishment, which quick calculation told me was within walking distance of the jail. Curtis didn't even have to spring for a taxi on release. I imagined that his was that one room without a ratty car parked out front. The occupants of the other units boasted Chevies and ten-year-old Cadillacs, vehicles favored by auto insurance defrauders, which is what they might have been. Curtis hadn't been out of jail long enough to engage in any illegal activities. Well, maybe littering, lewd conduct, and public spitting, but nothing *major.*

The Thrifty Motel looked like the sort of "auto court" where Bonnie and Clyde might have holed up. It was L-shaped, built of cinder block, and painted the strange green that yolks turn when they've been hard-boiled too long. There were twelve rooms altogether, each with a tiny porch a little bigger than a doormat. Someone had planted marigolds in matching coffee cans arranged in twos and threes by the front steps. The office at the entrance was dominated by a Coke machine and the front window was obscured by mock-ups of all the credit cards they took.

I was just about to cross the road and verify his presence when I spotted him emerging from the very room I'd mentally assigned him. He looked rested and freshly shaved, wearing jeans, a white T-shirt, and a denim jacket. He was in the process of running a pocket comb through his hair, which was damp from the shower and formed a curly fringe around his ears. He was simultaneously smoking and chewing gum, a refreshingly aromatic combination for the breath. I fired up the VW and followed at a distance.

I kept him in sight as he headed west, passing numerous small businesses: a pizza parlor, a gas station, a U-Haul rental, a home improvement "emporium," and a garden shop. Beyond these, where the road curved around to the left, was a combination bar and grill called the Wander Inn. The door was standing open. Curtis flipped his cigarette toward the pavement and disappeared through the front. I pulled into the gravel parking lot around at the back and left my car in one of ten empty slots. I entered the rear door, passing the rest rooms and the kitchen, where I could see the fry cook shaking the oil from a wire basket piled with golden fries.

The interior of the bar was all polyurethane and beer smell, illuminated by a wide shaft of daylight coming in the front. Already, the cigarette haze gave the room the misty quality of an old photograph. The only colors I could see were the vibrant primary hues of the pinball machine, where a cartoon spacewoman with big conical breasts straddled the earth in a formfitting blue space suit and thigh-high yellow boots. Behind her, a big red dildo-shaped spaceship was just blasting off for the moon.

At the bar, six men turned to look at me, but Curtis wasn't one. I spotted him in a booth, a beer bottle to his lips, Adam's apple thrusting up and down like a piston. He set the empty bottle on the table and paused to produce several noisy burps in succession, like a furious sea lion barking at his mate.

A waitress in a white blouse, black slacks, and crepe-soled deck shoes emerged from the kitchen with a tray of hot food, which she took to his booth. I waited until he'd been served a cheeseburger and a mound of fries, all of which he doctored with liberal doses of salt and ketchup. He piled lettuce, tomato, pickle, and onion on the burger, put the top of the bun back, and mashed it into place. He had to hold it with both hands in order to bite in. I approached the booth and slid into the seat across from him. He expressed as much enthusiasm as he could muster with his mouth full and his lips smeared with ketchup. "Hey, how are you? This is great! Glad to see you. I don't believe this. How'd you know I'd be here?" He swallowed his cheekful of burger and wiped the bottom half of his face with a paper napkin. I handed him a second napkin from the dispenser and watched him as he cleaned up his fingers, after which he insisted on shaking hands with me. I didn't see a polite way to refuse, though I knew my palm would smell like onions for an hour afterward.

118

I folded my arms, leaning on my elbows, to discourage any further contact. "Curtis, we have to talk."

"I got time. You want a beer? Come on and let me buy you one."

Without waiting for assent, he signaled the bartender by holding up his beer bottle and two fingers. "You want some lunch, too? Have some lunch," he said.

"I just ate."

"Well, have some fries. Help yourself. How'd you know I was out? Last time you seen me I'se in jail. You look great."

"Thanks. So do you. That was yesterday," I pointed out.

Curtis popped up and crossed to the bar to get the beers. While he was gone, I ate a couple of his french fries. They were wedge cut, with the skins on, and perfectly cooked. He returned to the booth with the beers and I saw him make a move as if to slide in on my side.

"No way," I said. He was acting like I was his date and I could see the guys at the bar begin to eye us with speculation.

I refused to give him room and he was forced to sit down again where he'd been. He handed me a beer and grinned at me happily. Curtis seemed to think that along with all the beer, cigarettes, and saturated fats, he might just get lucky and get laid this afternoon. He put his chin in his fist and tried his soulful, puppy-dog gaze on me. "You're not gonna be mean to me, now, are you, hon?"

"Finish your lunch, Curtis, and don't give me any more of that hangdog look. It just makes me want to hit you with a rolled-up newspaper."

"Damn, you're cute," he said. Love had apparently diminished his appetite. He pushed aside his plate and lit a cigarette, offering me a drag, like we were postcoital.

"I'm not cute at all. I'm a very cranky person. Now could we get down to business? I'm having a little problem with the story you told me."

He frowned to show he was serious. "How come?"

"You said you sat in on David Barney's trial—"

"Not the whole thing. I told you that. Crime might be exciting, but the law's a bore, right?"

"You said you talked to David Barney as he left court just after he'd been acquitted."

"I said that?"

"Yes, you did."

"Don't remember that part. What's the problem?"

"The problem is you were in jail at the time, waiting to be arraigned on a burglary charge."

"Nooo," he said with disbelief. "*I* was?"

"Yes, you were."

"Well, I'm burnt. You got me there. I forgot all about that. I guess I got my dates wrong, but the rest of it is gospel." He held his hand up as if he were taking an oath. "Swear to God."

"Cut the horseshit, Curtis, and tell me what's going on here. You didn't talk to him. You're lying through your teeth."

"Now wait. Just wait. I did talk to him. It just wasn't where I said."

"Where then?"

"At his house."

"You went to his *house*? That's baloney. When was this?"

"I don't know. Couple weeks after his trial, I guess."

"I thought you were still in jail."

"Naw, I'se out by then with time served and all that. My attorney cut a deal. I, like, copped to the lesser plea."

"Forget the jargon and tell me how you ended up at David Barney's house. Did you call him or did he call you?"

"I don't remember."

"You don't *remember*?" I said in a scathing tone of skepticism. I was being rude, but Curtis didn't seem to notice. He was probably accustomed to being addressed that way by all the hard-nosed prosecuting attorneys he'd faced in his short, illustrious career.

"I called him."

"How'd you get his telephone number?"

"Called Information."

"What made you think to get in touch with him?"

"It seemed like to me he wouldn't have many friends. I been there myself. Get in trouble with the law, a lot of people won't fool with you much after that. It's like they don't want to hang out with a jailbird."

"So you thought he needed a best friend and you were going to be it. What's the rest of it?"

His response was sheepish and he had the good grace to squirm. "Well, now, I knew where he lived—out in Horton Ravine—so I figured he was good for a meal or a couple drinks. We'd been cellmates and all and I thought he'd at least be polite."

"You went to borrow money," I said.

"You might put it that way."

So far, it was the only thing he'd said that rang true.

"I'd just got out. I didn't have no funds to speak of and this guy had lots. He's loaded—"

"Skip that. I believe you. Describe the house."

"He's living in the dead wife's house by then—up a hill, Spanish, with this courtyard and a terrace with this big black-bottom swimming pool—"

"Got it. Go on."

"I knock on the door. He's there and I say I was in the area and stopped by to congratulate him on gettin' off a murder rap. So he asks me in and we have a couple drinks—"

"What'd you drink?"

"He had some kind of pussy drink, vodka tonic with a twist. I had bourbon straight up with a water back. It was classy bourbon, too."

"So you're having drinks . . ."

"That's right. We're having these drinks and he's got this little old gal in the kitchen making up a tray of snacks. That green stuff. Guacamole and salsa and these triangle-shape chips that're gray. I said, 'What the hell are them?' and he said, 'They're blue corn tortilla chips.' Looked gray if you asked me. We set there and drank and carried on until almost midnight."

"What about dinner?"

"Wasn't any dinner. Just snacks is all, which is how we got so loaded."

"And then what?"

"And that's when he said what he said, about he done her."

"What'd he say exactly?"

"Said he knocked on the door. She come downstairs and flipped on the porch light. He waited until he seen her eye block the light in the little peephole? Then he fired away. Boom!"

"Why didn't you tell me this story to begin with?"

"It didn't look right," he said righteously. "I mean, I went up there to ask if he'd lend me some money. I didn't want it to seem like I was mad he turned me down. Nobody'd believe me if I told the story that way. Besides, he was nice about it and I didn't want to look like a dick. Pardon my French."

"Why would he admit he killed her?"

"Why not? Once he's acquitted, he can't be retried."

"Not in criminal court."

"Shoot. He's not going to worry about a damn civil suit."

"And you're prepared to go into court with this?"

"I don't mind."

"You will testify under oath," I said, trying to make sure he understood what this was about.

"Sure. Only . . . you know."

"Only you know what?"

"I'd like a little something back," he said.

"As in what?"

"Well, fair is fair."

"Nobody's going to pay you money."

"I know that. I never said money."

"Then what?"

"I'd like to see a little time off my parole, something like that."

"Curtis, nobody's going to make a deal with you. I have no authority whatsoever to do that."

"I never said make a deal, but I could use some consideration."

I looked at him long and earnestly. Why didn't I believe what he was telling me? Because he looked like a man who wouldn't know the truth if it jumped up and bit him. I don't know what made me blurt out the next question. "Curtis, have you ever been convicted of perjury?"

"Perjury?"

"Goddamn it! You know what perjury is. Just answer the question and let's get on with this."

He scratched at his chin, his gaze not quite meeting mine. "I never been *convicted*."

"Oh, hell," I said.

I got up out of the booth and walked away from him, heading for the rear of the restaurant. Behind me, I could hear him spring to his feet. I glanced back in time to see him fling some bills on the table as he hurried after me. I stepped out into the parking lot, nearly recoiling from the harsh sunlight on the white gravel.

"Hey! Now, wait up! I'm telling you the truth."

He grabbed at me and I pulled my arm out of reach. "You're going to look like crap on the stand," I said, without breaking stride. "You've got a record a mile long, including charges of perjury—"

"Not 'charges.' Just the one. Well, two, if you count that other business."

"I don't want to hear it. You've already changed your story once. You'll change it again the next time somebody asks. Barney's attorney is going to tear you apart."

"Well, I don't see why you have to take that attitude," he

said. "Just because I told one lie doesn't mean I can't tell the truth."

"You don't even know the *difference,* Curtis. That's what worries me."

"I do know."

I unlocked my car door and opened it, rolling down the window to break the air lock when I shut it. I got in the front seat and slammed the door smartly, nearly catching his hand on the doorpost where he was resting it. I reached over and flipped open the glove compartment. I got out one of my business cards and thrust it through the window at him. "Give me a call when you decide to tell the truth."

I started the car and pulled away from him, flinging up dust and gravel in my wake.

I drove back to the office with the radio blasting. It was 3:35 and, of course, parking was at a premium. It didn't occur to me that with Lonnie driving up to Santa Maria, his space would be free. I circled the area, increasing one block with each round, trying to snag a spot within reasonable walking distance of the office. Finally, I found a semiquestionable slot, with my rear bumper hanging out into somebody's driveway. It was an invitation for a parking ticket, but maybe all the meter maids had gone home by then.

I spent the rest of the afternoon doing busywork. My appointment with Laura Barney was coming up within the hour, but in truth, I was marking time until I had a chance to talk to Lonnie, who Ida Ruth kept assuring me was temporarily out of service. I found myself loitering in the vicinity of her desk, hoping I'd be nearby if he should happen to call in. "He never calls when he's working," she said patiently.

"Don't you ever call him?"

"Not if I'm smart. He gets annoyed when I do."

"Don't you think he'd want to hear about it if his prime witness turned sour?"

"What does he care? That's this case. He's tied up doing

something else. I've worked for him six years and I know what he's like. I can leave a message, but he'll just ignore it until this trial is over with."

"What am I supposed to do till he gets back? I can't afford to waste time and I hate spinning my wheels."

"Do whatever you want. You're not going to get anything from him until nine o'clock Monday morning."

I glanced at my watch. This was still Wednesday. It was 4:05. "I've got an appointment near St. Terry's in half an hour. After that, I think I'll go home and clean house," I said.

"What's with the cleaning? That doesn't sound like you."

"I spring clean every three months. It's a ritual I learned from my aunt. Beat all the throw rugs. Line-dry the sheets. . . ."

She looked at me with disgust. "Why don't you go on a hike up in Los Padres?"

"I don't hang out in nature if I can help it, Ida Ruth. There are ticks up in the mountains as big as water bugs. Get one of those on your ankle, it'd suck all your blood out. Plus, you'd probably be afflicted with a pustular disease."

She laughed, gesturing dismissively.

I dispensed with a few miscellaneous matters on my desk and locked my office in haste. I was curious about David Barney's ex-wife, but somehow I didn't imagine she'd enlighten me much. I went downstairs and hoofed it the three and a half blocks to my car. Happily, I didn't have a ticket sitting on my windshield. Unhappily, I turned the key in the ignition and the car refused to start. I could get it to make lots of those industrious grinding noises, but the engine wouldn't turn over.

I got out and went around to the rear, where I opened the hood. I stared at the engine like I knew what I was looking at. The only car part I can identify by name is the fan belt. It looked fine. I could see that some little doodads had come unhooked from the round thing. I said, "Oh." I stuck 'em back. I was just getting in the front seat when a car pulled halfway into the drive. I tried the engine and it fired up.

"Can I help?" The guy driving had leaned across the front seat and rolled the window down on the passenger side.

"No, thanks. I'm fine. Am I blocking your drive?"

"No trouble. There's room enough. What was it, your battery? You want me to take a look?"

What was this? The engine was running. I didn't need any help. "Thanks, but I've already got things under control," I said. To demonstrate my point, I revved the engine and shifted into neutral, temporarily perplexed about which way to go. I couldn't pull forward because of the car parked in front of me. I couldn't back up because his car was blocking my rear.

He turned his engine off and got out. I left mine rumbling, wondering if I had time to roll up my window without seeming rude. He looked harmless enough, though his face was familiar. He was a nice-looking man, in his late forties with light brown wavy hair graying at the temples. He had a straight nose and a strong chin. Short-sleeved T-shirt, chinos, deck shoes without socks.

"You live in the neighborhood?" he asked pleasantly.

I knew this guy. I could feel my smile fade. I said, "You're David Barney."

He braced his arms on the car and leaned toward the window. Subtly, I could feel the man invading my turf, though his manner remained benign. "Look, I know this is inappropriate. I know I'm way out of line here, but if I can just have five minutes, I swear I won't bother you again."

I studied him briefly while I consulted my internal warning system. No bells, no whistles, no warning signs. While the man had annoyed me on the telephone, "up close and personal" he seemed like ordinary folk. It was broad daylight, a pleasant middle-class neighborhood. He didn't appear to be armed. What was he going to do, gun me down in the streets with his trial a month away? At this point, I had no idea where my investigation was going. Maybe he'd provide some inspiration for a change. I thought about the professional implications of the conversation. According to the State Bar Rules of Court, an attorney is not permitted to communicate directly with the "represented party." A private investigator isn't limited by the same stringent code.

"Five minutes," I said. "I have to be somewhere after that." I didn't tell him the appointment was with his ex-wife. I turned the engine off and remained in my car with the window rolled down halfway.

He closed his eyes, letting out a big breath. "Thank you," he said. "I really didn't think you'd do this. I don't even know where to begin," he said. "Let me admit to something right up front. I pulled your distributor caps. It was a sneaky thing to do and I apologize. I just didn't think you'd agree to talk to me otherwise."

"You got that right," I said.

He looked off down the street and then he shook his head. "Did you ever lose your credibility? It's the most amazing phenomenon. You know, you live all your life being an up-right citizen, obeying the law, paying taxes, paying your bills on time. Suddenly, none of that counts and anything you say can be held against you. It's too weird. . . ."

I tuned him out briefly, reminded of a time, not that long ago, when my own credibility went south and I was suspected of taking bribes by the very company that had trusted me with its business for six years.

". . . really thought it was over. I thought I'd come through the worst of it when I was acquitted on the criminal charges. I just got my life back and now I'm being sued for everything I own. I live like a leper. I'm shunned. . . ." He straightened up. "Oh, hell, let's not even get into that," he said. "I'm not trying to generate sympathy—"

"What are you trying to do?"

"Appeal to your sense of fair play. This guy McIntyre, the informant—"

"Where'd you get that name?"

"My attorney took his deposition. I was floored when I heard what he had to say."

"I'm not at liberty to discuss this, Mr. Barney. I hope you understand that."

"I know that. I'm not asking. I just beg you to consider. Even if he'd actually been in the courthouse when the verdict came down, why would I say such a thing to him? I'd have to be nuts. Have you met . . . what's his name, Curtis? I was in a cell with the man less than twenty-four hours. The guy's a schmuck. He comes up to me on acquittal and I confess to murder? The story's crazy. He's an idiot. You can't believe that."

I was feeling oddly protective of Curtis. There was no way I was going to tell Barney the informant had changed his account. Curtis's testimony might still prove useful if we could ever figure out what the truth was. I didn't intend to discuss the details of his statement, however shaky it might appear. "This isn't such a hot idea," I said.

Barney went on, "Just think about it, please. Does he strike you as the type I'd confide my darkest secrets to? This is a frame-up. Somebody paid him to say that—"

"Get to the point. The talk about a frame-up is horseshit. I don't want to hear it."

"Okay, okay. I understand where you're coming from. That wasn't my intention anyway," he said. "When we spoke on the phone, I mentioned the business about this guy Shine. I was thrown by his death. It really shook me, I can tell you. I know you didn't take me seriously at the time, but I'm telling the truth. I talked to him last week and told him the same stuff I'm telling you. He said he'd check into a couple of matters. I thought maybe the guy was going to give me a break. When I heard he was dead, it scared the hell out of me. I feel like I'm playing chess with an invisible opponent and he just made a move. I'm getting boxed in here and I don't see a way out."

"Wait a minute. Did you think Morley Shine would do something your own attorney couldn't manage?"

"Hiring Foss on this one was a big mistake. Civil work doesn't interest him. Maybe he's burned out or maybe he's just tired of representing me. He's strictly painting by the numbers, doing what's expected, as far as I can see. He's got some investigator on it—one of those guys who generates a lot of paper, but doesn't inspire much confidence."

"So why don't you fire him?"

"Because they'll claim all I'm doing is impeding due process. Besides, I've got no money left. What little I have goes to pay my attorney, plus the upkeep on the house. I don't know what Kenneth Voigt thinks he's going to get out of the deal even if he makes this thing stick."

"I'm not going to argue the merits of the case. This is pointless, Mr. Barney. I understand you have problems—"

"Hey, you're right. I didn't mean to get off on that stuff. Here's the point: This case goes into court, all it's going to do is make both these attorneys rich. But Voigt's not going to back off. The guy's after my blood, so there's no way he'll agree to walk off with a handshake and a check for big bucks, even if I had it. But I'll tell you one thing—and here's what I do have—I've got an alibi."

"Really," I said, my voice flat with disbelief.

"Yes, really," he said. "It's not airtight, but it's pretty solid."

"Why didn't it come up during the criminal trial? I've read the transcripts. I don't remember any mention of an alibi."

"Well, you better go back and read the transcripts again because the testimony's right there. Guy named Angeloni. He put me miles from the crime scene."

"And you never testified in your behalf?"

He shook his head. "Foss wouldn't let me. He didn't want the prosecution to get a crack at me and it turned out he played it smart. He said it'd be 'counterproductive' if I took the stand. Hell, maybe he thought I'd alienate the jury if I got up there."

"Why tell me about it?"

"To see if I can put a stop to this before it goes to trial. The meter's ticking. Time is short. I figure my only chance is to make sure Lonnie Kingman knows the cards he's got out against him. Maybe he can talk to Voigt and get him to drop his suit."

"Have Herb Foss talk to Lonnie! That's what attorneys are supposed to do."

"I've asked him to do that. The guy is jerkin' me around. I finally decided it's time to circumvent the man."

"So you're tipping me off to your own attorney's *defense?*"

"That's right."

"Are you suicidal?"

"I told you I'm desperate. I can't go through this again. You don't have to take my word for it. Check the facts yourself," he said. "Now, do you want to hear me out or not?"

What I wanted was to bang my forehead against the steering wheel till it bled. Maybe the self-inflicted pain would help me clear my thought processes. Actually, I have to confess I was hooked. If nothing else, knowing Herb Foss's strategy would give Lonnie a big advantage, wouldn't it? "Jesus, all right. What's the story?" I said.

"Look, I know people don't believe I was out jogging the night Isabelle was killed, but I can tell you where I was. At one-forty, I was at the southbound off-ramp at San Vicente and the One-oh-one, which is probably eight miles from the house. If Iz was killed between one and two, there's no way I could have done it and still ended up at that intersection when I did. I mean, I've been running for years and I'm in pretty fair shape, but I'm not *that* good."

"How can you be so sure of the time?"

"I was running for time. That's how I train. And I'll tell you who else was there: Tippy Parsons, Rhe's daughter, driving a little pickup, and she was very upset. She came barreling down the off-ramp and turned left on San Vicente."

"Did she see you?"

"She nearly ran me down! I'm not sure she realized it, but she nearly knocked me ass over teakettle coming off the exit. I looked at my watch because I knew my times would be screwed up and it pissed me off."

"Did *anyone* see you?"

"Sure. Some guy working on a busted water main. They had a crew out there. You probably don't remember, but we had some heavy rainstorms over Christmas that year. With the ground saturated, the soil was shifting and those old pipes were disintegrating everyplace."

"You said the alibi wasn't airtight. What's that supposed to mean?"

He smiled slightly. "If you're dead or in federal custody, *that's* airtight. A hotshoe like Kingman can always find a way to twist facts. All I'm saying is, I was miles away and I've got a witness. And he's an honest, hardworking guy, not some piece of shit like what's-his-face, McIntyre."

"What about Tippy? She's never said a word about this as far as I know. Why didn't you confront her?"

"What the hell for? I figured if she'd seen me, she'd have spoken up by now. And even if she spotted me, it's my word against hers. She was sixteen years old and hysterical about something. She might have just broken up with her boyfriend, or her cat might have died. The bottom line is, I was miles from the house when Isabelle was killed. I didn't even know what had happened until an hour later when I jogged past the house again. All the cop cars were there, the place was blazing with lights—"

"What about the repair crew? Will they support your claim?"

"I don't see why not. The guy took the stand before. Fellow by the name of Angeloni. He's on the list of witnesses, probably right up at the top. He saw me for sure and I know he saw her truck. She scared me so bad I had to sit on the curb and get my heart back to normal. It took me five or six minutes until I was okay again. By then, I said to hell with it and headed on home."

"And you told the cops this?"

"Go read the report. Cops figured me for the murder so they didn't pursue it."

I was silent for a moment, wondering what to make of it. Two days ago, his claims would have seemed preposterous. Now I wasn't sure. "I'll pass this on to Lonnie when I talk to him. That's the best I can do." Jesus, was I going to have to go out and corroborate his alibi?

He started to say more and then seemed to think better of it. "Fine. You do that. That's really all I'm asking. I appreciate your time," he said. His eyes met mine briefly. "I thank you for this."

"It's all right," I said.

He returned to his car. I watched him in the rearview mirror while he started the engine and backed out of the drive. He pulled away and I listened to the sound of his transmission as he shifted gears. Curious story. Something rang a bell, but I couldn't think what it was. Was Tippy Parsons really at the intersection? It seemed as if there must be a way to find out. I remembered reading about the storm coming through about that time.

I started the VW and pulled away from the curb, heading for the appointment with his ex-wife.

The Santa Teresa Medical Clinic, where Laura Barney worked, was a small wood-frame structure in the shadow of St. Terry's Hospital, which was two doors away. The exterior was plain—ever so faintly shabby—the interior pleasant, but leaning toward the low-budget. The chairs in the waiting room had molded blue plastic seats and metal legs linked together in units of six. The walls were yellow, the floors a marbleized vinyl tile, tan with white streaks. There was a wide wooden counter at one end of the room. On the far side, through the wide archway, I could see four desks, straight-backed office chairs, telephones, typewriters . . . nothing high-tech, streamlined, or color-coded. The rear wall was lined with tan metal file cabinets. I gathered, from the scattering of toddlers, pregnant women, and wailing infants, that this was a combination maternity and well-baby facility. It was almost closing time and the patients still waiting had probably been backed up for an hour. Children's toys and ripped magazines were strewn across the floor.

I moved to the counter, spotting Laura Barney by her name tag, which read "L. Barney, R.N." She wore a white pants-suit uniform and white crepe-soled shoes. I judged her to be somewhere in her early forties. She had reached an age where she could still achieve the same fresh good looks she'd enjoyed ten years earlier—it just took a lot more makeup and the effect probably wore off after an hour or two. At this time of day, the layers of foundation and loose powder had become nearly translucent, showing skin underneath that was reddened from cigarette smoke. She looked like a woman who'd been forced to go out into the workplace and wasn't at all happy with the necessity.

She was currently in the process of instructing a new employee, probably the same young girl I'd spoken to on the phone. Laura was counting out money like a bank teller, flicking bills through her fingers almost faster than the eye could see, turning each bill so it was right side up. If she came across a denomination that was out of place, she would slide it into the proper sequence. "Every bill should face in the same direction and they should be arranged with the smallest bills in front. Ones, fives, tens, twenties," she was saying. "That way you'll never inadvertently make change with a ten-dollar bill when you mean to use a one. Look at this. . . ." She fanned them out like a magician performing a card trick. I almost expected her to say, "Pick a bill, any bill. . . ." Instead, she said, "Are you listening?"

"Yes, ma'am." The young woman might have been nineteen, fifteen pounds overweight, with dark curly hair, flushed cheeks, and dark eyes glinting with suppressed tears.

L. Barney, R.N., opened the cash drawer again and removed an unruly wad of bills, which she held out silently. The young clerk took them. Self-consciously, she began to sort through the handful of bills, turning one upright in an awkward imitation of Laura Barney's expertise. Several denominations were out of sequence and she held the wad against her chest while she tried to straighten them out, dropping two fives in an attempt to get them in the correct order. She stammered an apology, stooping quickly to retrieve them. Laura Barney watched her with a slight smile, eyes nearly glittering with the urge to snatch the money back and do it for her. She must have itched to demonstrate the smooth, seamless effort with which an experienced cashier could perform so elementary a task. The absorption with which she watched seemed to make the girl more clumsy.

Her own manner was brisk, efficient. She'd picked up a ballpoint pen, which she was clicking impatiently. She wasn't going to waste a lot of time and sympathy. Get 'em in, get 'em out. Payment is expected at the time services are rendered. Her smile was pleasant but fixed and probably ran only for the few seconds necessary to register the chill underneath. If you tried to complain later to the clinic doctor you'd be hard-pressed to put your finger on her failings. I'd dealt with people like her before. She was all form and no content, a stickler for detail, an avid enforcer of the rules and regulations. She was the kind of nurse who assured you your tetanus shot would feel like a little bee bite when in truth it'd raise a knot on your arm the size of a doorknob.

She looked up at me and the fixed smile returned. "Yes?"

"I'm Kinsey Millhone," I said. I half expected her to hand me a clipboard with a medical history to be completed.

"Just a moment, please," she said. Her manner suggested that I'd made an unreasonable demand for immediate service. She finished dealing with the clerk and then called two patients in rapid succession. "Mrs. Gonzales? Mrs. Russo?"

Two women rose from their respective chairs. One carried a swaddled infant, the other had a toddler affixed to one hip. Both had pre-school-age children in addition. Laura Barney held open the wooden gate that separated the waiting area from the corridor leading back to examining rooms. The two women and accompanying children passed in front of her, thus emptying the waiting room. She continued to hold the gate open. "You want to come with me?"

"Oh, sure."

She picked up two charts, like menus, and herded us into the rear, issuing instructions in rapid Spanish. Once everyone had been ushered into examining rooms, she continued on down the hall, crepe soles squeaking on the tile floor. The room she showed me into was a nine-by-nine generic office with one window, a scarred wooden desk, two chairs, and an intercom, the kind of setting where you're apt to receive the bad news about the lab tests they just ran. She shut the door and motioned to one chair while she cranked open the window and took a seat herself. She removed a pack of Virginia Slims and a pack of matches from her uniform pocket and lit a cigarette. She glanced surreptitiously at her watch, while pretending to adjust the band. "You came to ask about David. What exactly did you want to know?"

"I take it you're not on friendly terms with him."

"I get along with him fine. I hardly see the man."

"You also testified at his murder trial, didn't you?"

"Generally, I'm used to demonstrate what an unscrupulous bastard he is. You haven't read the transcripts?"

"I'm still in the process of reviewing all the paperwork. I was hired Sunday night. I've got a lot of ground to cover yet. It would be helpful if you could fill in some of the facts from your perspective."

"The facts. Well, let's see now. I met David at a party . . .

well, it was nine years ago this month. How's that for touching? I fell in love with him and we were married six weeks later. We'd been married about two years when he was offered a position with Peter Weidmann's firm. Of course, we were thrilled."

I interrupted. "How did that come to pass?"

"Through a friend of a friend. We were living in Los Angeles, very interested in getting out. David heard Peter had an opening so he applied. We'd been in Santa Teresa all of two months when Isabelle came on board. David didn't even like her. I thought she was very bright and very talented. I was the one who insisted we befriend her. After all, she was the light of Peter's eye. He was her mentor, in effect. It wasn't in David's best interest to be competitive when she was assigned to work on all the high-visibility projects. I encouraged David to cultivate her both socially and professionally so I guess you could say I engineered their entire relationship."

"How did you find out about their affair?"

"Simone let something slip. I forget now what it was, but suddenly everything made sense. I knew David had been distant. It was common knowledge that Isabelle and Kenneth were having problems. It took me a while to put two and two together, that's all. None so blind, et cetera. I confronted him, like a fool. I wish now I'd kept my mouth shut."

"Why is that?"

"I forced his hand. Their relationship didn't last. If I'd had the presence of mind to ignore what was happening, the affair might have blown over."

"Do you think he killed her?"

"It had to be someone who knew her pretty well." The intercom buzzed abruptly. She depressed the button. "Yes, Doctor."

The doctor sounded like he was calling from a public telephone booth. "We're going to do a pelvic on Mrs. Russo. Could you come in?"

She said "Yes, sir" to him and then to me, "I have to go. Anything else you want is going to have to wait."

She held the door open for me and I passed through.

Within seconds she was gone and I was left to find my own way out. I went back to my car and sat there for a minute while I dug my wallet from the depths of my leather shoulder bag. I removed all the paper money and carefully rearranged the bills, turning them so they all faced in the same direction, ones in front, a twenty bringing up the rear.

I drove back to the office and parked my car in Lonnie's slot, taking the stairs two at a time up to the third floor. If Ida Ruth was surprised to see me back, she kept it to herself. I unlocked my office and started going through the files, which were somewhat better organized, but still loosely arranged on every available surface. I found the file I was looking for and moved over to the desk, where I clicked on the light and settled down in my swivel chair.

What I pulled out were the photocopies of the six-year-old newspapers I'd pulled in preparation for canvassing the Barneys' neighbors. Sure enough, for the days in question there was ample reference to the heavy rainfall over most of California. There was also mention of emergency crews from the public works department working overtime to repair the rash of burst water pipes. The same weather pattern had spawned a minor crime spree—felons running amok, apparently stimulated by the shift in atmospheric conditions. I flipped through the pages, scanning item after item. I wasn't really sure what I was looking for . . . a link, some sense of connection to the past.

The questions were obvious. If Tippy Parsons could support David Barney's alibi, why hadn't she stepped forward with the information years ago? Of course, she might not have been there. He might have seen someone else or he might have manufactured her presence to suit his own purposes. If she *was* there, she might not have seen him—there was always that chance—but placing her at the scene would certainly lend credibility to his claims. And what about the guy Barney claimed was at the scene? Where was he in all this?

I reached for the telephone and dialed Rhe Parsons, hoping to catch her in her studio. The number rang four times, five, six. On the seventh ring she answered, sounding breathless and out of sorts. "Yes?"

"Rhe, this is Kinsey Millhone. Sorry to disturb you. It sounds like I caught you right in the middle of your work again."

"Oh, hi. Don't worry about it. It's my own fault, I guess. I should get a portable telephone and keep it out in the studio. Sorry for all the heavy breathing. I'm really out of shape. How are you?"

"I'm fine, thanks. Is Tippy there by any chance?"

"No. She works until six tonight. Santa Teresa Shellfish. Is there something I could help you with?"

"Maybe so," I said. "I was wondering where she was the night Isabelle was killed."

"She was home, I'm sure. Why?"

"Well, it's probably nothing, but somebody thought they saw her driving around in a pickup."

"A pickup? Tippy never had a pickup."

"It must be a mistake then. Was she with you when the police called?"

"You mean, about Isabelle's death?" There was a moment of hesitation, which I should have taken as a warning, but I was so intent on the question, I forgot I was dealing with a m-o-t-h-e-r. "She was living with her father during that period," she said with care.

"That's right. So you said. I remember that now. Did *he* have a truck?"

Dead silence. Then, "You know, I really resent the implications here."

"What implications? I'm just asking for information."

"Your questions sound very pointed. I hope you don't mean to suggest she had anything whatsoever to do with what happened to Iz."

"Rhe, don't be silly. I'd never suggest such a thing. I'm trying to disconfirm a report. That's all it is."

"What report?"

"Look, it's probably nothing and I'd rather not get into it. I can talk to Tippy later. I should have done that in the first place."

"Kinsey, if somebody's making some claim about my daughter, I'm entitled to know. Who said she was out? That's an outrageous accusation."

"*Accusation?* Wait a minute. It's hardly an accusation to say she was driving around in a pickup truck."

"Who told you such a thing?"

"Rhe, I'm really not at liberty to divulge my sources. I'm working for Lonnie Kingman and that information is privileged. . . ." This was not true, but it sounded good. Lawyer-client privilege didn't extend to me and had nothing to do with any witnesses I might approach. I could hear her try to get a grip on her temper.

"I'd appreciate it if you'd tell me what's going on. I promise I won't ask about your sources, *if* that's really an issue."

I debated briefly and decided there was no reason to withhold the information itself. "Someone claims to have seen her out that night. I'm not saying it has any bearing on Isabelle's death, but it struck me as odd that she's never spoken up. I thought she might have mentioned something to you."

Rhe's tone was flat. "She's never spoken up because she wasn't out."

"Great. That's all I need to know."

"Even if she was, it's no business of yours."

I cupped a mental hand behind my mental ear. " 'Even if she was' meaning what?" I said.

"Nothing. It's a turn of phrase."

"Would you ask her to call me?"

"I'm not going to ask her to call you!"

"Do what you like, Rhe. I'm sorry for the interruption." I banged down the receiver, feeling my face suffuse with heat. What was her problem? I made a note about a subpoena for Tippy Parsons if there wasn't one already. I hadn't attached that much credence to Barney's claim until I heard Rhe's reaction.

I buzzed Ruth on the intercom and asked her to order me a complete new set of transcripts from the criminal trial. Then I slouched down in my swivel chair, my feet up on the desk, fingers laced in front of me, as I thought about developments. No doubt about it, things were looking bad. Between Morley's sloppy records and his untimely death, we had a mess on our hands. Lonnie's prime witness suddenly seemed unreliable and now it looked as though the defendant actually had an alibi. Lonnie wasn't going to like this. It was better that he hear it now than on the first day of the trial when Herb Foss made his opening remarks to the jury, but it still wasn't going to sit well. He was going to get home Friday night and spend a lovely weekend with his wife. He'd been married for eight months to a *kenpo* karate instructor whom he had successfully defended against charges of felonious assault. I'm still trying to find out what Maria actually did, but all Lonnie would tell me is that the court case stemmed from a rape attempt by a man now retired from active life. I pulled my wandering thoughts back to the situation at hand. When Lonnie ambled into the office Monday morning, the dog-doo would start flying. Some of it was bound to land on me.

I went back through the list of prospective witnesses Lonnie'd acquired on discovery. A William Angeloni was listed, though his deposition hadn't been taken. I made a note of his address, checked the telephone book, and made a note of his number. I picked up the receiver and then set it down again. Better to do this in person so I could see what he looked like. Maybe he was some kind of sleazeball David Barney'd hired to lie for him. I shoved some papers in my briefcase and headed out again.

The address was over on the west side, the house a small stucco bungalow undergoing an extensive remodeling. The roof had been peeled back and the walls on one side had been ripped out. Big sheets of cloudy plastic were nailed across the studs, protecting whatever portions of the house remained untouched. Lumber and cinder block were neatly stacked to one side. There was a big dark blue Dumpster sitting in the drive, filled with broken drywall and ancient two-by-fours sporting bent and rusty nails. It looked as if the laborers had all left for the day, but there was a guy standing in the yard with a beer can in one hand. I parked my car across the street and got out, crossing to the borders of his now-scruffy lawn. "I'm looking for Bill Angeloni. Is that you, by any chance?"

"That's me," he said. He was in his midthirties, extraordinarily good-looking—dark, straight hair worn slightly long and brushed to one side, dark brows, dark eyes, strong nose, dimples, and a manly chin that probably took six swipes of a razor to shave properly. He wore jeans, muddy work boots, and a blue denim shirt with the sleeves rolled up. The hair on his forearms was dark and silky. He smelled of damp soil and metal. He looked like an actor who'd star in some movie about a doomed love affair between an heiress and a park ranger. I thought it was probably inappropriate to fling myself against him and bury my nose in his chest.

"Kinsey Millhone," I said, introducing myself. We shook hands briefly and then I told him who I worked for. "I just had a chat with David Barney and he mentioned your name."

Angeloni shook his head. "I can't believe that poor son of a bitch has to go to court again." He finished his beer, crushed the can, and fired a jump shot, tossing the empty container in the Dumpster with a plunking sound. He said "Two points" and made crowd sounds with his fist against his mouth. He had a nice smile, unpretentious.

"This time it's wrongful death," I said.

"Jesus. What about double jeopardy? Isn't that what it's called? I thought you couldn't be tried twice."

"That applies to criminal. This is civil."

"I'm glad I'm not him. You want a beer? I just got home from work and I always suck down a few. This place is a mess. You better watch out for loose nails."

"Sure, I'll have one," I said and followed him toward the kitchen, which I could see clearly through the plastic. His butt was cute, too. "How long has this been going on?"

"The remodel? About a month. We're adding a big family room and a couple bedrooms for the kids."

Scratch the wedding, I thought as we pushed into the kitchen.

He took two beers from a six-pack and popped the tops on both. "I gotta fire up the barbecue before Julianna gets home with the little rug rats in tow. My turn to cook," he said, dimpling.

"How many kids?"

He held up one hand and wiggled his fingers.

"Five?"

"Plus one in the hatch. They're all boys. We're looking for a little girl this time."

"Are you still with the water department?"

"Ten years in May," he said. "You're a private investigator? What's that like?"

I talked idly about my work while he dumped the ashes from the Weber grill. He had a flat electrical starter that he plugged into an extension cord, mounding on charcoal briquettes, which he rearranged with a set of long metal pincers. I knew I should press for information. All I needed was confirmation of David Barney's whereabouts the night of the murder—the possible identification of Tippy Parsons, too—

but there was something hypnotic about all the homely activity. I'd never been with a man who'd cared enough to fire up a Weber grill on my behalf. Lucky Julianna.

"Could you tell me about the night you saw David Barney?"

"There wasn't much to it. We were out digging up the street, trying to find a broken pipe. It had been pouring for days, but it wasn't raining right then. I heard a thump and looked up to see this guy in a running suit sprawled in the street. A pickup was turning left onto San Vicente and I guess it nearly nailed him. He picked himself off the pavement, limped over to where we were, and sat down on the curb. He was shaken, but not hurt. Mostly mad, you know how it is. We offered to call the paramedics, but he wouldn't hear of it. He sat till he caught his breath and then he took off again, kind of slow and limping. The whole business lasted maybe ten minutes or so."

"Did you see the driver of the truck?"

"Not really. It was some young girl, but I didn't get a clear look at her face."

"What about the license number? Did you catch that?"

He shrugged apologetically. "I never even thought to look. The truck was white. I know that."

"You remember the make?"

"Ford or Chevy, I'd guess. American, at any rate."

"How'd you find out who David Barney was? Did he introduce himself?"

"Not at the time. He got in touch with us later."

"How'd he know who you were?"

"He tracked us down through the department. Me and my buddy James. He knew the date, time, and location so it wasn't that tough."

"Can James confirm this?"

"Sure. We both talked to the guy."

"At the time Mr. Barney got in touch with you, did you know about his wife's murder?"

"I'd been reading about it in the paper. I didn't realize the connection until he told us who he was. Jesus, that was nasty. Did you hear about that?"

"That's why I'm here. The guy still swears he didn't do it."

"Well, I don't see how he could. He was miles away."

"You remember the time?"

"About one forty-five. Might have been a little earlier, but I know it wasn't later because I looked at my watch just as he was taking off."

"Didn't it seem odd to see someone out jogging at one-thirty in the morning?"

"Not a bit. I'd seen him jog along the same path the night before. Emergency work you see all kinds of things."

"You testified at the murder trial, didn't you?"

"Sure."

"What about this round? Will you testify again?"

"Absolutely. Glad to do it. The poor guy needs a break."

I thought back through Barney's story, trying to remember what he'd told me. "What about the cops? Did the police ever interview you?"

"Some homicide detective called and I told him everything I knew. He thanked me and that's the last I ever heard from him. I tell you one thing—they didn't like him. They had him tried and convicted before they even got him into court."

"Well, thanks. I appreciate this. You've given me a lot of information. I may get back in touch if I have any other questions." I gave him my card in case he thought of anything else. I crossed back to the car and sat there, making notes while his comments were still fresh.

I thought about Tippy, searching my memory. Rhe had told me those were Tippy's teen alcoholic years. If I remembered right, Rhe had sent her off to live with her father because she and Tippy had had a falling-out. So how would Rhe know if she was in that night or not? Maybe I should just ask Tippy and be done with it. "Do the obvious" had always been a working motto of mine.

I glanced at my watch. It was 5:35. Santa Teresa Shellfish

145

was out on the wharf—maybe two blocks from my apartment, which was not that far away. I headed for home, across the backside of Capillo Hill. If Tippy *was* out that night, I couldn't see why she wouldn't own up to it six years later. Maybe nobody'd ever asked her. What a happy thought.

I parked the car in front of my place, dropped off the briefcase, plucked my windbreaker off the back of the door, and walked the two blocks to the wharf. The sun wasn't quite down yet, but the light was gray. The days were marked by this protracted twilight, darker shadows gathering among the trees while the sky remained the color of polished aluminum. When the sun finally set, the clouds would turn purple and blue and the last rays of sun would pierce the gloom with shafts of red. Winter nights in California were usually in the fifties. Summer nights were often in the fifties, too, which offered the possibility of sleeping year-round beneath a quilt.

12

To my right, a quarter mile away, the long slender arm of the breakwater curved around the marina, cradling sailboats in its embrace. The ocean pounded on the seawall, the force of the waves creating a plume of spray that marched from right to left. Beneath my feet, the pier seemed to shift as if nudged by the waves. The smell of creosote rose like a vapor from heavy timbers saturated to a dark gloss. The tide was high, the water looking like dark blue ink, silver pilings stained with the damp. Cars rolled down the pier, the rumble of loose boards creating a continuous tremor along the length. The fog was rolling in, bringing with it the damp cloudy smell of seaweed. Darkened boats were moored just offshore in the poor man's marina.

On the wharf itself the lights were bright and cold against the deep shadows of the ocean. The Marina Restaurant was ablaze, the air around it scented with the savory aroma of char-grilled fish and steaks. One of the parking valets jogged toward the end of the small lot to retrieve a vehicle. Gulls rested on the peaked roof of the bait-and-tackle shop, the shingled slopes banked with snowy white where the bird droppings had collected. The fishermen were packing up, tackle boxes clattering, while a pelican waddled about beady-eyed, still hoping for a handout.

Looking back toward the town, I could see the dark hills carpeted in pinlights. The 101 was laid out parallel to the beach, the California coastline running an unexpected east to west in this stretch. Across the four lanes of the freeway, the one- and two-story buildings in the business district marched away up State Street, diminishing in size like a drawing lesson in perspective. The palm trees were a dark contrast to the artificial light that was just beginning to bathe the downtown with its pale yellow glow.

The sun had now dropped from sight but the sky wasn't completely dark, more the ashen charcoal gray of a cold hearth. I reached the brown-painted board-and-batten building that housed the Santa Teresa Shellfish Company. Eight wooden picnic tables and benches were secured to the pier out in front. The three employees inside were young, late teens—in Tippy's case, early twenties—wearing blue jeans and dark blue Santa Teresa Shellfish T-shirts, each emblazoned with a crab. Along the front of the booth, seawater tanks were filled with live crabs and lobsters, stacked on one another like sullen marine spiders. A glass-fronted display case was lined with crushed ice, fish steaks and fillets arranged in columns of gray and pink and white. A counter ran along the back. Beyond it, through a doorway, I could see an enormous fish being gutted.

They were in the process of closing up, cleaning off the counters. I watched Tippy for almost a minute before she spotted me. Her motions were brisk, her manner efficient as she waited to take an order from a fellow standing at the display case. "Last order of the day. We gotta close in five minutes."

"Oh, right. I'm sorry. I didn't realize it was so late." He scooted down toward the tank, pointing to the hapless object of his appetite. She tucked her order pad in her pocket and plunged her arm into the murky water. Deftly, she seized the lobster across its back and held it up for his approval. She plunked it on the counter, grabbed up a butcher knife, and inserted the tip just under the shell where the tail connected to the spiny body. I glanced away at that moment, but I could hear the thump as she pounded the knife and neatly severed the creature's spine. What a way to earn a living. All that death for minimum wage. She popped it in the steamer, slammed the door shut, and set the timer. She turned to me without really registering my identity.

"Can I help you?"

"Hi, Tippy. Kinsey Millhone. How are you?"

I saw belated recognition flash in her eyes. "Oh, hi. My mom just called and said you'd be stopping by." She turned her head. "Corey? Can I go now? I'll close out the register tomorrow if you can do it today."

"No problem."

She turned to the fellow waiting for his lobster dinner. "You want something to drink?"

"You have iced tea in a can?"

She took the can out of the cooler, put ice in a paper cup, and extracted a small container of coleslaw from the back of the display case. She scribbled the total across the bottom of the ticket and tore it off with a flourish. He gave her a ten and she made change with the same efficiency. The timer on the steamer began to peep. She reached in with a hot mitt and flopped the steaming lobster on the paper plate. The guy had barely picked up his order when she untied her apron and let herself out the Dutch door to one side.

"We can sit out at one of the tables unless you'd rather go somewhere else. My car's parked over there. You want to talk in the car?"

"We can head in that direction. I really just have a couple of quick questions."

"You want to know what I was doing the night Aunt Isabelle was killed, right?"

"That's right." I was sorry Rhe'd had time to call her, but what could I do? Even if I'd come straight over, Rhe would have had time to telephone. Now Tippy'd had sufficient warning to cook up a good cover story . . . if she needed one.

"God, I've been trying to think. I was at my dad's, I guess."

I stared at her briefly. "You don't remember anything in particular about that night?"

"Not really. I was still in high school back then so I probably had a lot of homework or something."

"Weren't you out of school? That would have been the day after Christmas. Most kids have the week off between Christmas and New Year's."

She frowned slightly. "I must have been, if you say so. I really don't remember."

"You have any idea what time your mother called to tell you about Isabelle?"

"Uh, I think about an hour later. Like an hour after it happened. I know she called from Aunt Isabelle's, but I think she'd been there awhile with Simone."

"Is there any chance you might have been out around one or one-thirty?"

"One-thirty in the morning? You mean, like doing something?"

"Yes, a date, or maybe just bopping around with your buddies."

"Nunh-unh. My dad didn't like me to be out late."

"He was home that night?"

"Sure. Probably," she said.

"Do you remember what your mom said when she called?"

She thought about that for a moment. "I don't think so. I mean, I remember she woke me up and she was crying and all."

"Does your dad have a truck?"

"Just for work," she said. "He's a painting contractor and he carries his equipment in the pickup."

"He had the same truck back then?"

"He's had the same truck ever since I can remember. He needs a new one actually."

"The one he has is white?"

That one slowed her down some. A trick question perhaps? "Yeah," she said reluctantly. "Why?"

"Here's the deal," I said. "I talked to a guy who says he saw you out that night, driving a white pickup."

"Well, that's screwed. I wasn't *out*," she said with just a touch of indignation.

"What about your father? Maybe he was using the truck."

"I doubt it."

"What's his name? I can check it out with him. He might remember something."

"Go ahead. I don't care. It's Chris White. He lives on West Glen, down around the bend from my mom."

"Thanks. This has been real helpful."

That seemed to worry her. "It has?"

I shrugged and said, "Well, sure. If your father can verify the fact that you were home, then this other business is probably just a case of mistaken identity." I allowed just the tiniest note of misgiving to sound in my voice, a little bird of doubt singing in a distant part of the forest. The effect wasn't lost.

"Who was it said they saw me?"

"I wouldn't worry about it." I looked at my watch. "I better let you go."

"You want a ride or something? It's no trouble." Little Miss Helpful.

"I walked over from my place, but thanks. I'll talk to you later."

"Night," she said. Her parting smile seemed manufactured, one of those expressions clouded with conflicting emotions. If she didn't watch it, those little frown marks were going to require cosmetic surgery by the time she was thirty. I glanced back and she gave me a halfhearted wave, which I returned in kind. I headed back down the pier, thinking "Liar, liar, pants on fire" for reasons I couldn't name.

I dined that night on Cheerios and skim milk. I ate, bowl in hand, standing at the kitchen sink, while I stared out the window. I made my mind a blank, erasing the day's events in a cloud of chalk dust. I was still troubled about Tippy, but there was no point in trying to force the issue. I turned the whole business over to my subconscious for review. Whatever was bugging me would surface in time.

At 6:40, I left for my appointment with Francesca Voigt. Like most of the principal players in this drama, she and Kenneth Voigt lived in Horton Ravine. I drove west on Cabana and up the long, winding hill past Harley's Beach, entering the Ravine through the back gate. The entire Horton property was originally two ranches of more than three thousand acres each, combined and purchased in the mid-1800s by a sea captain named Robertson, who, in turn, sold the land to a sheep rancher named Tobias Horton. The land has since been subdivided into some 670 wooded parcels, ranging from one-and-a-half-acre to fifty-acre estates, laced with thirty miles of bridal paths. An aerial view might show that two houses, seemingly miles apart, were really only two lots away from each other, separated more by winding roads than by any actual geographical distance. In truth, David Barney wasn't the only one whose property was in range of Isabelle's.

The Voigts lived on what must have been six or eight acres, if one could judge property lines by the course of the fifteen-foot hedges that snaked along the road and cut down along the hillside. The shrubs and flower beds were all carefully tended, towering eucalyptus grouped together at the fringes. The driveway was a half circle with a bed of thickly planted pansies massed together in its center, a blend of deep reds and purples, petals vibrant in the glow of the landscape lighting. Off to the right, I could see horse stalls, a tack room, and an empty corral. The air smelled faintly musty, a blend of straw, dampness, and the various by-products of horse butts.

The house was built low to the ground, white frame and white painted brick, with long brick terraces across the front, dark green plantation shutters flanking the wide mullioned windows. I left my car out in the drive, rang the bell, and waited. A stolid white maid in a black uniform opened the door. She was probably in her fifties and looked foreign for some reason—facial structure, body type . . . I wasn't really sure what it was. She didn't quite make eye contact. Her gaze came to rest right about at my clavicle and remained there as I indicated who I was and told her that I was expected. She made no reply, but she conveyed with body language that she comprehended my utterings.

I followed her across the polished white marble foyer and then trudged with her across white carpeting as thick and pristine as a heavy layer of snow. We passed through the living room—glass and chrome, not a knickknack or a book in sight. The room had been designed for a race of visiting giants. All the furniture was upholstered in white and over-size: big plump sofas, massive armchairs, the glass coffee table as large as a double-bed mattress. On a ponderous credenza, there was a bowl filled with wooden apples as big as softballs. The effect was strange, re-creating the same feelings I had when I was five. Perhaps, unbeknownst to myself, I'd begun to shrink.

We walked down a hallway wide enough for a snowplow. The maid paused at a door, knocked once, and opened it for me, staring politely at my sternum as I passed in front of her. Francesca was seated at a sewing machine in a room propor-tioned for humans, painted buttery yellow. One entire wall was covered by a beautifully organized custom-built cabinet that opened to reveal cubbyholes for patterns, bolts of fabric, trim, and sewing supplies. The room was airy, the interior light excellent, the pale hardwood floors sanded and varnished.

Francesca was tall, very slender, with short-cropped brown hair and a chiseled face. She had high cheekbones, a strong jawline, a long straight nose, and a pouting mouth with a pronounced upper lip. She wore loose white pants of some beautifully draped material, with a long peach tunic top that she had belted in heavy leather. Her hands were slender, her fingers long, her nails tapered and polished. She wore a se-ries of heavy silver bracelets that clanked together on her wrist like chains, confirming my suspicion that glamour is a burden only beautiful women are strong enough to bear. She looked like she would smell of lilacs or newly peeled oranges.

Francesca smiled as she held her hand out and we intro-duced ourselves. "Have a seat. I'm nearly finished. Shall I have Guda bring us some wine?"

"That would be nice."

I glanced back in time to see Guda's gaze drop to Francesca's belt buckle. I took this to mean she had heard and would obey. She nodded and moved out of the room on crepe-soled shoes. "Does she speak English?" I asked once the door was shut.

"Not fluently, but well enough. She's Swedish. She's only been with us a month. The poor dear. I know she's homesick, but I can't get her to say much about it." She sat back down at her machine, taking up a length of gauzy blue fabric that she had gathered across one end. "I hope this doesn't seem rude, but I don't like leaving work undone."

Expertly she turned the piece, adjusted a knob, and zig-zagged a row of stitches across the other end. The sewing machine made a soothing, low-pitched hum. I watched her, feeling mute. I didn't know enough about sewing to form a question, but she seemed to sense my curiosity. She looked up with a smile. "This is a turban, in case you're wondering. I design headwear for cancer patients."

"How did you get into that?"

She added a small square of Velcro and stitched around the edges, her knee pressing the lever that activated the machine. "I was having chemotherapy for breast cancer two years ago. One morning in the shower, all my hair fell out in clumps. I had a lunch date in an hour and there I was, bald as an egg. I improvised one of these from a scarf I had on hand, but it was not a great success. Synthetics don't adhere well to skulls as smooth as glass. The idea for the business got me through the rest of the chemo and out the other side. Funny how that works. Tragedy can turn your life around if you're open to it." She sent a look in my direction. "Have you ever been seriously ill?"

"I've been beaten up. Does that count?"

She didn't respond with the usual exclamations of surprise or distaste. Given what she'd been through, merely being punched out must have been an easy fix. "Call me if it ever happens to you again. I have cosmetics designed to cover any kind of bruise you might have. Actually, I have a whole line of products for the ravages of fate. The company's called Head-for-Cover. I'm the sole proprietress."

"How's your health at this point?"

"I'm fine. Thanks for asking. These days, so many of us make it. It's not like the past when any cancer diagnosis meant death." She added the other small square of Velcro, flipped the foot up, removed the garment, and clipped the threads. Deftly, she adjusted the turban around her head. "What do you think?"

"Very exotic," I said. "Of course, *you* could wrap your head in toilet paper and you'd look okay."

She laughed. "I like that. Disposable head wraps." She made a note to herself and then set the turban aside, shaking her hair loose. "Done. Let's go out on the terrace. We can use the heaters if it seems chilly."

The wide stone terrace at the rear of the house looked out over Santa Teresa with a view toward the mountains. In the town below, lights had come on, delineating the layout of city blocks in a grid of streets and intersections. We settled into wicker chairs padded with plump cushions in floral chintz. The pool was lighted, a glowing blue-green rectangle with a spa at one end. Wisps of steam drifted off the surface, creating a mild breeze scented with chlorine. The surrounding grass looked lush and dark, the house behind us a blaze of yellow.

Guda appeared with a bottle of chardonnay nestled in a cooler, two long-stemmed wineglasses, and a tray of assorted canapés. I put my feet up on a wicker ottoman and fed myself little treats. Guda served us water crackers as crisp and flavorless as slate, mounded with soft herb cheese infused with garlic. On the plate with the crackers, she'd arranged tuna-filled cherry tomatoes and flaky homemade cheese sticks. After a sumptuous supper of cold cereal, I had to restrain an urge to snatch at the food like a snarling mongrel. I tried a sip of the wine, a silky blend of apple and oak. Kick-ass private eyes hardly ever live like this. We're the Gallo aficionados of the jug-wine set. "Count your blessings," I said.

Francesca surveyed her surroundings as if seeing all of it through my eyes. "Odd that you should say that. I've been thinking of leaving Kenneth. I'll wait till the trial is over, but after that I can't think what would keep me."

I was surprised at the admission. "Really?"

"Yes, really. It's a matter of priorities. Winning his love used to seem so important. Now I realize my happiness has nothing to do with him. He did hang in there with me through the surgery and the chemo and I'm grateful for that. I've heard a lot of horror stories about spouses who can't handle the prolonged stresses of a battle with cancer. I'm the one who's undergone a shift. Gratitude doesn't make a marriage. I woke up one morning and realized I was out of control."

"What triggered the realization?"

"Nothing in particular. It's like being in a dark room with the lights suddenly flipped on."

"What will you do if you leave?"

"I'm not sure, but something simple. I probably feel the same sense of amazement at this place that you do. I wasn't born with money. My father was a grade-school custodian and my mother worked in a pharmacy, stocking shelves with dental floss and Preparation H."

I laughed at the image. "Well, you look like you belong here."

"I'm not sure that's a compliment. I'm a quick study. When Kenneth and I first started dating, I watched everybody in his crowd. I figured out who was really classy and did whatever they did, with embellishments of my own, of course, just to make it look original. It's just a series of tricks. I could teach you in an afternoon. It's mildly entertaining, but none of it really matters much."

"Don't you enjoy having all these things?"

"I suppose so. I mean, sure, it's nice, but I spend most days in the sewing room. I could do that anywhere."

"I can't believe you're saying this. I heard you were nuts about Kenneth."

"I thought so myself and I was, I suppose. I was totally infatuated with him in the early days of our relationship. It was like a form of craziness. I thought he was powerful and strong, knowledgeable, in charge. Very manly," she said in a deep voice. "He fit my image of what a man should be, but you know what? He turns out to be rather shallow, which is not to say I'm so profound myself. I woke up one day and thought, What am I doing? Really, it's a struggle to be around him. He doesn't read. He doesn't think about things. He has opinions, but no ideas. And most of his opinions he picks up from *Time* magazine. He's so shut down emotionally, I feel as if I'm living in a desert."

"That sounds like half the people I know," I said.

"Maybe so. It might just be me, but he's changed a lot in the last few years. He's so brooding and dark. You've met him, haven't you? What's your reaction?"

I shrugged noncommittally. "He seems okay," I said. I'd only met the man once, and though I didn't find him attractive, I'm wary about bad-mouthing one spouse to another. For all I knew, they'd reconcile later in the evening and all my remarks would be reported verbatim. I shifted the subject. "Speaking of reactions, what was yours to Isabelle? I take it that's part of what your testimony will be about."

Francesca made a face, stalling her response until she'd topped off our wineglasses. "That and the infamous gun disappearance. All of us were there. As for Isabelle, she was a bit like Kenneth in some ways—charismatic on the surface, but under that, nothing. She did have talent, but as a person she was hardly warm or caring."

"You and Kenneth connected up once she got involved with David Barney?"

"That's right. We met at a fund-raiser at the Canyon Country Club. I was there with a friend and someone introduced us. Isabelle had just left him and he was like a whipped puppy dog. You know how it is. There's nothing quite as irresistible as a man in need of help. I was smitten. I pursued him. I thought I'd die if I couldn't have him. I must have looked like a fool. People tried to warn me, but I wouldn't listen. The entire six months his divorce was in process, I nurtured and patted and petted and cooed."

"It worked, didn't it?"

"Oh, I got what I wanted for all the good it did me. We were married the minute he was free, but his heart wasn't in it. He was hung up on her, which kept me hooked for a long time. I knew he didn't love me so how could I resist the man? I had to fawn and grovel. I had to please him at any cost. Nothing worked, of course. I mean, basically he prefers women as rejecting of him as he is of me. Isn't that pathetic? He'll probably fall head over heels in love with me the day I serve him with papers."

"What changed your attitude, the cancer?"

"That was part of it. The lawsuit has had an effect on top of that. I realized, at a certain point, it was just his way of staying connected to Isabelle. He can be embroiled. He can suffer on her behalf. If he can't have her, at least he can have the money. That's what matters now."

"What about their daughter, Shelby? How does she fit into this?"

"She's a nice enough kid. He hardly sees her. She's hardly ever home. Once in a while—like, every two or three months —he goes to visit at school and takes her out for the day. They go to dinner and a movie and that's the extent of it."

"I thought the legal wrangle was for her, to make sure she's provided for."

"That's what he says, but it's ridiculous. He's heavily insured. If anything happened to him, Shelby'd get a million dollars. How much more does she need? He refuses to let go. That's all the lawsuit's about. God, do I sound like a bitch?"

"Not at all. I appreciate your candor. Frankly, I didn't think you'd tell me much."

"I'll tell you anything you want to know. I don't care about these people. I used to feel protective. There was a time I never would have said a word. I'd have felt guilty and disloyal. Now, it doesn't seem to matter much. I've begun to see them with great clarity. It's like being nearsighted and suddenly getting prescription lenses. It's all so much clearer it's astonishing."

"Such as what?"

"Just what I've been talking about . . . Kenneth and his obsession. The hard part for him was once Isabelle left him, he had to face the fact she was a flaming narcissist. With her dead, he can go back to believing she was perfect."

"She and David met at work, isn't that how it went? Peter Weidmann's firm?"

"That's right. It was 'love at first sight,' " she said, making quote marks with her fingers.

"You think he killed her?"

"David? I'm not sure how to answer that. During the trial I sure thought so, but now it doesn't make much sense to me. I mean, look at the situation. Hasn't it ever struck you how 'feminine' the murder was? It's always amazed me that no one's mentioned this before. I don't mean to sound sexist, but there's something almost 'sanitary' about shooting through a peephole. Maybe it's my prejudice, but I tend to think when men kill it's more forceful and direct. They strangle or bludgeon or stab. It's real straight-ahead stuff. Even when they shoot, there's nothing devious or sneaky. It's like BOOM! They blow your head off. They don't tiptoe around."

"In other words, men tend to kill face-to-face."

"Exactly. Shooting through a peephole, you wouldn't have to take responsibility. You wouldn't even have to *look* at the blood, let alone risk getting spattered. David may have harassed her, but he was so visible about it. Right out there in front of God and everyone. Restraining orders, cops, the two of them screaming at each other on the phone. If he really killed her, he must have known he'd be the first person they'd suspect. And that business about his jogging? What a stupid idea. Believe me, the man is smart. If he were guilty, then surely he could have come up with a better alibi than that."

"But what are you suggesting? You must have some kind of theory or you wouldn't be saying this."

"Simone's a possibility."

"Isabelle's twin *sister?*"

"Don't you know the story?"

"I guess not," I said, "but I'm sure you'll fill me in."

She laughed at my tone. "Well, look at the story. They never really got along. Isabelle did as she pleased and poor Simone was left holding the bag half the time. Isabelle had everything—ostensibly, at any rate—looks, talent, a darling child. Ah, and that was the sticking point. Simone wanted to have a baby more than anything. Her biological clock had jumped to daylight saving time. I take it you've met her?"

"I talked to her yesterday."

"And you noticed the limp?"

"Sure, but she didn't mention it and I didn't ask."

"It was a terrible accident. Isabelle's fault, I'm afraid. This was maybe seven years ago, about a year before Iz died. Iz was drunk and brought the car home and left it in the driveway without pulling the emergency brake. The car started to roll down that horrendous hill, smashing through the underbrush, picking up momentum. Simone was down at the mailbox and it crashed right into her. Crushed her pelvis, crushed her femur. They said she'd never walk again, but she defied 'em on that. You probably saw for yourself. She's really doing very well."

"But no kids."

"That's right. And what made things worse, she was engaged at the time and her fiancé broke it off. He wanted a family. End of story. For Simone, it really was the final straw."

I watched her face, trying to compute the impact of the information. "It's worth some thought," I said.

I stopped off at Rosie's on the way back to my place. I don't usually hang out in bars, but I was restless and I didn't feel like being alone just then. At Rosie's, I can sit in a back booth and ponder life's circumstances without being stared at, picked up, hit on, or hassled. After the wine at Francesca's, I thought a cup of coffee might be in order. It wasn't really a question of sobering up. The wine at Francesca's was as delicate as violets. The white wine at Rosie's comes in big half-gallon screw-top jugs you can use later to store gasoline and other flammable liquids.

Business was lively. A group of bowlers had come in, a noisy bunch of women who were

13

celebrating their winning of some league tournament. They were parading around the room with a trophy the size of *Winged Victory,* all noise and whistles and cheers and stomping. Ordinarily Rosie doesn't tolerate rowdies, but their spirits were contagious and she didn't object.

I got myself a mug and filled it from the coffeepot Rosie keeps behind the bar. As I slid into my favorite booth, I spotted Henry coming in. I waved and he took a detour and headed in my direction. One of the bowlers was feeding coins into the jukebox. Music began to thunder through the bar along with cigarette smoke, whoops, and raucous laughter.

Henry slid in across from me and put his head down on his arm. "This is great. Noise, whiskey, smoke, life! I'm so sick of being with that hypochondriac of a brother. He's driving me nuts. I swear to God. His health regimen occupied our entire day. Every hour on the hour, he takes a pill or drinks a glass of water . . . flushing his system out. He does yoga to relax. He does calisthenics to wake up. He takes his blood pressure twice a day. He uses little strip tests to check his urine for glucose and protein. He keeps up a running account of all his body functions. Every minor itch and pain. If his stomach gurgles, it's a symptom. If he breaks wind, he issues a bulletin. Like I didn't notice already. The man is the most self-obsessed, tedious, totally boring human being I've ever met and he's only been here one day. I can't believe it. My own brother."

"You want a drink?"

"I don't dare. I couldn't stop. They'd have to check me into detox."

"Has he always been like that?"

Henry nodded bleakly. "I never really saw it till now. Or maybe in his dotage he's become decidedly worse. I remember, as a kid, he had all these accidents. He tumbled out of trees and fell off swings. He broke his arm once. He broke a wrist. He stuck a pencil in his eye and nearly blinded himself. And the cuts. Oh my God, you couldn't let him near a knife.

He had all kinds of allergies and weird things going wrong with him. He had a spastic salivary gland . . . he really did. Later, he went through a ten-year period when he had all his internal organs taken out. Tonsils and adenoids, appendix, his gallbladder, one kidney, two and a half feet from his upper intestine. The man even managed to rupture his spleen. Out it came. We could have constructed an entire human being out of the parts he gave up."

I glanced up to find Rosie standing at my shoulder, taking in Henry's outburst with a placid expression. "He's having a breakdown?"

"His brother's visiting from Michigan."

"He don' like the guy?"

"The man is driving him nuts. He's a hypochondriac."

She turned to Henry with interest. "What's the matter with him? Is he sick?"

"No, he's not sick. He's neurotic as hell."

"Bring him in. I fix. Nothing to it."

"I don't think you quite understand the magnitude of the problem," I said.

"Is no problem. I can handle it. What's the fellow's name, this brother?"

"His name is William."

Rosie said "William" as she wrote it in her little notebook. "Is done. I fix. Not to worry."

She moved away from the table, her muumuu billowing out around her like a witch's cape.

"Is it my imagination or has her English gotten worse lately?" I asked.

Henry looked up at me with a wan smile.

I gave his hand a maternal pat. "Cheer up. Is done. Not to worry. She'll fix."

I was home by 10:00, but I didn't feel like continuing my cleaning campaign. I took my shoes off and used my dirty socks to do a halfhearted dusting of the spiral staircase as I went up to bed. Works for me, I thought.

. . .

I was awakened in the wee hours with a telegram from my subconscious. "Pickup," the message read. Pickup what? My eyes came open and I stared at the skylight above my bed. The loft was very dark. The stars were blocked out by clouds, but the glass dome seemed to glow with light pollution from town. The message had to be related to Tippy's presence at the intersection. I'd been brooding about the subject since David Barney first brought it up. If he was inventing, why attach her name to the story? She might have had a ready explanation for where she was that night. If he was lying about the incident, why take the chance? The repair crew had seen her, too . . . well, not really her, but the pickup. Where else had I come across mention of a pickup truck?

I sat up in bed, pushed the covers back, and flipped on the light, wincing at the sudden glare. In lieu of a bathrobe, I pulled on my sweats. Barefoot, I padded down my spiral staircase, turned on the table lamp, and hunted up my brief-case, sorting through the stack of folders I'd brought home from the office. I found the file I was looking for and carried it over to the sofa, where I sat, feet tucked up under me, leafing through old photocopies of the *Santa Teresa Dispatch*. For the third time in two days, I scanned column after column of smudgy print. Nothing for the twenty-fifth. Ah. On the front page of the local news for December 26 was the little article I'd seen about the hit-and-run fatality of an elderly man, who'd wandered away from a convalescent hospital in the neighborhood. He'd been struck by a pickup truck on upper State Street and had died at the scene. The name of the victim was being withheld, pending notification of his next of kin. Unfortunately, I hadn't made copies of the newspapers for the week after that so I couldn't read the follow-up.

I pulled out the telephone book and checked the yellow pages under Convalescent Homes & Hospitals. The sublistings were Homes, Hospitals, Nursing Homes, Rest Homes, and Sanitariums, most of which simply cross-referenced each other. Finally, under Nursing Homes, I found a comprehensive list. There was only one such facility in the vicinity of the accident. I made a note of the address and then turned the lights out and went back up to bed. If I could link that pickup to the one Tippy's father owned, it might go a long way toward explaining why she was reluctant to admit she was out. It would also verify every word David Barney'd said.

In the morning, after my usual three-mile run, a shower, breakfast, and a quick call to the office, I drove out to the South Rockingham neighborhood where the old man had been killed. At the turn of the century, South Rockingham was all ranchland, flat fields planted to beans and walnuts, harvested by itinerant crews who traveled with steam engines, cookhouses, and bedroll wagons. An early photograph shows some thirty hands lined up in front of their cumbersome, clanking machinery. Most of the men are mustachioed and glum, wearing bandannas, long-sleeved shirts, overalls, and felt hats. Staunchly they lean on their pitchforks while a dusty noon sun beats down. The land in such pictures always looks pitiless and flat. There are few trees and the grass, if it grows at all, seems patchy and sparse. Later aerial photos show the streets radiating from a round hub of land, like the spokes of a wagon wheel. Beyond the outermost rim, the squares of young citrus groves are pieced together like a quilt. Now South Rockingham is a middle-class neighborhood of modest custom-built homes, half of which went up before 1940. The balance were constructed during a miniboom in the ten years between 1955 and 1965. Every parcel is dense with vegetation, houses crowded onto every available lot. Still, the area is considered desirable because it's quiet, self-contained, attractive, and well kept.

I located the convalescent hospital, a one-story stucco structure flanked on three sides by parking lots. From the outside, the fifty-bed facility looked plain and clean, probably expensive. I parked at the curb and climbed four concrete steps to the sloping front walk. The grass on either side was in its dormant stage, clipped short, a mottled yellow. An American flag hung limply from a pole near the entrance.

I pushed through a wide door into a comfortably furnished reception area, decorated in the style of one of the better motel chains. Christmas hadn't surfaced yet. The color scheme was pleasant: blues and greens in soothing, noninflammatory shades. There was a couch covered in chintz and four matching upholstered chairs arranged so as to suggest intimate lobby chats. The magazines on the end tables were neatly fanned out in an arc of overlapping titles, *Modern Maturity* being foremost. There were two ficus trees, which on closer inspection turned out to be artificial. Both might have used a dusting, but at least they weren't subject to whitefly and blight.

At the desk, I asked to see the nursing home director and was directed to the office of a Mr. Hugo, halfway down the corridor to my left. This wing of the building was strictly administrative. There were no patients in evidence, no wheelchairs, gurneys, or medical paraphernalia. The very air was stripped of institutional odors. I explained my business briefly, and after a five-minute wait Mr. Hugo's personal secretary ushered me into his office. Nursing home directors must have a lot of holes to fill in their appointment books.

Edward Hugo was a black man in his midsixties with a curly mix of gray and white hair and a wide white mustache. His complexion was glossy brown, the color of caramel. The lines in his face suggested an origami paper folded once, then flattened out again. He was conventionally dressed, but something in his manner hinted at obligatory black-tie appearances for local charity events. He shook my hand across his desk and then took his seat again while I took mine. He folded his hands in front of him on the desk. "What can I help you with?"

"I'm trying to learn the name of a former patient of yours,

an old gentleman who was killed in a hit-and-run accident six years ago at Christmas."

He nodded. "I know the man you're referring to. Can you explain your interest?"

"I'm trying to verify an alibi in another criminal matter. It would help if I could find out if the driver was ever found."

"I don't believe so. Not to my knowledge, at any rate. To tell you the truth, it's always bothered me. The gentleman's name was Noah McKell. His son, Hartford, lives here in town. I can have Mrs. Rudolph look up his number if you'd like to speak to him."

He went on in this manner, direct, soft-spoken, and mat-ter-of-fact, managing in our ten-minute conversation to give me all the information I needed in a carefully articulated format. According to Mr. Hugo's account of the night in question, Noah McKell had removed his IV, disconnected himself from a catheter, dressed himself in his street clothes, and left his private room by the window.

I was surprised by that. "Aren't the windows kept locked?"

"This is a hospital, Miss Millhone, not a prison. Bars would constitute a danger if a fire ever broke out. Aside from that, we feel our patients benefit from the fresh air and a view of some greenery. He'd left the premises on two other occasions, which was a matter of great concern to us, given his condition. We considered the use of restraints for his pro-tection, but we were reluctant to do so and his son was ada-mant. We kept the bed rails up and we had one of the aides look in on him every thirty minutes or so. The floor nurse went in at one-fifteen and discovered the empty bed.

"Of course, we moved very quickly once we realized he was gone. The police were alerted and the security people here began an immediate search. I received a call at home and came right over. I live up on Tecolote Road so it didn't take me long. By the time I got here, we'd heard about the hit-and-run. We went to the scene and identified the body."

"Were there any witnesses?"

"A desk clerk at the Gypsy Motel heard the impact," he said. "She ran out to help, but the old man was dead. She was the one who called the police."

"You remember her name?"

"Not offhand. Mr. McKell would be able to tell you, I'm sure. It's possible she's still there."

"I think I better talk to him in any event. If the driver was found, I won't need to take any more time with the questions."

"I'd like to think he would have told us if that were the case. Please give me a call and let me know what you find. I'd feel better about it."

"I'll do that, Mr. Hugo, and thanks for your help."

I called Hartford McKell from a public telephone booth that was located near a hamburger stand on upper State. There was no point in going back to the office when the accident site was only two blocks away. I pulled out a pen and a notepad, prepared to take notes.

The man who answered the phone identified himself as Hartford McKell. I explained who I was and the information I needed. He sounded like a man without humor—direct, impatient, with a tendency to interrupt. In the matter of his father's death, he made it clear he wasn't interested in commiseration of any sort. The story seemed to spill out, his anger unabated by the passage of time. I refrained from comment except for an occasional question. The driver of the vehicle had never been found. The Santa Teresa Police had conducted an intense investigation, but aside from the skid marks, there hadn't been much in the way of evidence at the scene. The only witness—the motel desk clerk, whose name was Regina Turner—had given them a sketchy description of the truck, but she hadn't seen the license plate. It was one of those traffic fatalities that outraged the community and he'd offered a twenty-five-thousand-dollar reward for information leading to the arrest and conviction of the driver. "I brought Pop down here from San Francisco. He'd had a stroke and I wanted him close. You know where he was headed every time he left? He thought he was still up there, just a few blocks from his place. He was trying to get home because he was worried about his cat. Animal's been dead now for fifteen years, but Pop wanted to make sure his cat was okay. It makes me crazy to think someone's gotten away with murder."

"I can understand—"

He cut me off. "No one can understand, but I'll tell you one thing: You don't run over an old man and then drive on without a backward glance."

"People panic," I said. "One in the morning, the streets are virtually empty. The driver must have figured no one would ever know the difference."

"I don't really care what the reasoning was. I want to nail the son of a bitch. That's all I care about. Do you have a line on this guy or not?"

"I'm working on it."

"You find the driver and that twenty-five thousand is yours."

"I appreciate that, Mr. McKell, but that's not my prime interest in the matter. I'll do what I can."

We terminated the conversation. I got back in the car and drove the two blocks down State Street to the intersection where the elder McKell was killed. The + formed by the two cross streets was bounded by a motel, a vacant lot, a garden-style medical complex, and a small bungalow, which looked like a private residence, converted now to real estate offices. The Gypsy was an unassuming block of units, with all the architectural grace of a two-by-four, bounded on all sides by strip parking. An accordion-pleated metal portico jutted out in front. The two-story building had probably gone up in the sixties and seemed to rely heavily on concrete and aluminum-frame sliding doors. I parked in the portion of the motel lot set aside for registration. The office was glass-enclosed with ready-made mesh drapes blocking out the early afternoon sun. A blinking neon sign out in front alternated NO and VACANCY.

The woman behind the desk was big—not the giant but the large economy size. She had a big well-shaped nose, a large mouth rosy with lipstick, ice-blond hair pulled up in a braid on top, the coil of hair wrapped around itself until it formed a rope. She wore mauve glasses with beveled frames, the lower portion of both lenses smudged slightly with peachy foundation makeup. Her street clothing was obscured by a pink nylon smock of the sort worn by cosmetologists.

I took out a business card and placed it on the counter. "I wonder if you can help me. I'm looking for Regina Turner."

"Well, I'll try. I'm Regina Turner. Glad to meet you," she said. We shook hands. Our conversation was put on hold briefly when the telephone rang; she held one finger up as a digital marker while she verified some reservations. "Sorry for the interruption," she said when she'd hung up. She gave my card a perfunctory glance and then focused a sharp look on my face. "I don't answer questions about the folks who stay here."

"This is about something else," I said. I was halfway through my explanation when I saw her clock out. I could tell she'd already leapfrogged to the end of the conversation. "You can't help me," I said.

"I wish I could," she replied. "The police talked to me just after that poor old man was killed. I felt awful, honestly, but I told them everything I know."

"You were working that night?"

"I work most nights. Anymore, you can't get good help, especially around the holidays. I was right here at the desk when the accident occurred. I heard the squeal . . . that's an awful sound, isn't it? And then a thump. This pickup must have barreled around the big bend out there at sixty miles an hour. Truck caught the old fella in the crosswalk and flung him right up in the air. Looked like somebody been gored by a bull. You know how in the movies you see 'em get tossed like that? He came down so hard I could hear him hit the pavement. I looked out the front window and saw the truck pull away. My view of the intersection is excellent. You can see for yourself. I dialed nine-one-one and went out to see what I could do. By the time I got to him, the poor man was dead and the truck had taken off."

"Do you remember the time?"

"Eleven minutes after one. I had that same little digital clock sitting on the counter and I remember seeing that the time was one-one-one, which is my birthday. January eleventh. I don't know why, but something like that will stick with you for years afterwards."

"You didn't see the driver?"

"Not at all. I saw the truck. It was white, with some kind of dark blue logo on the side."

"What kind of logo?"

She shook her head. "That I can't help you with."

"This is good though. Every little bit helps," I said. There were probably only six thousand white trucks in California. The particular pickup involved in the accident might have been junked, repainted, sold, or taken out of state. "I appreciate your time."

"You want your card back?" she asked.

"You keep it. If you think of anything that might help, I hope you'll get in touch."

"Absolutely."

At the door, I hesitated. "Do you think you could identify the truck if I brought you some pictures?"

"I'm pretty sure I could. I may not remember it, but I think I'd recognize it if I saw it again."

"Great. I'll be back."

I returned to my car, aware of the little rush of hope I was having to subdue. I wanted to make an assumption here. I'm not a fool. I could see the probability that the white pickup truck involved in McKell's death was the same pickup that had bumped into David Barney approximately thirty minutes later and approximately eight miles away. There was too much at stake to jump to conclusions about who was driving it. Better to play it by the book as I'd been taught. The first step was to take pictures of several similar vehicles, including the truck owned by Tippy's father, Chris White. If Regina Turner could make a positive ID, then I'd have something concrete to start with. Step two, of course, was to figure out who had actually been at the wheel.

I went back to the office, again parking my car in Lonnie's slot. As usual, I took the stairs two at a time all the way to the third floor and spent a moment leaning against the wall gasping while I recovered my breath. I let myself into the law office through the plain unmarked door halfway down the hall from the entrance. It was an exit we used as a shortcut to the bathrooms across the hall from us. Originally, the third floor consisted of six separate suites, but Kingman and Ives had gradually assimilated all the available space except for the rest rooms, located in the corridor so as to be accessible to the public.

I unlocked my door and checked for mes-

14

sages. Louise Mendelberg had called, wondering if there was any way I could get Morley's keys back to them that afternoon. Morley's brother was due in and they wanted to make his car available. Any time would be fine if it was not too much trouble.

I decided to get my desk organized and then Xerox the files I'd picked up at Morley's house so I could return them at the same time. I sat down and went through the mail, putting bills in one pile and junk in the wastebasket. I opened all the bills and did some quick mental arithmetic. Yes, I could pay them. No, I couldn't quit my job and retire on my savings, which were nil anyway. I peeked at the balance in my checkbook and paid a bill or two just for sport. Take that, Gas & Electric. Ha ha ha! Foiled again, Pacific Telephone.

I gathered up the stack of folders and went down to use the copier. It took me thirty minutes to Xerox all the data and reassemble the files. I put the originals back in the grocery bag Louise had given me for the purpose, set aside a box of files to review at home, and then removed my 35-millimeter camera from the bottom drawer and loaded it with a roll of color film. I hauled out the telephone book and looked up Tippy's father in the yellow pages under Painting Contractors. Chris White's company, Olympic Painting, was featured in a substantial quarter-page box ad that listed his name, company address, telephone number, license number, and the scope of his work: "complete painting services, water blasting (we provide the water), custom colors and matching, fine wood finishing, wallpapering." I jotted down all the information relevant to my purposes. After I dropped off the files, I was going to go find five or six white pickup trucks and take pictures. I had a quick chat with Ida Ruth and then went out by the same door I'd entered, hauling the grocery bag and a cardboard box.

The drive to Colgate was pleasant enough. The day was clear and chilly and I flipped on the VW's heater so that it would blow hot breath on my feet. I was beginning to give serious thought to the possibility that David Barney might be innocent. Up to this point, we'd all been operating on the assumption that he was the one who shot Isabelle. He was the obvious suspect, with the means, the motive, and the opportunity to have killed her, but murder is an aberrant deed, often born of passions distorted by obsessiveness and torment. Emotion doesn't travel in a straight line. Like water, our feelings trickle down through cracks and crevices, seeking out the little pockets of neediness and neglect, the hairline fractures in our character usually hidden from public view. Beware the dark pool at the bottom of our hearts. In its icy, black depths dwell strange and twisted creatures it is best not to disturb. With this investigation, I was once again uncomfortably aware that in probing into murky waters I was exposing myself to the predators lurking therein.

Morley Shine's driveway was empty, the red Ford rental car nowhere in evidence. The Mercury still sat on the grass in the side yard. I stood on the porch and studied the pattern of rust spots on the fender while I waited for someone to answer my knock. Two minutes passed. I knocked again, this time louder, fervently hoping that I wasn't rousing Dorothy Shine from her sickbed. After five minutes, it seemed safe to assume that no one was home. Maybe Louise had taken Dorothy to the doctor or the two had been required to put in an appearance at the funeral home to pick out a casket. Louise had told me they left the back door unlocked so I made my way around the side of the house, passing through the breezeway between the garage and house. The door to the utility room was not only unlocked, but slightly ajar. I rapped again at the glass and then waited the requisite few minutes in case someone was home. Idly, I surveyed the premises, feeling vaguely depressed. The property looked as though it was ready for the auction block. The backyard was neglected, the winter grass dry and frost-cropped. In the weedy flower beds that bordered the yard, last autumn's annuals were still planted in dispirited clumps. Once-sunny marigolds had turned brown, a garden of deadheads with leaves limp and withered. Morley probably hadn't sat out here with his wife for a year. I could see a built-in brick barbecue, the cook surface so rusty the rods on the grill nearly touched each other.

I pushed the door all the way open and let myself in. I wasn't sure why I was being so meticulous. Ordinarily, I'd have popped right in and had a look around, just because I'm nosy and the opportunity was presented. This time I really didn't have the heart to snoop. Morley was dead and what remained of his life should be safe from trespass. I left the grocery bag of files on the washing machine as instructed. The very air smelled medicinal, and from the depths of the house I could hear the ticking of a clock. I pulled the door shut behind me and returned to the street.

As I took out my car keys, I realized with a flash of irritation that I'd meant to leave Morley's keys in the bag with the files. I turned on my heel and retraced my steps at a half trot. As I passed the Mercury, I could feel my steps slow. Wonder what he has in the trunk, my bad angel said. Even my good angel didn't think it would hurt to look. I'd been given ready access to both his offices. I had his very keys in hand and in the interest of thoroughness it seemed only natural to check his vehicle. It was hardly trespassing when I had implied permission. By the time I reached that phase of my rationalization, I had popped open the trunk and was staring down in disappointment at the spare tire, the jack, and an empty Coors beer can that looked as if it had been rolling around in there for months.

I closed the trunk and moved around to the driver's side, where I unlocked the car and searched the interior, starting with the rear. The seats were covered in a dark green suede cloth that smelled of cigarette smoke and ancient hair oil. The scent conjured up a quick flash of Morley and a sharp jolt of regret. "God, Morley, help me out here," I said.

The floor in the back netted me a gas receipt and a bobby

pin. I wasn't really sure what I was looking for . . . an invoice, a pack of matches, or a mileage log, anything to indicate where Morley had gone and what he'd done in the course of his investigation. I slid into the driver's seat and placed my hands on the steering wheel, feeling like a kid. Morley's legs were longer than mine and I could barely reach the brakes. Nothing in the map pockets. Nothing on the dashboard. I leaned over to my right to check the glove compartment, which I found crammed with junk. This was more my speed. Cleaning rags, a lady's hairbrush, more gas receipts (all local and none recent), a crescent wrench, a pack of Kleenex, a used windshield wiper blade, proof of insurance and registrations for the last seven years. I removed item after item, but nothing seemed pertinent to the case itself.

I returned everything to the glove compartment, tidying the contents in the process. I straightened up and put my hands on the steering wheel again, imagining I was Morley. Half the time when I search I don't find jackshit, but I never give up hope. I'm always thinking something's going to come to light if I just open the right drawer, stick my hand in the right coat pocket. I checked the ashtray, which was still full. He'd probably spent a lot of time in the Merc. In this business, where you're on the road a lot, your car becomes a traveling office, a surveillance vehicle, the observation post for a nightlong stakeout, even a temporary motel if your travel funds run short. The Mercury was perfect, aging and nondescript, the sort of vehicle you might note in your rearview without really seeing it. I checked the car above eye level.

On the sun visor, he'd attached a "leather-finish" vinyl utility valet with a mirror, a slot for sunglasses, and a pencil and blank memo pad that looked unused. The valet was attached to the visor by two flimsy metal clamps. I reached up and pulled the visor down. On the underside, Morley'd slipped a six-inch strip of paper under one of the clamps. It was the perfect place to tuck such things; "To Do" lists, receipts for cleaning, parking lot tickets. The strip had been

179

torn from a perforated flap for one of the film envelopes used by a One-Hour Foto Mart in a Colgate shopping mall. The strip showed an order number, but no date, so it might have been up there for months. I slipped the paper in my pocket, got out of the car, and locked it up again. I completed the return trip to the utility porch, where I dropped the keys in the brown bag with the files I'd left.

I drove the five blocks to the mall. An Asian fellow, wearing rubber gloves, was visible through the plate glass window of the One-Hour Foto Mart, removing strips of film from the developer. Prints on a conveyor moved slowly down one side of the window and across the front. Fascinated, I paused, watching as a surprise fortieth birthday party progressed from cake and wrapped presents on a table to a crowd of grinning well-wishers looking smug and self-satisfied while the birthday boy in sweaty tennis togs pretended to be a good sport.

I was stalling, postponing the inevitable. I wanted the photo order to be pivotal. I wanted the pictures to relate to the investigation in some terribly meaningful and pithy way. I wanted to believe Morley Shine was as good a private eye as I'd always believed he was. Oh well. I pushed the door open and went in. Might as well get it over with. Chances were I'd be looking at a set of snapshots from his last vacation.

The interior of the shop smelled of acrid chemicals. The place was empty of customers and the young clerk who waited on me took no time at all coming up with the order. I paid $7.65 and he assured me that I'd be reimbursed for any prints I didn't like. I left the envelope sealed until I reached my car. I sat in the VW and rested the envelope on the steering wheel. Finally, I opened the top flap and slid the prints into the light.

I made a startled sound . . . not a real word, but something punctuated with an audible exclamation point.

There were twelve prints altogether, each marked at the bottom with last Friday's date. What I was looking at were six white pickup trucks, two views each, including one with a dark blue logo with five interlocking rings. The company was Olympic Painting Contractors; Chris White's name was printed underneath with a telephone number. Morley had been on the same track I was, but what did it mean?

I sorted back through the photographs. It looked as though he'd done exactly what I meant to do. He'd apparently visited various businesses and used-car lots around town and had taken pictures of six- and seven-year-old white pickups, some with logos, some without. In addition to Chris White's company truck, there was one utilized by a gardening firm and one used by a catering company with a camper shell on top. Clever touch. Because he'd incorporated a variety of trucks in the "lineup," it was possible that a more detailed recollection might be triggered from the one and only witness we had.

I stared out the car window, pondering the implications. If he'd talked to Regina Turner at the Gypsy Motel, she'd never mentioned it to me. Surely she'd have brought it up if she'd been queried twice about the same six-year-old fatal accident. But how else could he have known about the logo and color of the vehicle, if not from her? David Barney might have told him about the truck that nearly knocked *him* down. Morley might have thought to check old issues of the newspaper just as I had myself. Maybe he acquired a copy of the original police report on the hit-and-run and then decided to take the pictures with him when he interviewed the only witness. A description of the truck plus Regina's name and place of business would have been noted by the first officer on the scene. The problem was, I hadn't spotted the police report among the files I'd found, nor had I seen any photocopies of the newspapers to indicate that he was curious about other incidents on the night Isabelle was killed. When I'm working a case, I tend to take a lot of notes. If anything happened to me, the next investigator coming down the pike would know what I'd done and where I'd meant to go next. Clearly, Morley didn't work that way. . . .

Or did he?

I'd always given him credit for being both smart and efficient. The guy who trained me in the business was a nut about details, and since he and Morley had been partners, I'd assumed it was an attitude they shared. I suspect that's why I was so dismayed when I finally saw Morley's offices. It was the chaotic state of his paperwork that made me question his professionalism. What if he wasn't as disorganized as he seemed?

A sudden image intruded.

When I was a kid, there was a novelty item that circulated through our elementary school. It was a fortune-telling device, a "crystal ball" that consisted of a sealed sphere with a little window, the whole of it filled with dark water in which a many-sided cube floated. The cube had various messages written on it. You would pose a question and then turn the ball upside down in your hand. When you righted it, the cube in the water would float to the surface with one of the printed messages uppermost. That would be the answer to your query.

In my gut, I could feel a message begin to rise to the surface. Something was off here, but what? I thought about what David Barney'd said when he'd suggested Morley's death was a shade too convenient. Was there something to that? It was a question I couldn't stop and pursue at the moment, but it had a disquieting energy attached to it. I set the notion aside, but I had a feeling it was going to stick to me with a certain burrlike tenacity.

At least with the pictures, Morley had saved me a step, and I was grateful for that. I took comfort from the fact that we were thinking along the same lines. I could go straight back to the Gypsy and show these to Regina.

"Well, that was quick," she said when she caught sight of me.

"I was lucky," I said. "I came across a batch of snapshots that should do the job."

"I'll be happy to take a look."

"I have one question first. Did you ever hear from an investigator named Morley Shine?"

Her face clouded briefly. "Nooo, I don't think so. Not that I recall. In fact, I'm sure not. I'm good with names—my return customers like to be remembered—and his is unusual. I'd know if I'd talked to him, especially about this. What's the connection?"

"He was working on a case until two days ago. He died Sunday evening of a heart attack, which is why I was called in. It looks like he saw a link between the same two incidents."

"What was the other one? When you were here earlier, you said a near miss of some sort."

"A white pickup truck bumped a guy at an exit off the southbound One-oh-one. This was about one forty-five. He claims he knew the driver, though he had no idea there'd been a hit-and-run earlier." I held out the envelope. "Morley Shine dropped these off to be developed. If he meant to talk to you, he was probably waiting until he picked up the prints for ID purposes." I placed the envelope on the counter.

She adjusted her glasses and removed the twelve snapshots. She studied them thoughtfully, giving each picture her undivided attention before she laid it on the counter, making a line of trucks, like a motorcade that marched across the blotter. I watched for a reaction, but when Tippy's father's truck crossed her line of vision, there was no alteration in her expression, no remark indicating surprise or recognition. She studied the six trucks with care and then put an index finger on the Olympic Painting pickup. She said, "This is the one."

"You're sure of that."

"Positive." She picked up the print and held it closer. "I never thought I'd see this again." She flashed me a look. "Maybe we'll finally see someone brought to justice after all these years. And wouldn't that be nice."

I had a brief image of Tippy. "Maybe so," I said. "Anyway, you'll hear from the police as soon as I talk with them."

"Is that where you're off to?"

I shook my head reluctantly. "I have something else to do first."

I made a quick call to Santa Teresa Shellfish, but Tippy'd traded shifts and wasn't going to be in that day. I left the motel and headed for Montebello, hoping I could catch Tippy at home . . . preferably without her mother hovering in the background. In essence, I'd put the woman on notice. Rhe knew something was up, though she probably didn't have a way to guess just how serious it was.

West Glen is one of the primary arteries through Montebello, a winding two-lane road lined with tall hedges and low stone walls. Morning glories spilled over the fence tops in a waterfall of blue. The gnarled branches of the live oaks were laced together overhead, the sycamores interplanted with eucalyptus and acacia trees. Thick patches of hot pink geraniums grew by the road like weeds.

The small stucco cottage that Rhe and Tippy occupied was a two-bedroom bungalow built close to the road. I squeezed my car in on the shoulder and walked up the path to the porch, where I rang the bell. Tippy appeared almost instantly, shrugging into her jacket, purse and car keys in hand. She was clearly on her way out. She stared at me blankly with her hand on the doorknob. "What are you doing here?"

"I have a couple more questions, if you don't mind," I said.

She hesitated, debating, then she checked her watch. Her expression denoted a little impromptu wrestling match—reluctance, annoyance, and good manners doing takedowns. "God, I don't know. I'm meeting this friend of mine in about twenty minutes. Could you, like, really make it quick?"

"Sure. Can I come in?"

She stepped back, not thrilled, but too polite to refuse. She was wearing jeans and high-heeled boots, a portion of a black leotard visible under her blue denim jacket. Her hair was down today and it trailed halfway down her back, strands still showing waves where the French braid had been undone. Her eyes were clear, her complexion faintly rosy. Somehow it made me feel bad that she looked so young.

I took in the cottage at a glance.

The interior consisted of a combination living room/dining room, tiny galley-size kitchen visible beyond. The walls were hung with original art, probably Rhe's handiwork. The floors were done in Mexican paving tiles. The couch was upholstered in hand-painted canvas, wide brushstrokes of sky blue, lavender, and taupe, with lavender-and-sky-blue pillows tossed carelessly along its length. The side chairs were inexpensive Mexican imports, caramel-colored leather in a barrel-shaped rattan frame. There was a wood-burning fireplace, big baskets filled with dried flowers, lots of copper pots hanging from a rack in the kitchen area. Dried herbs hung from the crossbeams. Through French doors, I could see a small courtyard outside with a pepper tree and lots of flowering plants in pots.

"Your mom here?"

"She went up to the market. She'll be back in a minute. What did you want? I'm really really in a hurry so I can't take too long."

I took a seat on the couch, a bit of a liberty as Tippy hadn't really offered. She chose one of the Mexican chairs and sat down without enthusiasm.

I handed her the pictures without explanation.

"What're these?"

"Take a look."

Frowning, she opened the envelope and pulled out the prints. She shuffled through with indifference until she came to the Olympic Paint truck. She looked up at me with alarm. "You went and took a picture of my dad's pickup?"

"Another investigator took those."

"What for?"

"Your father's truck was seen twice the night your aunt

Isabelle was murdered. I guess the other P.I. meant to show the pictures to a witness for identification."

"Of what?" I thought a little note of dread had crept into her voice.

I kept my tone flat, as matter-of-fact as I could make it. "A hit-and-run accident in which an old man was killed. This was on upper State in South Rockingham."

She couldn't seem to formulate the next question, which should have been, Why tell me? She knew where I was headed.

I went on. "I thought we ought to talk about your whereabouts that night."

"I already told you I didn't go out."

"So you did," I said with a shrug. "So maybe your father was the one driving."

We locked eyes. I could see her calculate her chances of squirming out from under this one. Unless she fessed up to the fact that she was driving, she'd be pulling her father right into the line of fire.

"My dad wasn't driving."

"Were you?"

"No!"

"Who was?"

"How should I know? Maybe somebody stole the truck and went joyriding."

"Oh, come on, Tippy. Don't give me that. You were out in the truck and you fuckin' know you were so let's cut through the bull and get down to it."

"I was not!"

"Hey, face the facts. I feel for you, kiddo, but you're going to have to take responsibility for what you did."

She was silent, staring downward, her manner sullen and unresponsive. Finally she said, "I don't even know what you're talking about."

I nudged her verbally. "What's the story, were you drunk?"

"No."

"Your mom told me you'd had your license suspended. Did you take the truck without permission?"

"You can't prove any of this."

"Oh, really?"

"How are you going to prove it? That was six years ago."

"For starters, I have two eyewitnesses," I said. "One actually saw you pull away from the scene of the accident. The other witness saw you at the southbound off-ramp on San Vicente shortly afterward. You want to tell me what happened?"

Her gaze flickered away from mine and the color came up in her cheeks. "I want a lawyer."

"Why don't you tell me your side of it. I'd like to hear."

"I don't have to tell you anything," she said. "You can't make me say a word unless I have an attorney present. That's the law." She sat back in the chair and crossed her arms.

I smirked and rolled my eyes. "No, it's not. That's *Miranda*. The cops have to Mirandize you. I don't. I'm a private eye. I get to play by a different set of rules. Come on. Just tell me what happened. You'll feel better about it."

"Why would I tell you anything? I don't even like you."

"Let me take a guess. You were living at your dad's and he was out and these friends of yours called you up and just wanted to go out for a little while. So you borrowed the truck and picked them up and the three of you or the four of you, however many it was, were just messing around, drinking a couple of six-packs down at the beach. Suddenly it was midnight and you realized you better get home before your father did so you quick took everybody home. You were barreling home yourself when you hit the guy. You took off in a panic because you knew you'd be in big trouble if you got caught. How's that sound? Close enough to suit?"

Her face was still stony, but I could see that she was fighting back tears, working hard to keep her lips from trembling.

"Did anybody ever tell you about the fellow you hit? His

name was Noah McKell. He was ninety-two years old and he'd been staying at that convalescent hospital up the street. He had the wanderlust, I guess. His son told me he was probably trying to get home. Isn't that pathetic? Poor old guy used to live in San Francisco. He thought he was still up there and he was worried about his cat. I guess he forgot the cat had been dead for years. He was heading for home to feed it, only he never got there."

She put a finger to her lips as if to seal them. The tears began. "I've tried to be good. I really have. I'm AA and everything and I cleaned up my act."

"Sure you did and that's great. But your gut must send you little messages, doesn't it? Eventually, you'll get back into booze just to silence that voice."

Her voice shifted up into the squeaky range. "God, I'm sorry. I really am. I'm so sorry. It was an accident. I didn't mean to do it." She hugged herself, bending over, the sobs as noisy as those of a child, which is what she was. I watched with compassion, but made no move to comfort her. It wasn't up to me to make life easier. Let her experience remorse, all the grief and guilt. I didn't know that she'd ever let herself assimilate the full impact of what she'd done. The tears came in uncontrollable waves, great gut-wrenching sobs that seemed to shake her from head to toe. She sounded more like a howling beast than a young girl filled with shame. I let it happen, almost unable to look at her until the pain subsided some. Finally, the storm passed like a fit of helpless laughter that peters out at long last. She groped in her purse and pulled out a wad of tissues, using one to mop her eyes and blow her nose. "God." She clutched the fistful of tissues against her mouth for a moment. She nearly lost it again, but she collected herself. "I haven't had a drop of alcohol since the night it happened. That's been hard." She was feeling sorry for herself, maybe hoping to stimulate pity or compassion or amnesty.

"I'll bet it has," I said, "and I applaud that. You've done a lot of hard work. Now it's time to tell the truth. You can't skip over that and expect recovery to work."

"You don't have to lecture me."

"Apparently I do. You've had six years to think about this, Tootsie, and you haven't done the right thing yet. I'll tell you this: It's going to look a lot better if you walk into the police station of your own accord. I know you didn't mean to do it. I'm sure you were horrified, but the truth is the truth. I'll give you some time to think, but by Friday I intend to have a conversation with the cops. You'd be smart to get your butt in there and talk to them before I do."

I got up and slung my big leather bag across my shoulder. She made no move to follow. When I reached the front door, I looked back at her. "One more thing and then I'll leave you to your conscience. Did you see David Barney that night?"

She sighed. "Yes."

"You want to expand on that?"

"I nearly ran into him coming off the freeway. I heard this thump, and when I looked out the window, he was staring right at me."

"You do understand you could have cleared him years ago if you'd admitted that." I didn't wait for her response. She was beginning to sound martyred about the whole business and I didn't want to deal with that.

15

I stopped off at my place after I left Tippy and grabbed a hasty lunch, which I ate without much interest. There was precious little in the refrigerator and I was forced to open a can of asparagus soup, which I think I bought originally to put over something else. I've been told novice cooks are chronically engaged in this hoary ruse. Cream of celery soup over pork chops, baked at 350 for an hour. Cream of mushroom soup over meat loaf, same time, same temp. Cream of chicken soup over a chicken breast with half a cup of rice thrown in. The variations are endless and the best part is you have company once, you never see them again. Aside from the aforementioned, I can scramble eggs and make a fair tuna salad, but that's about it. I eat a lot of sandwiches, peanut-butter-and-pickle and cheese-and-pickle being two. I also favor hot sliced hard-boiled egg sandwiches on whole wheat bread with lots of salt and Best Foods mayonnaise. As far as I'm concerned, the only reason for cooking is to keep your hands busy while you think about something else.

What was bugging me at this point was this question of Morley's death. What if David Barney's paranoia was justified? He'd been right about everything else. What if Morley was getting too close to the truth and had been eliminated as a consequence? I was torn between the notion of murder as too farfetched and the worry that someone was actually getting away with it. I went back and forth, exploring the possibilities. His curiosity might well have been stimulated by his conversation with David Barney. Maybe he'd inadvertently stumbled across something significant. Had he been silenced? I could feel myself shy away from the idea. It was so damn melodramatic. Morley had died of a heart attack. The death certificate had been signed by his family doctor. I didn't doubt there were drugs that could trigger or simulate the symptoms of cardiac arrest, but it was hard to picture how such a drug might have been administered. Morley wasn't a fool. Given his health problems, he wasn't going to take medications not prescribed by his own physician. It almost had to be poison, but I hadn't heard the possibility mentioned. Who was I to step in and distress his ailing widow? She had problems enough and all I had to offer was conjecture.

I finished my soup, washed the bowl, and left it in the dish rack with my solitary spoon. If I kept up this cycle of cereal and soup, I could eat for a week without dirtying another dish. I wandered idly around the apartment, feeling restless and uneasy. I wanted desperately to talk to Lonnie, but I didn't see a way to do it, short of driving the hour up to Santa Maria. Ida Ruth seemed to feel he'd resent the intrusion, but I thought he should be apprised of what was going on. Currently, his case was in complete disarray, and I didn't see a way to clean it up before he came home. He was going to love me.

This was now Thursday afternoon. Morley's funeral was on Friday, and if I had questions to raise about the cause of death I was going to have to move quickly. Once he was buried, this whole issue would be buried with him. Since his death was attributed to natural causes, my guess was that nobody'd bothered to question his activities the last couple of days of his life. I still had no idea where he'd gone or whom he'd seen. The only thing I was sure about was that he'd taken those pictures. I was assuming his actions had been prompted by his conversation with David Barney, but I couldn't be certain. Maybe he'd talked to Dorothy or Louise about the case.

I put a call through to the house. Louise answered on the first ring. "Hi, Louise. This is Kinsey. You found the bag I left?"

"Yes, and thank you. I'm sorry we weren't here, but Dorothy wanted to go over to the funeral home to see Morley. We realized you'd stopped by as soon as we got back."

"How's Dorothy holding up?"

"About as well as could be expected. She's a pretty tough old bird. We both are if it comes to that."

"Uhm, listen, Louise, I know this is an imposition, but is there any way I could talk to the two of you this afternoon?"

"About what?"

"I'd really prefer to discuss it in person. Is Dorothy up for a visit?"

I could hear her hesitation.

"It's important," I said.

"Just a minute. I'll check." She put a hand over the mouthpiece and I could hear the murmur of their conversation. She came back on the line. "If you can make it brief," she said.

"I'll be out there in fifteen minutes."

For the third time in two days, I drove out to Morley's house in Colgate. The early afternoon sun was just making an appearance. December and January are really our best months. February can be rainy and it's usually gray. Spring in Santa Teresa is like spring anywhere else in the country. By early summer, we're swathed in a perpetual marine layer so that days begin in the bright white-gray of fog and end in a curious golden sunlight. So far December had been a blend of the two seasons, spring and summer alternating inexplicably from day to day.

Louise answered my knock and let me into the living room, where Dorothy had been ensconced on the couch.

"I'm going to make us a pot of tea," Louise murmured and then excused herself. Moments later, I could hear her rattling dishes as she took them from the cupboard.

Dorothy was still dressed in a skirt and sweater from her recent outing. She'd taken off her shoes and a quilt had been tucked around her legs for warmth. One narrow foot, looking as fragile as porcelain, extended from the swaddling. She and Louise might have looked more like sisters before her illness had drained her face of color. Both were small-boned with blue eyes and fine-textured skin. Dorothy was sporting a platinum-blond wig in a blowsy bedroom style. She caught my eye and smiled, reaching up to adjust the Dynel pouf. "I always wanted to be a blonde," she said ruefully and then held out her hand. "You're Kinsey Millhone. Morley told me all about you." We shook hands. Hers felt light and cold, as leathery as a bird's claw.

"Morley talked about me?" I said with surprise.

"He always thought you had great promise if you could learn to curb your tongue."

I laughed. "I haven't quite managed that, but it's nice to hear. I was sorry he and Ben never patched up their differences."

"They were both much too stubborn," she said with mock disgust. "Morley never could remember what they fought about. Have a seat, dear. Louise will bring us some tea in just a minute."

I chose a small chair covered in a tapestry. "I don't want to be a bother. I appreciate this. You must be tired."

"Oh, I'm used to that. If I fade, you'll just have to forgive me and carry on with Loo. We were just over at the funeral home for the 'viewing,' as they refer to it."

"How does he look?"

"Well, I don't think the dead ever look *good*. They seem flat somehow. Have you ever noticed that? Like they've had half the stuffing taken out," she said. Her tone was matter-of-fact, as if she were discussing an old mattress instead of the man she'd been married to for forty-odd years. "I hope that doesn't sound heartless. I loved the man dearly and I can't tell you what a shock it was to have him go like that. This past year, we talked quite a lot about death, but I always assumed mine was the one under discussion."

Louise returned to the room. "The tea will just be another minute. In the meantime, why don't you tell us what's on your mind." She perched on the arm of Morley's leather chair.

"I need some answers to a few questions and I thought you might help. Did Morley talk to you about this case he was working on? I don't want to give you background if you already know the setup."

Dorothy adjusted her quilt. "Morley told me about every case. As I understand it, this fellow Barney had already been tried for murder. The lawsuit was an attempt on the part of the victim's ex-husband to prove him guilty of wrongful death so that he couldn't inherit the woman's estate."

"Exactly," I said. "David Barney got in touch with me twice yesterday. He said he'd talked to Morley on Wednesday of last week. He implied Morley was going to look into a couple of questions for him. Did Morley tell you what he was doing? I'm trying to piece this together and I don't want to jump to conclusions if I can help it."

"Well, let's see now. I know the fellow got in touch with him, but he never went into any detail. I had my chemo Wednesday afternoon and I was in bad shape. Usually we spent time together in the evenings, but I was completely exhausted and ended up in bed. I slept right through the evening and most of Thursday."

I glanced at Louise. "What about you? Did he talk to you about it?"

She shook her head. "Not anything specific. Just the fact that they'd talked and he had work to do."

"Did he seem to believe what David Barney had told him?"

Louise thought about that and shook her head. "I'm not really sure. He must have given him some credit or he wouldn't have done anything."

Dorothy spoke up. "Well, now that's not quite true, Loosie. Whatever the man said, he was trying to keep an open mind. Morley said it was foolish to make assumptions before all the facts were in."

I said, "That's certainly what I was taught." I reached into my shoulder bag and retrieved the pack of photographs. "It looks like he took these sometime on Friday. Did he tell you what he was up to?"

"That one I can answer," Louise said promptly. "We had an early lunch together. Since he was dieting, he liked to have his meals here at the house. Less temptation, he said. He left here about noon and went out to the office to pick up his mail. He had an early afternoon appointment and then he spent the rest of the day out looking for trucks. He dropped the film off on his way home and said he'd pick the prints up Saturday, which was when he started feeling poorly. He probably forgot all about it."

"How'd he know what to look for?"

"You mean what kind of truck it was? He didn't say anything about that. He thought the same truck might have been involved in some kind of accident, but he didn't say what it was or how he came to that conclusion. He'd picked up a description of it from the original police report."

I thought about the timing. Everything must have come on the heels of his conversation with David Barney. "What happened on Saturday?"

"With his work?" Louise asked.

"I mean with anything." I looked from Louise to Dorothy, inviting either one to answer.

Dorothy took my cue. "Nothing unusual. He went into the office and did some things out there. Mail and whatnot from the sound of it."

"Did he have an appointment?"

"If he was seeing anyone, he didn't say who. He came home around noon and just picked at his lunch. He usually took his meals in my room so we could visit while he ate. I asked him then if he was feeling all right. He said he had a headache and thought he was coming down with something. I thought that was more than Louise had bargained for—two invalids for the price of one. I sent him to bed. I couldn't believe he actually listened, but he did what I said. Turned out he had that terrible flu that's been going around. The poor thing. Nausea, vomiting, diarrhea, stomach cramps."

"Could it have been food poisoning instead?"

"I don't see how, dear. All he had for breakfast was cereal with skim milk."

"Morley really ate that? It doesn't sound like him," I said.

Dorothy laughed. "His doctor put him on a diet at my insistence—fifteen hundred calories a day. Saturday lunch, he had a little soup and a few bites of dry toast. He said he was a little nauseated and didn't have much appetite. By midafternoon, he was sick as a dog. He spent half the night with his head in the commode. We joked about taking turns if I started feeling worse. Sunday morning he was better, though he didn't look good at all. His color was terrible, but the vomiting had stopped and he was able to keep a little ginger ale down."

"Tell me about Sunday dinner. Did you fix it yourself?"

"Oh dear no, I don't cook. I haven't cooked for months. Do you remember, Loosie?"

"I made us a cold plate, poached chicken breast with salad," she said. From the kitchen came the piercing shriek of the kettle. She excused herself and headed off in that direction while Dorothy took up the narrative.

"I was feeling better by then so I came out to the table just to keep them both company. He did complain some of chest pain, but I assumed it was indigestion. Louise was concerned, but I remember teasing him. I forget what I said now, but I was sure it wasn't serious. He pushed his plate back and got up. He had his hand to his chest and he was gasping for breath. He took two steps and went down. He was gone almost at once. We called the paramedics and we tried mouth-to-mouth, but it was pointless."

"Mrs. Shine, I don't know how to say this, but is there any way you might consider having the body autopsied? I know the subject is painful and you may not feel there's any necessity, but I'd feel better if we were really sure about the cause of death."

"What's the nature of your concern?"

"I'm wondering if someone, uhm, tampered with his food or medications."

Her gaze settled on my face with a look of almost luminous clarity. "You think he was murdered."

"I'd like to have it ruled out. It may be a long shot, but we'll never know otherwise. Once he goes in the ground . . ."

"I understand," she said. "I'd like to talk it over with Louise and perhaps Morley's brother, who's arriving tonight."

"Could I call you later this evening? I'm really sorry to have to press. I know it's distressing, but with services tomorrow, time is very short."

"Don't apologize," she said. "Of course you may call. At this point, I don't suppose an autopsy would do any harm."

197

"I'd like to have a conversation with the coroner's office to alert them to the situation, but I don't want to do anything without your permission."

"I have no objections."

"To what?" Louise asked as she came around the corner with a fully laden tea tray. She placed the tray on the coffee table. Dorothy filled her in, summing up the possibilities as succinctly as she'd summed up the wrongful death suit.

"Oh, let her go ahead with it," Louise said. She filled a cup and passed it over to me. "If you discuss it with Frank, you'll never hear the end of it."

Dorothy smiled. "I thought the same thing myself, but I didn't want to say so." To me she said, "Go ahead and do whatever you think best."

"Thank you."

Detective Burt Walker, of the coroner's bureau, was a man in his early forties with receding auburn hair and a close-clipped beard and mustache in a blend of red and blond. His face was round, his complexion ruddy, his coloring suggestive of Scandinavian heritage. His glasses were small and round with thin metal frames. He wasn't heavyset, but he looked like a man who was becoming more substantial as the years went on. The weight looked good on him. He wore a brown tweed jacket, beige chinos, blue shirt, a red tie with white polka dots. While I detailed the circumstances surrounding Morley's death, he leaned an elbow on his desk and variously nodded and rubbed his forehead. I verbalized my suspicions, but I couldn't tell if he was taking me seriously or simply being polite.

When I finished, he stared at me. "So what are you saying?"

I shrugged, embarrassed when it came right down to articulating my hunch. "That he actually died from some kind of poisoning."

"Or maybe it was a poison that precipitated his fatal heart attack," Burt said.

"Right."

"Well. It's not inconceivable," he said slowly. "Sounds like he could have been dosed. I don't guess there's any chance he might have done it himself, despondent, depressed about something."

"Not really. His wife does have cancer, but they'd been married forty years and he knew she depended on him. He'd never abandon her. They were very devoted from what I gather. If he was poisoned, it'd almost have to be something he ingested without knowing."

"You have a theory about the chemical agent involved?"

I shook my head. "I don't know anything about that stuff. I've talked to his wife about his last couple of days and she can't pinpoint anything in particular. Nothing overt or obvious, at any rate. She said his color was bad, but I really didn't quiz her about what she meant by that."

"Couldn't have been anything corrosive or you'd know right off," he said. He sighed, shaking his head. "I don't know what to tell you. I'm not going to ask a toxicologist to run any kind of 'general unknown.' You got nothing to work with. A request like that is too broad. You look at the number and variety of drugs, pesticides, industrial products . . . man oh man . . . even the substances you handle casually at home. From what you're telling me—I mean, let's assume you're right, just for the sake of argument—the problem's compounded by the fact he was in such poor shape."

"You knew Morley?"

He laughed. "Yeah, I knew Morley. Great old guy, but he's living in the fifties when everybody thought drinking a fifth a day and smoking three packs of cigarettes was just something you did for sport. Guy like Morley whose liver or kidney functions were probably already hampered by disease will be more severely affected by any kind of toxic agent because they got no efficient way to excrete such a substance and they probably can't tolerate as much as a healthy individual. Few things we can probably eliminate right off the bat," he said. "Acids, alkalies. I take it she didn't mention any kind of smell to his breath."

"No, and she'd have noticed. They tried mouth-to-mouth resuscitation at first and then figured out it was pointless."

"Takes out cyanide, paraldehyde, ether, disulfide, and nicotine sulfate. You couldn't palm those off on a person anyway."

"Arsenic?"

"Well, yeah. Symptoms you described would fit that pretty well. Except him feeling better. I don't like that much. Too bad he never went over to ER. They'd have tagged it."

"I guess with his wife sick, he didn't want to be a bother," I said. "Everybody's had the flu. He probably thought that's all it was."

"Which it might have been," Burt said. "On the other hand, if it's something he ate and you're talking about the gastrointestinal tract as the portal of entry, then you're talking about a period of time here when you got both chemical transformation and elimination. Generally speaking, chemicals that enter a living organism are either metabolized, eliminated, or both, which means you're progressively reducing the amount of detectable poison. Digestive system goes to work. Hell, he's throwing up the evidence. If the poison kills quickly, there's almost always quantities present on autopsy. It doesn't help he's been embalmed. In a situation like that, when you've got embalming fluid injected in the circulatory system with resultant visceral profusion, toxicologist's problems are blown way bad."

"But would it still be possible to identify?"

"Probably. We'd have to analyze samples of clean embalming fluids, too, check those against whatever foreign elements and compounds are found in the viscera. I tell you what would be the biggest help if you want to get serious about this: Bring me any household products you can find on the premises. Check the garbage for suspect foods. Pill bottles, rat poison, roach powder, cleaning and disinfecting agents, garden insecticides, that kind of thing. I can have a conversation with the funeral director and see if he has anything to contribute. Those guys are pretty sharp once they know what you're after."

"So you'll do it?"

"Well, if she signs the papers, we'll give it a shot."

I could feel excitement bubble up, mixed with equal parts fear. If I was wrong, I was going to feel like a fool.

"What's the grin for?" he asked.

"I didn't think you'd take me seriously."

"I'm paid to take people seriously when it comes right down to it. Lot of times, presumption of death by poisoning only comes about because of suspicion on the part of decedent's friends and relatives. We'll bring Morley out here and take a look."

"What about the funeral?"

"They can go ahead with the services. We'll have him brought out here after that and get right on it." He paused, giving me a speculative look. "Got a suspect in mind if it turns out you're right?"

"I literally don't have a clue," I said. "I'm still trying to figure out who killed Isabelle Barney."

"I wouldn't try too hard if I were you."

"How come?"

"That kind of curiosity might have been what killed Morley."

16

I couldn't believe I had to go back to Morley's again, but that's where I was headed. Burt Walker had asked me to bring him any household products that were possible poison candidates. Louise was out in front, standing at the mailbox, when I pulled up. If she was surprised to see me she gave no indication. She waited patiently while I parked the car and got out. We began walking toward the house as companionable as old friends.

"Where's Dorothy?" I asked.

"She's gone to her room to rest."

"Was she upset?"

Her look was frank. "My sister is a realist.

Morley's gone. If someone poisoned him, she wants to know. Of course it's upsetting. Why wouldn't it be?"

"I hated to add to her burden, but I didn't see a way around it."

"There's nothing either one of us can do about that. What brings you back?"

I told her about my conversation with the coroner. "He doesn't seem optimistic, but at least he's willing to check into it if I round up some possibilities. I'm going to need some sort of carrier for the items we find."

"How about a kitchen garbage bag? Ours are the small ones with a drawstring at the top."

"Perfect," I said.

I followed her to the kitchen and together we gathered up everything that seemed pertinent. The storage area under the sink turned out to be a rich lode of toxic substances. It was sobering to realize that the average housewife spends her days knee-deep in death. Some items I declined, like the Drano, reasoning there was no way he could have sucked down a fatal dose of hair-ball solvent without being aware of it.

Louise had a sharp eye, pointing out items I might have overlooked otherwise. Into the bag went oven cleaner, Raid, Brasso, household ammonia, denatured alcohol, and a box of ant motels. I had a brief incongruous image of Morley with his head back, slipping ant motels down his gullet like a succession of live goldfish. There were several of Morley's prescriptions lined up along the kitchen window sill and we tossed those into my trick-or-treat bag.

In the bathroom, we emptied the medicine cabinet of everything with Morley's name on it, plus a few over-the-counter medications that might be lethal in quantity. Aspirin, Unisom, Percogesic, antihistamines. None of it felt particularly ominous or threatening. We checked all the wastebaskets, but came up with nothing the slightest bit suspicious. The garage netted us a few containers, but not nearly as many as I'd anticipated. "Not many insecticides or fertilizers," I remarked idly. Louise was loading my bag with turpentine and paint thinner.

"Morley hated working in the garden. That was Dorothy's bailiwick." She stood back from the shelves, doing a slow turn as she scanned the premises. "That looks like it. Well, motor oil," she said. She turned and looked at me.

"You might as well put it in the bag," I said. "I can't believe he OD'd on Sears heavyweight, but anything's possible. What about the office? Does he have a medicine cabinet in the bathroom there?"

"I hadn't even thought about that. He sure does. Here, let me rustle up his keys while we're at it."

"Don't worry about it. I can have the woman in the beauty shop let me in from her side."

We returned to the front of the house, where I got out my car keys. "Thanks for your help, Louise."

"Let us know what they find," she said.

"It'll be a while yet. Toxicology reports sometimes take a month."

"What about the autopsy? That should tell them something."

"Nothing's going to happen till after the funeral."

"Will we see you at the service?"

"As far as I know."

Driving over to Morley's office I found myself nearly overwhelmed with uncertainty. This was ridiculous. Morley wouldn't have eaten anything laced with Brasso or Snarol. He was hardly an epicurean, but he surely would have noticed the first time he slurped up a spoonful of malathion or Sevin. I couldn't speak to the issue of his medications. None of the bottles had been empty, or even low, so it didn't look as if he'd overdosed, accidentally or otherwise. The two prescriptions that came in capsule form could have been tampered with, of course. I gathered that most days the back door was left unlocked and open. Anyone could have walked in and replaced his pills with something fatal.

I reached Morley's office and parked in the driveway. I rounded the bungalow and moved toward the front door, toting my plastic garbage bag like a vagrant Santa Claus. On second viewing, the place seemed even more depressing than it had at first. The exterior siding was painted the bright turquoise of Easter eggs, the window frames and roof trim done in sooty white. Various signs in the plate glass window, tucked in among the snowdrifts, announced that the salon was now stocking Jhirmack and Redken. I went in.

This time the shop was empty and Betty, whom I took to be the owner, was having coffee and a cigarette at the back while she worked on her accounts. "Where is everybody?"

"They're all out at lunch. Jeannie has a birthday and I said I'd mind the phones. What can I do for you?"

"I need to get back into Morley's office."

"Help yourself," she said and shrugged.

Someone had pulled the shades down. The light in the room was tawny, overcast sun filtered through cracked paper. Along with the smell of mildew and carpet dust, I picked up the scent of old cigarette butts mingling with the smell of scorched coffee and fresh smoke that wafted through the heating vent from the salon adjacent.

A cursory check of the desk drawers and file cabinets netted me nothing in the way of toxic substances. In the bathroom, I found a can of Comet so close to empty the remaining cleanser had formed pellets that rattled around the bottom like dried peas. The medicine cabinet was empty except for a half-empty bottle of Pepto-Bismol. I added that to my plastic bag in case the contents had been infused with rat poison, powdered glass, or mothballs. Having staged this little melodrama, I felt obliged to play it all the way out to the end. The bathroom waste can was empty. I returned to the office to check the wastebasket under Morley's desk but there was no sign of it. I looked around in puzzlement. I'd seen it in here my first trip.

I opened the connecting door and stuck my head into the salon. "Where'd Morley's wastebasket disappear to?"

"Out on the porch."

"Thanks. Can you do me another favor?"

"I can try," she said.

"Morley's office might turn out to be a crime scene; we won't know for another couple days. Can you keep it secure?"

"Meaning what? Don't let anybody in?"

"Right. Don't touch anything and don't throw anything away."

"That's how Morley kept it in the first place," she said.

I closed the door again and retrieved the wastebasket from the front porch, where the Ho Chi Minh of ant trails now meandered across the concrete. Gingerly, I poked through, brushing ants away. I sat down on the top step and began to empty the contents. Discarded papers, catalogues, used Kleenex, Styrofoam coffee containers. The cardboard box, with the half-eaten pastry in it, had now become sole food source for the teeming colony of ants. I set the box on the porch beside me and did a quick study of the contents. Morley must have stopped off at the bakery on his way into the office, picked up a sweetie, and brought it back with him. He'd eaten half of it and then tossed the rest in the trash, probably feeling guilty about breaking his diet. I peered at the pastry closely, but I had no idea what I was looking at. It didn't appear to be fruit, but what else do you make strudel with? I gathered the remnants carefully and wrapped them in the paper that had come with the box.

There was nothing else of interest. I piled everything back in the wastebasket and tucked it just inside the door, which I locked behind me. I returned to my car and took the entire collection of detritus to the coroner's office, where I left it with the secretary to pass along to Burt.

I was ready to pack it in for the day and head home. The whole case was making my stomach hurt. I was feeling bummed out and depressed. The only thing I'd actually accomplished so far was to dismantle Lonnie's case. Thanks to my efforts, the informant's testimony had now been called into question and the defendant himself had an alibi. If I made many more of these sterling contributions, Barney's attorney would have grounds for dismissal. I could feel the anxiety begin to churn in my chest and I felt the kind of gut-level fear I hadn't experienced since grade school. Not to whine about it, but in some ways I could see that my being fired from CF was generating a crisis of confidence. I had always acted from instinct. I was often frustrated in the course of an investigation, but I operated with a sort of cocky self-assurance, buoyed up by the belief that in the end I could do the job as well as the next man. I'd never felt quite as insecure as I was feeling now. What would happen if I had my ass fired for the second time in six weeks?

I went home and cleaned my apartment like Cinderella on uppers. It was the only thing I could think of to offset my anxiety. I grabbed some sponges and the cleanser and attacked the bathroom off the loft. I don't know how men cope with life's little stresses. Maybe they play golf or fix autos or drink beer and watch TV. The women I know (the ones who aren't addicted to junk food or shopping) turn to cleaning house. I went to town with a rag and a johnny mop, mowing down germs with copious applications of disinfectants, variously sprayed and foamed across every visible surface. Any germs I didn't kill, I severely maimed.

At 6:00 I took a break. My hands smelled of bleach. In addition to sanitizing my entire upstairs bathroom, I'd dusted and vacuumed the loft, and changed the sheets. I was just about to tackle my dresser drawers when I realized it was time to stop and grab a bite to eat. It might even be time to knock off altogether. I took a quick shower and then donned fresh jeans and a clean turtleneck. My stab at domesticity didn't extend to home cooking, I'm afraid. I snagged my shoulder bag and a jacket and headed up to Rosie's.

I was somewhat taken aback to find the place just as busy as it had been the night before. This time, instead of bowlers, there appeared to be a softball team—guys in sweatpants and matching short-sleeved shirts that sported the name of a local electrical supply firm in stitching across the back. Much cigarette smoke, many raised beer steins and bursts of the sort of raucous laughter that drinking unleashes. The place looked like one of those beer commercials where people seem to be having a much better time than they actually do in real life. The jukebox was pounding out a cut so distorted it was difficult to identify. The television set at one end of the bar was turned to ESPN, the picture showing laps of some dusty and interminable stock car race. No one was paying the slightest attention, but the sound was turned up to compete with the din.

Rosie looked on, beaming complacently. What was happening to the woman? She'd never tolerated noise. She'd never encouraged the patronage of sports buffs. I'd always worried the tavern would be discovered by the yuppies and turned into an upscale drinking establishment for business executives and attorneys. It never crossed my mind I'd be rubbing elbows with a bunch of Ben-Gay addicts.

I spotted Henry and his brother William. Henry was wearing cutoffs, a white T-shirt, and deck shoes, his long tanned legs looking muscular and sturdy. William still wore his suit, but he'd removed the matching vest. While Henry slouched in his chair with a beer in front of him, William sat bolt upright, sipping mineral water with a slice of lemon. I gave Henry a wave and headed for my favorite back booth, which was miraculously empty. I stopped at the halfway point. Henry's gaze had settled on mine with such a look of mute pleading that I found myself opting for his table instead.

William rose to his feet.

Henry shoved a chair toward me with his foot. "You want a beer? I'll buy you a beer."

"I'd really prefer white wine if it's all the same to you," I said.

"Absolutely. No problem. White wine it is."

Since I'd seen the two of them the day before, I could have sworn they'd regressed. I could almost picture them as they'd been at eight and ten years old respectively. Henry was all elbows and knees, conducting himself with a sullen-younger-brother belligerence. He'd probably spent his youth being victimized by William's fastidious and lofty manner. Maybe their mother had assigned Henry to his brother's care, forcing the two of them into unwanted proximity. William looked like the sort who would lord it over Henry, tormenting his younger brother when he wasn't tattling on him. Now at eighty-three, Henry looked both restless and rebellious, unable to assert himself except in clowning and asides.

He was searching now for Rosie while William sat down again. I turned to William and raised my voice so he could hear me over all the ruckus in the place. "How was your first day in Santa Teresa?"

"I'd say the day was fair. I suffered a little episode of heart palpitations. . . ." William's voice was powdery and feeble.

I put a hand to my ear to indicate I was having trouble hearing him. Henry leaned toward me.

"We spent the afternoon at the Urgent Care Center," Henry yelled. "It was fun. The equivalent of the circus for those of us on Medicare."

William said, "I had a problem with my heart. The doctor ordered an ECG. I can't remember now what he called my particular condition. . . ."

"Indigestion," Henry hollered. "All you had to do was burp."

William didn't seem dismayed by Henry's facetiousness. "My brother's uncomfortable at any sign of human frailty."

"Hanging around you all my life, I ought to be used to it."

I was still focused on William. "Are you feeling okay?"

"Yes, thank you," he replied.

"Here's how I feel," Henry said. He crossed his eyes and hung his tongue out the side of his mouth, clutching his chest.

William didn't crack a smile. "Would you care to have a look?"

I wasn't sure what he was offering until he took out the tracing from his electrocardiogram. "They let you keep this?" I asked.

"Just this portion. The remainder is in my chart. I brought my medical records with me, in case I needed them."

The three of us stared at the ribbon of ink with its spikes at regular intervals. It looked like a crosscut of ocean with four shark fins coming straight at us through the water.

William leaned close. "The doctor wants to keep a very close eye on me."

"I should think *so*," I said.

"Too bad you can't take a day off work," Henry said to me. "We could take turns checking William's pulse."

"Mock me if you like, but we all have to come to grips with our own mortality," William said with composure.

"Yeah, well, tomorrow I've got to come to terms with somebody else's mortality," I said. And to Henry I added, "Morley Shine's funeral."

"A friend of yours?"

"Another private investigator here in town," I said. "He used to be pals with the guy who trained me so I've known him for years."

"He died in the line of duty?" William asked.

I shook my head. "Not really. Sunday night he dropped dead of a heart attack." The minute I said it, I wished I'd kept my mouth shut. I could see William's hand stray to his chest.

He said, "And what age was the man?"

"Gee, I'm not really sure." I was lying, of course. Morley was a good twenty years younger than William. "Golly, there's Rosie." I can "Gee" and "Golly" with the best of 'em in a pinch.

Rosie had just emerged from the kitchen and was staring

at us from across the room. She approached, her face set in an expression of determination. As she passed the bar, she reached over and muted the volume on the TV set. Henry and I exchanged significant looks. I was sure he was thinking the same thing I was: She was going to take care of William and no two ways about it. I found myself almost feeling sorry for the man. The jukebox shut down and the noise level dropped. The quiet was a blessing.

William pushed his chair back and rose politely to his feet. "Miss Rosie. What a pleasure. I hope we can persuade you to join us."

I looked from one to the other. "You've been introduced?"

Henry said, "She came over to the table when we first got here."

Rosie's gaze strayed to William and then dropped modestly. "You might be engaged in conversation," she said, fishing for reassurance as usual. This from a woman who bullies everybody unmercifully.

"Oh, come on. Have a seat," I said, adding my invitation to William's. He remained standing, apparently waiting for her to sit, which she showed no signs of doing.

Rosie barely acknowledged Henry and me. Her glance at William shifted from coquettish to quizzical. She focused on the ECG tracing. She tucked her hands beneath her apron. "Sinus tachycardia," she announced. "The heart is suddenly beating one hundred times a minute. Is horrible."

William looked at her with surprise. "That's it. That's correct," he said. "I suffered such an incident just this afternoon. I had to see the doctor at an urgent care facility. He's the one who ran this test."

"There's nothing they can do," she said with satisfaction. "I have similar condition. Maybe some pills. Otherwise is hopeless." She settled herself gingerly on the edge of the chair. "You sit."

William sat. "It's much worse than fibrillation," William said.

"Is much more worse than fibrillation and palpitations put together," Rosie said. "Let me see that." She took the tracing. She adjusted her glasses low on her nose, rearing back to see it better. "Look at that. I can' believe this."

William peered over at it again as if the strip of paper might have been injected with a whole new meaning. "It's that serious?"

"Terrible. Not as bad as mine, but plenty serious. These wavy lines and these spiky points?" She shook her head, her mouth pulling down. She handed the tracing back abruptly. "I get you a sherry."

"No, no. Out of the question. I don't imbibe spirits," he said.

"This Hungarian sherry. Is completely different. I take myself at first sign of attack. Boomb! Is gone. Just like that. No more wavy lines. No more spike."

"The doctor never mentioned anything about sherry," he said uneasily.

"And you want to know why? How much you pay to see this doctor today? Plenty, I bet. Sixty, eighty dollars. You think he don' want you come running beck? You got that kind of money? I'm telling you, do what I say and you'll be just like new in no time. You try. You don' feel better, you don' pay. I guarantee. I give you the first. On the house. Ebsolutely free."

He seemed torn, debating, until Rosie turned a steely gaze on him. He held his thumb and his index finger an inch apart. "Perhaps just a bit."

"I pour myself," she said, getting to her feet.

I raised my hand. "Could I have a glass of white wine, please? Henry's treating."

"A round of blood pressure medication for the bar," he said.

Rosie ignored his attempt at humor and moved off toward the bar. I didn't dare look at Henry, because I knew I'd smirk. Rosie had William eating out of her hand. While

Henry had been mocking and I'd been polite, Rosie was treating William with the utmost seriousness. I had no idea where she intended to go from here, but William seemed to be thoroughly disarmed by the approach.

"Doctor never said anything about spirits," he repeated staunchly.

"It can't hurt," I supplied just to keep the game afloat. Maybe she meant to get him drunk, soften his defenses so she could tell him the truth—for a man his age, he was as healthy as a horse.

"I wouldn't want to do anything counterproductive to my long-term treatment," he said.

"Oh, for God's sake. Have a drink," Henry snapped.

Under the table, I placed my foot on top of Henry's and applied some pressure. His expression shifted. "Yes, well, that just reminded me. Grandfather Pitts partook of occasional spirits. You remember that, don't you, William? I can still picture him on the front porch, sitting in his rocking chair, sipping his tumbler of Black Jack."

"But then he *died,*" William said.

"Of course he died! The man was a hundred and one years old!"

William's expression shut down. "You needn't shout."

"Well, shit! People in the Bible didn't live as long as he did. He was healthy. He was hale and hearty. Everybody in our family—"

"Hennnnrrry, you're losing it," I sang.

He was abruptly silent. Rosie was returning to the table with a tray in hand. She'd brought a glass of white wine for me, a beer for Henry, plus two liqueur glasses and a small ornate bottle filled with amber liquid. William had obediently risen to his feet again. He pulled a chair out for her. She put the tray down and sent him a simpering smile. "Such a gentleman," she said and actually batted her eyes. "Very nice." She passed the wine to me, the beer to Henry, and then sat down. "Permit me, please," she said to William.

"Just the tiniest amount," he said.

"I'm telling you the amount," she said. "I'm showing you how to drink. Like this." She poured sherry to the rim of the small glass and placed it to her lips. She tossed her head back and drained the contents. She dabbed the corners of her mouth daintily with the knuckle of her index finger. "Now you," she said. She filled a second liqueur glass and handed it to William.

He hesitated.

"Do what I'm telling you," she said.

William did as she was telling him. As soon as the alcohol hit the back of his throat, he began to shudder . . . a wonderful involuntary spasm that started in his shoulders and traveled rapidly down his spine. "My stars!"

" 'My stars!' is correct," she said. She studied him slyly and her chuckle was positively lascivious. She poured them both another round, tossing her shot down like some old cowboy in a John Wayne movie. Having got the hang of it, William did likewise. A bit of color had come up in his cheeks. Henry and I were watching with mute amazement.

"Done!" Rosie banged a hand on the table and gathered herself together. She stood, placing the sherry bottle and the two glasses carefully on her tray again. "Tomorrow. Two o'clock. Is like medicine. Very strict. Now I bring you dinner. I know just what you need. Don't argue."

I could feel my heart sink. I knew dinner would consist of some incredible concoction of Hungarian spices and saturated fats, but I didn't have the nerve to flee.

William watched her depart. "That's remarkable," he said. "I believe I can actually feel my blood pressure drop."

I slept badly that night and jogged Friday morning in a halfhearted fashion. Morley's funeral was scheduled for 10:00 and I was dreading it. There were still too many questions up in the air and I felt as if I'd been responsible for most of them. Lonnie would be coming back from Santa Maria as soon as he wrapped up his court case. I still had a batch of subpoenas Morley'd never served, but it didn't make sense to try to get those out until I knew where things stood. Lonnie might not be going into court at all. I showered and then dug around in my underwear drawer, searching for a pair of panty hose that didn't look like kittens had been climbing up the legs. The drawer was a jumble of old T-shirts and mismatched socks. I was really going to have to get in there and get it organized one day. I put on my all-purpose dress, which is perfect for funerals: black with long sleeves, in some exotic blend of polyester you could bury for a year without generating a crease. I slipped my feet into a pair of black flats so I could walk without hobbling. I have friends who adore high heels, but I can't see the point. I figure if high heels were so wonderful, men would be wearing them. I decided to skip breakfast and get into the office early.

It was 7:28 and mine was the first car in the lot. With no access to daylight, the interior stairwell was intensely dark. The little flashlight on my keychain provided just enough illumination to prevent my tripping and falling flat on my face. When I reached the third floor, I let myself in by the front entrance. The place was gloomy and cold. I spent a few minutes turning lights on, creating the illusion that the workday had begun. I set up a pot of coffee and flipped the switch to On. By the time I'd unlocked my office, the scent of perking coffee was beginning to permeate the air.

I checked my answering machine and found the light blinking insistently. I pressed the button for messages and was greeted by an annoyed-sounding Kenneth Voigt. "Miss Millhone. Ken Voigt. It's . . . uh . . . midnight on Thursday. I just got a call from Rhe Parsons, who's very upset over this business with Tippy. I've put a call through to Lonnie up in Santa Maria, but the motel switchboard is closed. I'll be at the office by eight tomorrow morning and I want this straightened out. Call me the minute you get in." He left the telephone number at Voigt Motors and clicked off.

I checked my watch. It was 7:43. I tried the number he'd left, but all I got was a recording, advising in cultured tones that the dealership was closed and giving me an emergency number in case I was calling to announce that the building was going up in flames. I was still wearing my jacket and it didn't make sense to settle in at my desk. Might as well face the music. Ida Ruth was just arriving so I told her where I was going and left the place to her. I went back down to the parking lot, where I retrieved my car. I'd only met Kenneth Voigt once, but he'd struck me as the sort who'd enjoy being on the sending end of a good chewing out. I really didn't want to discuss the latest developments in the case. For one thing, I hadn't told Lonnie what was happening and I figured it was his place to deliver bad news. At least he could advise Voigt about the legal consequences.

Traffic on the freeway was still fairly light and I made it to the Cutter Road off-ramp by five minutes after eight. Voigt Motors was the authorized dealer for Mercedes-Benz, Porsche, Jaguar, Rolls-Royce, Bentley, BMW, and Aston Martin. I parked my VW in one of ten empty slots and moved toward the entrance. The building looked like a Southern plantation, a glass-and-concrete tribute to gentility and taste. A discreet sign, hand-lettered in gold, indicated that business hours were Monday–Friday 8:30am to 8pm, Saturday 9am to 6pm, and Sunday 10am to 6pm. I cupped a hand against the smoky glass, looking for signs of activity in the shadowy interior. I could see six or seven gleaming automobiles and a light at the rear. To the right, a staircase swept up and out of sight. I tapped a key against the glass, wondering if the tiny clicking sound carried far enough to be effective.

Moments later, Kenneth Voigt appeared at the top of the stairs and peered over the railing. He came down and crossed the gleaming marble floor in my direction. He wore a dark pin-striped business suit, a crisp pale blue dress shirt, and a dark blue tie. He looked like a man who'd built up one of the most prosperous high-end car dealerships in Santa Teresa County. He detoured briefly, taking time to flick on interior lights, illuminating a fleet of pristine automobiles. He unlocked the front door and held it open for me. "I take it you got my message."

"I was in early this morning. I thought we might as well talk in person."

"You'll have to hang on a minute. I was just putting a call through to New York." He crossed the showroom, moving toward a row of identical glass-fronted offices where business was conducted during working hours. I watched as he took a seat in somebody else's swivel chair. He punched in a number and leaned back, keeping an eye on me while he waited for his call to go through. Someone apparently picked up on the other end because I saw his interest quicken. He began to gesture as he talked. Even from a distance, he managed to look tense and unreasonable.

Don't blow this, I thought. Do not mouth off. The man was Lonnie's client, not mine, and I couldn't afford to antagonize him. I ambled around the showroom, hoping to stifle my natural inclination to bolt. Getting fired had taken some of the cockiness out of me. I focused on my surroundings, taking in the aura of elegance.

The air smelled wonderfully of leather and car wax. I wondered what it felt like to have enough in a checking account to make a down payment on a vehicle that cost more than two hundred thousand dollars. I pictured lots of chuckles and not a lot of haggling. If you could afford a Rolls-Royce, you had to know it would set you back plenty walking in the door. What was there to negotiate, the trade-in on your Bentley?

My gaze settled on a Corniche III, a two-door convertible with a red exterior. The top was down. The interior was upholstered in creamy white leather piped in red. I glanced back at Voigt. He was now fully engrossed in his telephone conversation so I opened the door on the driver's side of the Rolls and got in. Not bad. A copy of the car's specs was printed on parchment, bound in leather, and tucked in the glove box. It looked like the wine list in an expensive restaurant. There wasn't anything as vulgar as a price in evidence, but I did learn that the "kerb weight" for the motorcar was 2430 kg and the "luggage boot capacity" was 0,27 m³. I studied all the dials and switches on the instrument panel, admiring the inlaid walnut. I did some serious driving, turning the steering wheel this way and that while I made tire-squealing noises with my mouth. James Bond in drag. I was in the process of navigating a hairpin turn on a mountainous road above Monte Carlo when I looked up to find Voigt standing beside the car. I could feel the color rise in my face like heat. "This is beautiful," I murmured. I knew I only said it as a way of sucking up to him, but I couldn't help myself.

He opened the door and slid in on the passenger side. He surveyed the dashboard lovingly and then touched the supple leather on the bucket seat. "Fourteen hides for every Corniche interior. Sometimes after closing, I come down here and sit."

"You own this place and you don't drive one yourself?"

"I can't afford it quite yet," he said. "I made up my mind if we won this lawsuit I was going to buy one of these, just for the thrill of it." His expression was pained. "From what Rhe tells me, you've stirred up a hornets' nest. She's talking about suing the shit out of you and Lonnie both."

"On what grounds?"

"I have no idea. People who sue hardly need a reason these days. God only knows how it's going to impact my case. You were hired to serve subpoenas. You weren't instructed to go off on any tangents."

"I can't assess the situation from a legal standpoint—that's really Lonnie's job. . . ."

"But how did it happen? That's what I don't get."

Trying not to sound defensive, I told him about my conversation with Barney and what I'd found out since then, detailing Tippy's involvement in the death of the elderly pedestrian. Voigt didn't let me get to the end of it.

"That's ludicrous. Absurd! Morley worked on this case for months and he never came up with any information about Tippy and this hit-and-run accident."

"Actually, that's not true. He was pursuing the same lead I was. He'd already taken pictures of her father's pickup, which was my next step. I showed the photographs to the witness, who's identified it as the vehicle at the scene."

His brow furrowed. "Oh, for God's sake. So what? After all these years, that doesn't constitute proof. You're jeopardizing millions and what's the point?"

"The point is I talked to Tippy and she told me she did it."

"I don't see the relevance. Just because David Barney claims he saw her that night? This is bullshit."

"You might not see the relevance, but a jury will. Wait until Herb Foss gets hold of it. He'll play the timing for all it's worth."

"But suppose it was earlier? You can't be sure about what time it was."

"Yes, I can. There's a corroborating witness and I've talked to him."

He wiped his face with one hand, palm resting across his mouth briefly. He said, "Jesus. Lonnie's not going to be happy. Have you talked to him?"

"He'll be back tonight. I can talk to him then."

"You don't know how much I have wrapped up in this. It's cost me thousands of dollars, not to mention all the pain and suffering. You've undone all of that. And for what? Some six-year-old hit-and-run accident?"

"Wait a minute. That pedestrian is just as dead as Isabelle. You think his life doesn't matter just because he was ninety-two? Talk to his son if you want to discuss pain and suffering."

A look of impatience flitted across his face. "I can't believe the police will press charges. Tippy was a juvenile at the time and she's led an exemplary life since. I hate to seem callous, but what's done is done. In Isabelle's case, you're talking cold-blooded murder."

"I don't want to argue. Let's just see what Lonnie says. His point of view may be entirely different. Maybe he'll come up with a whole new strategy."

"You better hope so. Otherwise, David Barney's going to get away with murder."

"You can't very well 'get away with' something if you didn't do it in the first place."

A telephone began to ring in one of the sales offices. Unconsciously, we both paused and looked in that direction, waiting for the machine to pick up. By the fifth ring, Voigt flashed a look of irritation at the rear. "Oh, hell, I must have turned off the answering machine." He got out and crossed the showroom at a quick clip, snatching up the receiver on the seventh or eighth ring. When it was clear that he'd been caught up in another lengthy conversation, I got out of the Rolls and let myself out the side door.

I spent the next hour in a Colgate coffee shop. In theory, I was having breakfast, but in truth, I was hiding. I wanted to feel like the old Kinsey again . . . talkin' trash and kickin' butt. Being cowed and uncertain was really for the birds.

The Wynington-Blake mortuary in Colgate is a generic sanctuary designed to serve just about any spiritual inclination you might favor in death. I was given a printed program as I entered the chapel. I found a seat at the rear and spent a few minutes contemplating my surroundings. The construction was vaguely churchlike: a faux apse, a faux nave with a big stained-glass window filled with blocks of rich color. Morley's closed coffin was visible up in front, flanked by funeral wreaths. There were no religious symbols—no angels, no crosses, no saints, no images of God, Jesus, Muhammad, Brahma, or any other Supreme Being. Instead of an altar, there was a library table. In lieu of a pulpit, there was a lectern with a mike.

We were seated in pews, but there wasn't any organ music. The hallowed equivalent of Muzak was being piped in, hushed chords vaguely reminiscent of Sunday school. Despite the secular tones of the environment, everybody was dressed up and looking properly subdued. The place was filled to capacity and most of those gathered were unknown to me. I wondered if the etiquette followed that of weddings

—the deceased's friends on one side, the survivor's on the other. If Dorothy Shine and her sister were present, they'd be seated in the little family alcove to the right, hidden from public view by a partial wall of glass block.

There was a quiet stirring to my left and I became aware that two gentlemen had just entered the pew from the side aisle. As soon as they'd been seated, I felt a gentle nudge to my elbow. I glanced to my left and experienced a disorienting moment when I caught sight of Henry and William sitting next to me. William was wearing a somber charcoal suit. Henry had forsaken his usual shorts and T-shirt and was quite respectably attired in a white dress shirt, tie, dark sport coat, and chinos. And tennis shoes.

"William wanted you to have support in this your hour of need," Henry murmured to me under his breath.

I leaned forward. Sure enough, William had a mournful eye fixed on me. "Actually, I could use it, but what made him think of it?"

"He loves funerals," Henry was whispering. "This is like Christmas morning for him. He woke up early, all excited—"

William leaned over and put a finger to his lips.

I gave Henry a nudge.

"It's the truth," he said. "I couldn't talk him out of it. He insisted I put on this ridiculous outfit. I think he's hoping for a really tragic cemetery scene, widow flinging herself into the open grave."

There was a rustling sound. At the front of the chapel, a middle-aged man in a white choir robe had appeared at the lectern. Under the robe, you could see he was wearing an electric blue suit that made him look like some kind of television evangelist. He seemed to be organizing his notes in preparation for the service. The microphone was on and the riffling of paper made a great clattering.

Henry crossed his arms. "The Catholics wouldn't do it this way. They'd have some boy in a dress swinging a pot of incense like he had a cat by the tail."

William frowned significantly, cautioning Henry to silence. He managed to behave himself for the next twenty minutes or so while the officiating pastor went through all of the expected sentiments. It was clear he was some kind of rent-a-reverend, brought in for the day. Twice, he referred to Morley as "Marlon" and some of the virtues he ascribed to him bore no relation to the man I knew. Still, we all tried to be good sports. When you're dead, you're dead, and if you can't have a few lies told about you when you're in your grave, you've just about run out of shots. We stood and we sat. We sang hymns and bowed our heads while prayers were recited. Passages were read from some new version of the Bible with every lyrical image and poetic phrase translated into conversational English.

"The Lord is my counselor. He encourages me to go birding in the fields. He leads me to quiet pools. He restores my soul and takes me along the right pathways of life. Yes, even if I pass by Death's dark wood, I won't be scared. . . ."

Henry sent me a look of consternation.

When we were finally liberated, Henry took me by the elbow and we moved toward the door. William lingered behind, filing with a number of others toward the closed casket, where final respects were being paid. As Henry and I passed into the corridor, I glanced back and saw William engaged in an earnest chat with the minister. We went through the front door to the covered porch that ran the width of the building. The crowd had subdivided, half still in the chapel, the other half lighting up cigarettes in the parking lot. The scent of sulfur matches permeated the air. This was funeral weather, the morning chilly and gray. By early afternoon, the cloud cover would probably clear, but in the meantime the sky was dreary.

I looked to my right, inadvertently catching sight of a departing mourner with a slight limp. "Simone?"

She turned and looked at me. Now I'm an haute couture ignoramus, but today she was wearing an outfit even I recognized. The two-piece "ensemble" (to use fashion magazine talk) was the work of a designer who'd amassed a fortune making women look ill-shapen, overdressed, and foolish. She turned away, her body rocking as she hobbled toward her car.

I touched Henry's arm. "I'll be right back."

Simone wasn't actually running, but it was clear she didn't want to talk to me. I pursued her at a hard walk, closing down the distance between us. "Simone, would you wait up?"

She stopped in her tracks, letting me pull abreast.

"What's your hurry?"

She turned on me in cold fury. "I got a call from Rhe Parsons. You're going to ruin Tippy's life. I think you're a shit and I don't want to talk to you."

"Hey, wait a minute. I got news for you. I don't make up the facts. I'm being paid to investigate—"

She cut in. "Oh, right. That's a good one. And who paid you? David Barney, by any chance? He's good-looking and single. I'm sure he'd be willing to cut you in on the deal."

"Of course it wasn't David. What's the matter with you? If she committed a crime—"

"The girl was sixteen years old!"

"The girl was drunk," I said. "I don't care what age she was. She has to take responsibility—"

"Don't try that righteous tone on me. I don't have time for this," she said and began to walk away. She reached her car and fumbled with her keys. She got in and slammed the door shut.

"You're pissed because this gets David Barney off the hook."

She rolled the window down. "I'm pissed because David Barney is a horrible man. He's despicable. I'm pissed because good people have to suffer while the bad people walk away with everything."

"You think just because you don't like some guy it's okay to see him falsely convicted of murder?"

"He hated Iz." She put the key in the ignition, turned the engine over, and released the hand brake.

"That doesn't mean he killed her. You were not exactly without a motive yourself."

"Me?"

"The accident you were involved in was her fault, wasn't it? I heard she was drunk and left the car in the drive without the brake pulled on. Because of her, you lost any hope of having children. That's a big price to pay when you'd been cleaning up after her for most of your life. It couldn't have sat well with you—"

"That's ridiculous. People don't murder other people over things like that."

"Of course they do. Pick up the newspaper any day of the week."

"David Barney's full of shit. He'd do anything to shift the blame."

"This didn't come from him. It came from someone else."

"And who was that?"

"I'd rather not go into that. . . ."

"Well, you're a fool if you believe it."

"I didn't say I believed it, but the point is a good one."

"Which is what?"

"Other people had a motive for wanting her dead. We've all been so busy believing David Barney did it, we haven't looked at anyone else."

She seemed momentarily stumped by the thought and then her gaze shifted slyly. "Well, then. Why don't you look in the right direction?"

"What are you saying?"

"I'm saying Yolanda Weidmann. Isabelle wrecked Peter's business pulling out when she did. He really promoted her career. He put in a lot of time and money when no one else would lift a finger. You have to understand just how crazy Isabelle was. Erratic, self-destructive, all the booze and the dope. She didn't have a degree. She didn't have a reputation until Peter took her up. He was her mentor and she shafted him royally. She turned her back on him after all he did. And then, that heart attack of his. That was the finishing touch. In theory, it was brought on by stress and overwork. The truth is, she broke his heart. That's the long and short of it."

"But he didn't seem bitter when I talked to him."

"I didn't say *he* was bitter. Yolanda's the one. She's really a spider, not a woman you'd want to cross."

"I'm listening."

"You've met the woman. You tell me."

I shrugged. "Personally, I couldn't stand her. I spent half an hour over there and she put him down constantly, all these barbs and zingers, little ha-has at his expense. I'd rather see a knock-down, drag-out fight. At least it's honest. She seemed . . . I don't know . . . wily."

Simone smiled slightly. "Ah, yes. She's very cunning. Under it all, I assure you, she's fiercely protective. She can treat him any way she likes, but you try it and look out! I think it makes her a very good candidate."

"But the woman must be sixty-five years old if she's a day. It's hard to believe she'd turn to murder."

"You don't know Yolanda. I'm surprised she didn't do it sooner. As for her age, she's in better shape than I am." She broke off eye contact and her manner became brisk. "I have to go. I'm sorry I blew my stack." She put the car in reverse and backed out of the slot. I stared after her with interest as she pulled away.

I retraced my steps, moving toward the entrance. I could see Henry heading off across the parking lot toward his car. The first cluster of mourners had dispersed to some extent and those who remained in the chapel were just emerging. William appeared from the cool depths of the funeral home, looking somehow offended and confused. He was holding his fedora, which he placed squarely on his head with a slight adjustment to the brim. "I don't understand what denomination that was."

"I think the service is meant to cover all bets," I said.

He looked back over his shoulder at the facade with disapproval. "The building looks like a restaurant."

18

"Well, you know, eating out is close to a religion these days," I said dryly. "People used to tithe to the church. Now the ten percent goes to the waiter instead."

"It wasn't very satisfactory as funerals go. In Michigan, we conduct these services properly. I understand there's not even going to be a graveside ceremony. Very disrespectful, if you ask me."

"It's just as well," I said. "From what I know of Morley, he didn't have a highly developed spiritual side and he probably wouldn't have wanted any kind of fuss made about his death. Anyway, his wife is ill and might not have been up for more than this." I didn't mention that the body would probably be whisked over to the coroner's office within the hour.

"Where did Henry go?" William asked.

"He's bringing the car around, I think."

"Will you be coming back to the house with us? We're having a light lunch on the patio and we'd be happy to have you join us. We invited Rose, hoping to reciprocate her many courtesies."

"I wish I could, but I have something to take care of. I'll stop by a little later and see what you're up to."

Henry pulled up beside us in his five-window coupe. It's a 1932 Chevrolet that he's had since it was new. It's been meticulously maintained, boasting the original paint, headliner, and upholstery. If William were driving it, I suspect the car would seem prissy. With Henry at the wheel, there was something rakish and sexy about the vehicle. You have to keep an eye on Henry as he's still very appealing to "babes" of all ages, including me. I could see people turning to admire the car, checking him out afterward to see if he was someone famous. Because Santa Teresa is less than two hours away from Hollywood, a number of movie stars live in town. We all know this, but it's still disconcerting when some guy at the car wash who looks just like John Travolta turns out to be John Travolta. I saw Steve Martin driving through Montebello once and nearly rammed into a tree trying to get a good look at him. He's Technicolor handsome, in case you're wondering.

William got into Henry's car and the two rumbled off. There was still not a hint about the trap Rosie meant to spring. Whatever her intention, it was still early in the game. William did seem less self-absorbed today. We'd actually made it through a three-minute conversation without reference to his health.

I drove back into town, taking the freeway south on 101. I got off at the Missile off-ramp and headed east until I reached State Street, where I hung a right. The Axminster Gallery, where Rhe Parsons's show would be opening that night, was located in a complex that included the Axminster Theater and numerous small businesses. The gallery itself was located along a walkway that ran behind the shops. I parked on a side street and cut through a public lot. The entrance was marked by a hand-forged iron sign. A panel truck had been backed in close to the door and I could see two guys unloading blocks wrapped in heavily quilted moving pads. The door was standing open and I followed the workmen in.

The entry was narrow, probably scaled down for effect, because I quickly passed into a large room with a thirty-foot ceiling. The walls were a stark white and light cascaded down through wide skylights, currently cranked open to admit fresh air. A complicated arrangement of canvas, cording, and pulleys was affixed at ceiling height so that the fabric shades could be drawn across the opening if the light needed to be cut. The floors were gray concrete carpeted with Oriental rugs, the walls hung with batiks and framed watercolor abstracts.

Rhe Parsons was consulting with a woman in a smock, the two of them apparently discussing the placement of two final pieces the workmen were bringing in. I circled the room while the discussion continued. Tippy was perched on a stool near the back wall, commenting on the overall effect from her vantage point. Rhe's show consisted of sixteen pieces arranged on pedestals of varying heights. She was working in resins, casting large polished pieces—maybe eighteen inches on a side—which at first seemed identical. I inspected five in range of me. I could see that the translucent material was formed into subtly tinted layers, with sometimes an object buried at the heart—a perfectly preserved insect, a safety pin, a locket on a chain, a ring of brass keys. With the light shining through, the effect was of peering through blocks of ice, except that the resin looked solid and indestructible. It wasn't hard to imagine these totems being dug up at some point in the future, along with bleach bottles, pull tabs, and disposable diapers.

Rhe must have seen me, but she gave no sign of recognition. She was wearing jeans and a heavy mohair sweater in shades of pale blue and mauve. Her dark hair was banded at the nape of her neck, a long silky tassel reaching almost to her waist. Tippy wore a jumpsuit in a lightweight denim. Unseen by her mother, she greeted me with a wiggle of her fingers, which I took to mean "Hi." It was heartening to realize that the person whose life I'd allegedly ruined was alive and well and still speaking to me.

Rhe murmured something to her companion, who turned to stare at me. The woman picked up a clipboard and clopped off across the room, stack heels resounding on the concrete floor.

"Hello, Rhe."

"What the hell do you want?"

"I thought we should talk. I didn't mean to cause you any trouble."

"Wonderful. That's great. I'll tell my attorney you said so."

Out of the corner of my eye, I saw Tippy hop down from the stool and cross the room toward us. Rhe made the kind of gesture an owner uses with a dog. She snapped her fingers and held her hand flat, meaning "Stay" or "Lie down."

Tippy wasn't that well trained. She said "Mom . . ." in a tone that embraced both outrage and insult.

"This doesn't concern you."

"It does too!"

"Wait for me in the car, baby. I'll be there in a minute."

"Can't I even listen to the conversation?"

"Just do as I tell you!"

"Well, God!" Tippy said. She rolled her eyes and sighed hard, but she did as her mother asked.

As soon as she'd left, Rhe turned on me with a chill fury. "Do you have any idea the damage you've done?"

"Hey, I came here to discuss the situation, not to take abuse. What did I do?"

"Tippy *just* got herself squared away. She's finally on track and now you come along with this trumped-up allegation."

"I wouldn't call it trumped up. . . ."

"Let's not get into semantics. The point is, even if it's true, which I greatly doubt, you didn't have to turn it into a big deal—"

"What big deal?"

"Besides which, if you're convinced she's guilty of some kind of criminal behavior, she's entitled to an attorney. You had no right to confront her without my being present."

"She's twenty-two, Rhe. In the eyes of the law, she's an adult. I don't want to see her charged with anything. There might have been an explanation, and if so, I wanted to hear it. All I did was talk to her, trying to get information, and I did that without going to the cops first, which I could easily have done. If I'm aware a crime's been committed, I can't look the other way. The minute I cover for her, I become an accessory."

"You intimidated her. You were threatening and manipulative. By the time I got home, she was hysterical. I really don't know what your story is, but you had better take a good hard look at yourself. You are not judge and jury here—"

I raised my hands. "Wait a minute. Just wait. This isn't about me. This is about Tippy, who seems to be dealing with reality a lot better than you are. I understand you feel protective—I would, too—but let's not lose sight of the facts."

"What facts? There aren't any facts!"

"Let's skip it. Never mind. Discussion isn't possible. I can see that now. I'll have Lonnie talk to your attorney as soon as he gets back."

"Good. You do that. And you better be prepared for the worst."

Trying to get the last word in was almost irresistible, but I closed my mouth and removed myself from the room before I said something I might regret later. As I left the gallery, Tippy approached and fell into step with me. "I wouldn't let your mother see us together if I were you."

"What'd she say?"

"Just about what you'd expect."

"Don't worry, okay? I know she was really mad, but she'll get over it. She's been under a lot of pressure lately, but she'll come around."

"Let's hope so for your sake," I said. "Listen, Tip, I'm really sorry this had to happen. I feel like a dog, but I didn't see a way around it."

"It's not your fault. I'm the one who fucked up. I'm the one who should feel bad about it, not you."

"How are you doing?"

"Pretty good," she said. "I talked to one of my AA counselors last night and she was really great. As soon as we finish here I'll go talk to her, and then later this afternoon I'll talk to the police."

"Your mother's right. It's probably a good idea to see an attorney before you do. You need some advice about presenting your side of it."

"I don't care about that. I just want to get it over with."

"It still might be smart. They'll want your attorney there anyway before you make a statement. You want me to go with you?"

She shook her head. "I can handle it, but thanks."

"Good luck."

"You, too." She glanced back toward the gallery reluctantly. "I better split. I don't guess we'll see you at the opening tonight."

"Probably not, but I do like her work," I said. "Call if you need me."

She smiled and waved, walking backward, then turned and went back to the gallery.

I got in my car and sat there for a minute, feeling heavyhearted. Tippy was a good person. I wished there were some way to spare her what she would have to go through. She'd be okay in the end, I was confident of that, but I didn't relish having been the impetus for her pain. I could argue she'd actually brought it on herself, but the truth was, she'd found a way to live with the situation for six years now. I had to guess she'd experienced remorse and regret in privacy. Maybe there simply wasn't any way to avoid public penance. In the meantime, I was left with feelings of my own. I really couldn't deal with any more angry people. I'd had it with accusations, threats, and bullying. My job was to figure out what was going on and I intended to do that.

I reached for the ignition key and fired up the VW, then did an illegal U-turn. There was a drugstore a block up and I pulled into the tiny lot, ducking in just long enough to buy three packages of three-by-five index cards—one white, one green, and one a pale orange. After that, I went home. I still had a batch of files from Morley's Colgate office in my car. I found a parking spot across the street from the apartment. I unloaded the backseat and proceeded through the gate, weighted down like a pack mule. I eased around to the backyard and fumbled with my keys.

In the glass-enclosed breezeway that links Henry's place with mine, I caught sight of the luncheon in progress. The December sun was weak, but with so many windows the space functioned like a greenhouse. William and Rosie had their heads bent together in earnest conversation. The subject was probably pericarditis, colitis, or the perils of lactose intolerance. Henry's face was dark and I could have sworn he was sulking, a behavior utterly unlike the Henry I knew. I anchored the stack of files against the doorframe with my hip while I unlocked my apartment and let myself in. I dumped everything on the counter. I turned around to find Henry coming in behind me with a plate piled with food—lemon chicken, ratatouille, green salad, and homemade rolls.

"Hi, how are you? Is that for me? It looks great. How's it going?" I asked.

He put the plate down on the counter. "You won't believe it," he said.

"What's the matter? Hasn't Rosie found a way to whip William into shape?"

Henry squinted his eyes and tapped his temple with his index finger. "It's funny you should mention that. The penny finally dropped. Do you know what she's doing? She's flirting with him!"

"Rosie always flirts."

"But William's flirting back." He opened a kitchen drawer and pulled out a knife and fork, which he handed me with a paper napkin.

"Well, there's no harm in that," I said, and then saw his look. "Is there?"

"You eat while I talk. Suppose the two of them get serious? What do you think's going to happen?"

"Oh, come on. They've known each other one day." I tried a bite of roll first, tender and buttery.

"He's going to be here two weeks. I hate to think what the next thirteen days are going to bring at this rate," he said.

"You're jealous."

"I'm not jealous. I'm terrified. He was fine this morning. Obsessed with his bowels. He took his blood pressure twice. He had several mysterious symptoms that occupied him for an hour. Then we went off to the funeral and he still seemed okay. We get home and he had to go and rest for a while. Same old William. No sweat, I can handle it. I put lunch together and then Rosie shows up wearing rouge on her cheeks. Next thing I know, the two of them are in there with their heads together, laughing and nudging like a couple of kids!"

"I think it's sweet. I like Rosie." I had moved on to the chicken, tucking into lunch in earnest. I hadn't realized I was hungry until I started chowing down.

"I like her, too. Rosie's fine. She's great. But as a *sister-in-law?*"

"It won't come to that."

"Oh, it won't? You ought to go in and listen to 'em talk. It would make your stomach turn."

"Come on, Henry. You're overreacting. William's eighty-five years old. She's probably sixty-five, if she'd ever admit to it."

"My point exactly. She's too young for him."

I started laughing. "I can't believe you're serious."

"I can't believe you're not! What if they get 'involved' in some flaming affair? Can you imagine the two of them in my back bedroom?"

"Is that your objection, that William might have a sex life? Henry, you astonish me. That's not like you."

"I think it's tacky behavior," he said.

"He hasn't done anything yet! Besides, I thought you wanted him to quit harping on his health. What better way? Now he can harp on something else."

Henry stared at me, his expression suddenly tinged with uncertainty. "You don't think it's vulgar? Romance at his age?"

"I think it's great. You had a romance of your own not that long ago."

"And look how that turned out."

"You survived it."

"But will he? I keep picturing Rosie flying back to Michigan for Christmas. I hate to sound snobbish, but the woman has no class. She picks her teeth with a bobby pin!"

"Oh, quit worrying."

His mouth formed a grudging line as he reconsidered his position. "I don't suppose it would do any good to protest. They'd just act as if they didn't know what I was talking about."

I kept my mouth shut, concentrating on the food instead. "This is great," I said.

"There's some for later if you want it," he remarked. He pointed to the cards. "You have work to do?"

I nodded. "As soon as I finish this."

He blew out a breath. "Well, enough of this nonsense. I better let you get to it."

"Keep me posted on developments."

"Absolutely," he said.

We made the usual departing mouth noises and then he disappeared. I closed the door behind him and made a beeline for the loft, where I kicked off my flats and peeled out of the all-purpose dress and panty hose. I pulled on my jeans, turtleneck, socks, and Nikes. Heaven.

I went downstairs, popped open a Diet Pepsi, and got down to business. I spread all the material on the counter: Morley's files, his calendar, his appointment book, and his rough-draft reports. I made a list of all the people he'd talked to, the dates, and the details of what was said, according to his notes. I opened the first pack of index cards and started making notes of my own, laying out the story as I understood it. I used to use this technique for every case I worked, pinning the cards on my bulletin board so I could see how the story looked. I learned the practice from Ben Byrd, who'd taught me the business when I was first starting out. Now that I thought about it, Ben had probably learned the method from Morley, who'd been in partnership with him until their falling-out. I smiled to myself. They'd called the agency Byrd–Shine; two old-fashioned gumshoes with whiskey bottles in their desk drawers and endless hands of gin rummy. Their specialty had been "matrimonial inquiries," i.e., extramarital sex. In those days, adultery was considered a shocking breach of morality, good breeding, common decency, and taste. Now you couldn't qualify for a talk show appearance on grounds that tame.

The index cards permitted a variety of approaches: timetables, relationships, the known and the unknown, motives and speculations. Sometimes I shuffled the pack and laid the cards out like solitaire. For some reason, I hadn't employed the routine of late. It felt good to get back to it. It was restful, reassuring, a welcomed time-out in which to get the facts down.

I left my perch and went over to the storage closet, where I hauled out my bulletin board and propped it up on the counter. At this stage, I make no attempt to organize the cards. I censor nothing. There's no game plan. I simply try to record all the information, writing down everything I can think of in the moment. All the cards for Isabelle's murder were green. Tippy's accident was on the orange cards, the players on the white. I found the box of pushpins and began to tack the cards up on the board. By the time I finished the process, it was 4:45. I sat on a kitchen stool, elbows propped on the counter, my chin in my hands. I studied the effect, which really didn't look like much . . . a jumble of colors, forming no particular pattern.

What was I looking for? The link. The contradiction. Anything out of place. The known seen in a new light, the unknown rising to the surface. At intervals, I took all the cards down and put them up again, ordered or random, arranging them according to various schemes. I thought idly about Isabelle's murder, letting my mind wander. How delicious it must have been for the killer to watch this whole drama unfold. It was even possible that David Barney's harassment had suggested the possibility. Shoot Isabelle and who's the first person they'd suspect? The killer had to be someone who knew David Barney's habits, someone close enough to the scene to keep watch. Of course, half of the people who knew Isabelle were in that position, I thought. The

Weidmanns lived within a mile of the house, as did her sister, Simone, whose cottage was on the property. Laura Barney was an interesting possibility. She certainly knew David's penchant for late-night runs. On the face of it, she had little or nothing to gain. I'd tended to assume that the motive was money, but among the killing set there were probably many other satisfactions besides greed to be derived from homicide. What could be more perfect than killing the woman who'd wrecked her marriage and having the blame for it fall on her ex-husband?

There was something here. I was almost sure of it. Maybe it was the angle of approach, some elusive piece of information, some new interpretation of the facts as I knew them.

When the telephone rang, I jumped, my heart banging abruptly into cardiac arrest range.

It was Ida Ruth. "Kinsey. I hope I'm not interrupting anything, but you just got a call from the coroner's office, a Mr. Walker. I guess he left a message on your office machine and then tried this one. He wants you to call him as soon as you can."

I tucked the phone against my shoulder while I picked up a pen and reached for a scratch pad. "What's Burt's number, did he give it to you?"

She gave me the number. As soon as she hung up, I dialed his office.

"Coroner's office. Detective Walker."

"Hello, Burt. This is Kinsey. Ida Ruth said you wanted me to get in touch."

"Oh, good. Glad she found you. Hang on a second, let me grab my notes." In the background, I heard paper rustling. He put a palm across the receiver, engaging in a brief muffled conversation before he came back. "Sorry. We just finished the post on Morley. Turned out he died of acute renal failure, with evidence of liver damage, cardiovascular damage with circulatory collapse, tubular necrosis—"

"Caused by what?"

"I'm getting to that. I called Wynington-Blake after we talked yesterday? I had a chat with the funeral director. I wanted to tell him what was going on and I was curious if he'd picked up on anything. He says when Morley was brought in, he was 'markedly jaundiced.'"

"From the drinking?"

"That was my first thought, but then I did a little research. I got to picking through that bunch of household and garden items you dropped off. The pastry specimen bothered me because it was vegetable material. Most of that other stuff I couldn't see how anybody could ingest without being aware of it. I checked some reference books here and I'll tell you what popped up. The autopsy confirms this. Did you ever hear about *Amanita phalloides*?"

"Sounds like a sex act. What the hell is it?"

"The death cap mushroom. *Amanita verna* is another possibility. That's another species from the same family, also known as the fool's mushroom. Both are deadly. Judging from this pastry—whatever you want to call it—it looks like somebody baked him an *Amanita* strudel."

"Sounds grim."

"Oh, it is. Listen to this. One fifty-millionth of a gram of phalloidine injected into a mouse is fatal in one to two days. Takes less than two ounces to kill a human being."

"Jesus."

"And either type would do just about what you describe of Morley's symptoms. Interestingly enough, ingestion can be followed by what they call a latent period of six to twenty hours. Then what you'd see is nausea, abdominal pain, vomiting and diarrhea, and cardiovascular collapse."

"So if he got sick midday on Saturday, he could have conceivably eaten the stuff anywhere from early Saturday morning to some time on Friday."

"Looks like it."

"Where would somebody find the damn things? Do they grow in this area?"

"Book says eastern North America and Pacific Coast, late summer and fall. It'd be late for that, but I suppose it's possible. *Verna* is said to be common in hardwood and coniferous forests. They can grow singly, or in clumps or rings. Says they're rare on the West Coast, but somebody might have brought 'em in from some other part of the country. Dried or frozen, something like that. Where'd you find the pastry, at his house?"

"In the wastebasket in his office out in Colgate. I saw the bakery box the first time I was there, but I didn't think anything about it until I went out again."

"Any idea how he got it?"

"I didn't even think to ask. I just tucked it in the bag along with everything else. Actually, I was assuming he'd stopped at the bakery and picked it up himself. Betty, in the beauty shop, says he sneaked all kinds of food in. He'd been on a strict diet for a week, but she'd seen him with doughnuts and Chinese, all kinds of fast food, so the bakery box wasn't inconsistent. Maybe somebody brought it out to him and left it on his doorstep—"

Burt cut in. "I'll tell you something else. According to the data I'm looking at? There's a brief calm period sets in. Remember telling me he got to feeling better? With *Amanita* poisoning, it sometimes looks like the patient's condition is improving."

"You're talking about Sunday morning," I said.

"Right. The truth is, the damage would have been done by then. This toxin tears up your liver, dissolves blood corpuscles, causes hemorrhaging in the digestive tract. He was probably experiencing bloody stools and bloody vomitus, though from what you've said he never mentioned it. Either he didn't think anything about it or he didn't want to alarm his wife. Actually, even if he'd gone into the emergency room, they couldn't have done anything to save him."

"He must have felt like shit. Why didn't he try to get some help?" I asked.

"It's hard to know. Severity of symptoms probably depends on how much he ate. He might have tried some, decided it was spoiled or something, and tossed the rest in the trash. You ever watch Morley eat? He was quick. Man prided himself on how fast he could put food away."

"Somebody knew him pretty well," I said.

"Not necessarily. He made no secret of it. Same with his health. He was always talking about his heart problems and his weight."

"What about the mushrooms? Can they be identified on sight?"

"Not unless you know what to look for. I'll read you what it says. '*A. verna* is pure white. *A. phalloides* is yellowish green to greenish. Spores in both are white and not attached to the stem.' Yada, yada, yada. Let's see. This particular type of mushroom starts out enclosed in what they call a universal veil that leaves a cup at the stem base. When you're picking mushrooms, you have to dig around some because it's sometimes hidden in the dirt. The illustration looks like a toadstool busting out of an egg. Says it's slimy, too. You want more?"

"I got the basics. If the killer had a batch of 'em growing in the yard, the rest would be gone by now anyway. What happens next?"

"I've sent the pastry up to Foster City, the Chemical Toxicology Institute, for analysis. Might be a while until we hear back from them, but I have a feeling they're going to confirm our suspicion. I've put a call through to Homicide, but you might want to talk to Lieutenant Dolan yourself. Believe me, the hard work has just started. Tough thing about homicidal poisoning is proving *legally* that a crime was committed. You have to demonstrate that the death was caused by a poison that was administered with malicious and evil intent to the deceased by the accused. And that means 'beyond a reasonable doubt.' How are you going to link the killer to the crime in this case? Somebody bakes a cake and drops the damn thing off. Morley gets to his office, 'Oh, hey, is this for me?' Odds are nobody even saw where it came from, so what the whole thing's going to boil down to is all circumstantial. We don't even have a suspect."

"Yeah, I know," I said.

"Well, you have to start someplace. I'll give you a call as soon as we have more. In the meantime, I wouldn't eat anybody's home-baked goodies."

"I'll try not to. And thanks, Burt."

By the time I hung up the telephone, my hands were cold. In the past several months, Morley had talked to a number of people associated with the murder of Isabelle Barney. What had he discovered that precipitated his death, too? It must have been significant. A poisoner is considered one of the smartest and most devious of murderers, largely because poison, as a method, requires knowledge, skill, premeditation, and cunning. One doesn't poison in the heat of passion. Poisoning is not an impulsive, spur-of-the-moment crime. The covertness and deliberation suggest the kind of cruelty that makes a charge of first-degree murder nearly automatic in such cases. Morley Shine had died of an internal violence that probably left no outward mark, yet his death had been as agonizing as a stabbing or gunshot wound. I had a sudden flash of the killer with a supply of deadly mushrooms, leafing through a cookbook for a little appetizer Morley might enjoy. I pictured pastry dough being rolled out, the filling gently sautéed with butter, the strudel lovingly assembled, packed in a bakery box, and delivered to Morley's doorstep. The killer might have sat and chatted with him while he ate the lethal savory. Even if it had tasted strange, Morley might not have complained. Too hungry from his diet. Too polite to protest. And then the hours that had passed while he became aware that he wasn't feeling well. He probably didn't even associate the nausea and the stomach pain with the pastry he'd consumed so many hours before. . . .

I'd seen toadstools somewhere. The image flickered in my memory . . . a wooded area . . . toadstools growing in a circle . . .

There weren't that many places it could have been. Simone's . . . the house where David Barney had lived at the time of Isabelle's death, though I didn't remember anything about the landscaping there. The house had overlooked the ocean—few trees in the vicinity. The Weidmanns'. I'd accompanied Yolanda to the patio where Peter Weidmann was napping—a formal garden with the lawn stretching off toward the trees.

Methodically, I removed the index cards from my bulletin board and put them up again. What had Morley seen that I wasn't seeing? I pulled out his Month at a Glance from one of the stacks of files sitting on my counter. I started with the month of October, trying to get a feel for what he'd been doing the last two months. Most squares were empty. November was similarly blank except for a couple of notations: two doctor's appointments, a haircut one Wednesday afternoon. This month, December, had been slightly busier and it looked like he'd actually conducted a couple of interviews. Lonnie would be thrilled to hear he'd done *some*thing for his pay. Yolanda and Peter Weidmann's names appeared twice. The first appointment must have been canceled because he had a line drawn through the time and a big penciled arrow extended from that date to the same day and time a week later. I remembered Yolanda complaining about what a pest he'd made of himself, so he must have been there more than once.

On December 1, a week ago Thursday, he'd penciled in the initials F.V. at 1:15. Voigt? Had he talked to Francesca? She'd told me she'd never met the man. I'd come across a folder made up with her name on the tab, but the file had been empty. Of course, the F.V. could have been a witness on another case, but it didn't seem likely. The Voigts' home phone number was noted at the top of the page. Had she lied about seeing him? There was also the notation on Saturday morning of the appointment with Laura Barney. She'd told me about the appointment herself, claiming Morley never showed. But Dorothy said he'd gone out to the office to pick up his mail. If my theory was right, the fatal pastry could have been delivered as early as Friday afternoon, probably no later than Saturday morning, since he became ill shortly after lunch. Might bear checking out. Working in a medical clinic, Laura Barney would certainly have access to information about poisons. Maybe I'd start with her and work my way back through the list.

I locked up the apartment and went out to the car. I fired up the engine and headed toward the freeway overpass. I cut under the 101 on Castle, turning right on Granita and then left on Bay. It was just past 5:00 when I reached Santa Teresa Medical Clinic, which was in a pleasant treelined neighborhood of medical buildings and single-family dwellings. I was hoping I hadn't missed Laura. The clinic probably closed at 5:00, which meant I was going to arrive to find the door locked and the personnel gone for the weekend. I didn't have her home address, and though I could probably find it, I was impatient at the delay. To my astonishment, I spotted her, head bent, a light coat over her uniform, white crepe-soled shoes moving rapidly as she crossed the street in front of me. I tooted my horn. She shot me a look of annoyance, apparently assuming that I was chiding her for jaywalking.

I waved and leaned over to roll down my car window on the passenger side. "Can I talk to you?"

"I just got off work," she said.

"It won't take long."

"Can't it wait? I'm exhausted. I was looking forward to a big glass of wine and a hot bath. Come back in an hour."

"I have to be someplace else."

She broke off eye contact. I could see her debate, not really wanting to give in. She made a slight face, staring at the sidewalk with annoyance.

"It'll take five minutes if that," I said.

"Oh, hell. All right," she said. She cocked her head at the house behind her, a Victorian structure that had apparently been converted into apartments. "This is where I live. Why don't you go find a place to park and come on up. That'll give me time to get out of this uniform and take my shoes off. It's apartment six, down the hall at the back."

"I'll be right there."

She turned and walked quickly up the porch steps, disappearing through the front door. I found a parking spot six doors down, on the far side of the street. In a little flicker of paranoia, I wondered if she really lived somewhere else. I pictured her entering the building, then leaving by a back exit before I could catch up with her. I went up the wooden porch steps and opened a glass-paneled door into a shadowy hallway. The place was quiet. To the left, there was a hall table with a lamp that hadn't been turned on yet. Mail was piled up, along with several copies of the day's paper. Doors along the corridor had been closed off. What had once been the front parlor and the dining room probably now formed one unit, with a second at the back, with maybe a studio at the rear. I was guessing three apartments down, another three above. A set of stairs angled up on the right.

I went upstairs as instructed. This was not the cheeriest place I'd ever been, I thought, but it was clean enough. The wallpaper looked new, chosen for its Victorian flavor, which is to say saccharine. Nosegays and trailing ribbons led the eye on a merry chase. The effect was depressing despite all the pink and green and mauve activity.

I knocked at the door marked with an oversize brass 6. Laura appeared a moment later, tying a cotton kimono at the waist. I could see her white nursy shoes on the floor near an upholstered chair where she'd tossed her white uniform. I could hear bathwater running, which seemed pointed enough. The apartment consisted of two very large rooms with a cramped bathroom, probably converted from a linen closet. I could see the space heater from the front door and the rim of an ancient tub. The ceilings were high and there was lots of woodwork of the sort that somehow smells of shel-

246

lac even if it hasn't been touched by a brush for years. The place was sparsely furnished, but what she had was good. She watched me survey the living room/bedroom combination with a trace of amusement. "Does it suit you?"

"I'm always curious to see how other single people live."

"How do you live?"

"About like this. I try to keep it simple," I said. "I don't like working just to pay a bunch of bills every month."

"I hate being single. Have a seat if you like."

"You do?"

"Of course, don't you? It's lonely. And who wants to live like this?" She made a gesture that embraced more than the physical surroundings. She moved into the bathroom and turned off the water. Belatedly, I picked up the damp herbal scent of Vitabath.

"Looks great to me. Besides, nobody's going to take care of you," I said.

She returned to the room. "Well, I hope that's not true. I'm not resigned, I must say."

"Togetherness is an illusion. We're all on our own."

"Oh, spare me. I hate talk like that," she said. "You want to tell me what you came for?"

"Sure. It's about Morley Shine. You had an appointment last Saturday."

"That's right, but he never showed."

"His wife says he went to his office that day."

"I was there at nine. I waited half an hour and then I left," she said.

"Where'd you wait? Were you actually in his office?"

"I was out in the drive. Why? What difference does it make?"

"None, I suppose. I was curious about a delivery," I said. "That box from the bakery."

"You were there when that arrived?"

"Sure, I was out in my car. The bakery truck pulled up beside me. Some guy got out with this white bakery box. As he passed me he asked if I was Marla Shine. I told him the name was Morley and the guy was late arriving. The sucker tried to give *me* the box, but I'd waited long enough and I was out of there. I hate being stood up. I got better things to do."

"What'd the guy do with it?"

"The box? I don't know. He probably took it in the front. Maybe he left it on the porch."

"What bakery?"

"I didn't see. The truck was red. Might have been a messenger service, come to think of it. Why the quiz?"

"Morley was murdered."

She said, "Really." And her surprise seemed genuine.

"It was probably the strudel in the box you saw. I just talked to the guy in the coroner's office."

"He was poisoned?"

"Looks like it."

"Where does that leave you?"

"I don't know yet. Morley knew something. I'm not sure what it was, but I think I'm close."

"Too bad he didn't leave you the answer."

"In a way, he did. I know how his mind worked. He and the fellow who taught me the business were in partnership for years."

"What else do you need from me?"

"Nothing, at this point. I'll let you get to your bath."

I headed over to the freeway, driving north on 101 until I reached the Cutter Road off-ramp. I turned left, driving into Horton Ravine through the front gateposts. I felt as if I'd spent the whole week trekking back and forth between Colgate, downtown Santa Teresa, and the Ravine itself. The afternoon was turning gray, typical December with the temperature dipping close to fifty, the kind of cold snap only Californians could complain about. I parked in the circular drive and rang the bell. Francesca came to the door herself. She wore a wool shirtwaist dress in a chocolate brown, black tights, and boots, with a black crewneck sweater across her shoulders like a shawl.

She said, "Well, Kinsey. You're the last person in the world I expected to see." She hesitated, focusing fully on my face. "Is something wrong? You don't look right. Have you had bad news?"

"Actually, I have, but I don't want to go into it. Do you have a minute to spare? I want to talk to you about something."

"Sure. Come on in. Guda's gone off to the market to pick up a few items. I was just having coffee by the fire in the den. Let me grab a mug and you can join me. It seems nasty out."

It's nasty everywhere, I thought. I followed her to the kitchen, which was done in black and white, with oversize windows on three sides. The appliance fronts were black, as well as the cabinet facings, which were a gleaming lacquer. The counters were Corian, snow white and seamless. Racks and accessories were polished aluminum. The only touches of color were bright red dish towels and bright red oven mitts. She took a mug from the cupboard and indicated we could reach the den through the dining room. "You take cream and sugar? I've got both on the tray. There's skim milk if you prefer."

"Milk is fine," I said. I didn't want to tell her about Morley just yet. She was looking back at me with curiosity, clearly troubled by my manner. Bad news is a burden that only sharing seems to lift.

The den was paneled in birch, the furniture upholstered in saddle-colored leather. She resettled herself on the leather sofa where she'd been. She was in the process of reading a hardback, a Fay Weldon novel she'd nearly finished judging by the bookmarker. It had been ages since I was able to take a day off and shut myself in under a quilt with a good book. There was a plump pot of coffee on the brass table to one side. She poured coffee into the mug and passed it over to me. I took it with a murmured "Thank you," which she acknowledged with a wary smile. She pulled a pillow into her lap, holding on to it like a teddy bear.

I noticed she didn't press to find out why I'd stopped by. Finally I said, "I checked Morley's appointment book. According to his notes, you talked to him last week. You should have told me when I asked."

"Oh." She had the good grace to flush and I could see her debate about how to respond. She must have decided the lie wasn't worth telling twice. "I guess I was hoping you wouldn't have to know."

"You want to fill me in?"

"I'm embarrassed about it really, but I called first thing Thursday morning and set it up myself."

There was silence. I said, "And?"

She lifted one shoulder uncomfortably. "I was angry with Kenneth. I'd come across some information . . . something I'd been unaware of. . . ."

"Which was what?"

"I'll get to that in a minute. You have to understand the context. . . ."

I couldn't wait to hear this. "Context" is what you mention when you're rationalizing bad behavior. You don't need to talk about "context" when you've done something good. "I'm listening."

"I finally realized just how sick I was of Isabelle's murder. I'm sick of the whole subject and all the drama attached. It's been six years and that's all Kenneth talks about. Her murder, her money, her talent. How beautiful she was. The tragedy of her death. He's obsessed with the woman. He's more in love with her dead than he was when she was alive."

"Not necessarily. . . ."

She went on as if I hadn't spoken. "I told Morley I hated Iz, that I was thrilled to pieces when she died. I was just, you know, spewing out all this emotional . . . garbage. What's weird is when I thought about it later, I understood how twisted my thinking had become. Kenneth's, too. I mean, look at us. This is really a very neurotic relationship."

"You came to this conclusion after talking to Morley?"

"That was part of what triggered the realization that it was time to get out. If I'm ever going to be healthy, I've got to separate myself from Ken, learn to stand on my own two feet for a change—"

"And that's when you decided you were leaving him? Just last week?"

"Well, yes."

"So it had nothing to do with the cancer two years ago."

She shrugged. "I'm sure that played a part. It was like waking up. It was like suddenly understanding what my life was about. Honestly, until I talked to Morley, I thought I was happily married. Really. I thought everything was fine. I mean, more or less. After that, I understood it was all an illusion."

"Must have been a hell of a conversation," I said.

I waited briefly, but she had lapsed into silence.

"What was the 'more or less' part?" I asked.

She looked up at me. "What?"

"You want to tell me what you discovered? You said something made you angry. I gather that's why you got in touch with Morley in the first place."

"Oh. Yes, of course. I was tidying up the study and came across an account Ken had been keeping from me."

"A bank account?"

"Like that. A ledger sheet. He'd been, uhm, assisting someone financially."

"Assisting someone," I repeated blankly.

"You know. Regular cash payments from month to month. This has been going on for three years. Being a good businessman, of course he kept a record. It must not have occurred to him that I'd lay hands on it."

"What's it about? Does Kenneth have a mistress?"

"That's what I thought at first, but in a way it's worse."

"Francesca, would you just quit screwing around and tell me what's going on?"

It took her a moment. "He's been giving money to Curtis McIntyre."

"To *Curtis?*" I said. I could barely take that in. "What for?"

"That's what I asked. I was appalled of course. The minute he came home, I confronted him."

I stared at her. "And what did he say?"

"He says it was like walking-around money. To help with his rent. A few bucks to get some of his bills paid off. Things like that."

"Why would he do such a thing?" I asked.

"I have no idea."

"How much?"

"About thirty-six hundred dollars so far."

"Well, there goes that," I said. "Here I've been feeling guilty because I came up with information that throws a monkey wrench into Lonnie's case and now I find out the plaintiff has been keeping the prime witness on retainer. Wait till Lonnie hears. He's going to have a fit!"

"That's what I told Ken. He swears he was just trying to help the guy out."

"Doesn't he know how that's going to look if it comes to light? It's going to look like he's paying Curtis for his testimony. Trust me, Curtis is not that reliable as it is. How are we going to pass him off as an impartial witness doing his civic duty?"

"He doesn't see anything wrong with it. He says Curtis was having trouble finding a job. I guess Curtis told him he might have to leave the area and go somewhere else. Kenneth wanted to make sure he'd be available—"

"That's what subpoenas are for!"

"Well, don't get mad at me. Ken swears it's not what it looks like. Curtis came to him after David was acquitted—"

"Oh, stop it, Francesca. What's a jury supposed to think?

How convenient. Curtis's testimony is going to directly benefit the man who's been paying him now for three years. . . ."
I stopped where I was. Something in the way she was clutching at the pillow made me study her more closely. "What's
the rest?"

"I gave Morley the ledger. I was worried Kenneth would
destroy it so I left it with Morley for safekeeping till I could
decide what to do."

"When was this?"

"When I found the ledger? Wednesday night, I guess. I
took it over to Morley on Thursday, and when Kenneth got
home later, we had a huge fight. . . ."

"Did he know you'd taken it?"

"Yes, and he was furious. He wanted it back, but there was
no way I was going to do that."

"Did he know you'd given it to Morley?"

"I never said that. He might have figured it out, but I
don't see how. What makes you ask?"

"Because Morley was murdered. Somebody baked him a
strudel filled with poisoned mushrooms. I found the white
bakery box in the wastebasket."

Her face was blank. "Surely you don't think it was *Ken*."

"Let's put it this way: I've been through both Morley's
offices. There's no ledger at all and the files are incomplete.
I've been operating on the assumption that his housekeeping
was sloppy or he was ripping Lonnie off, billing him for work
that was never done. Now I'm wondering if someone stole
files to cover the theft of something else."

"Kenneth wouldn't do such a thing. He wouldn't do any
of it."

"What happened Thursday when you couldn't produce
the ledger? Did he drop the subject?"

"He asked me repeatedly, but I wouldn't tell him. Then he
said it didn't matter anyway because it wasn't a crime. If he
lent Curtis money, it was between the two of them."

"But doesn't it strike you as interesting? Here's Kenneth

Voigt paying Curtis McIntyre, whose testimony just happens to incriminate David Barney in a lawsuit that just happens to benefit Kenneth Voigt. Don't you see the symmetry? Or maybe it was blackmail. Now there's a thought."

"Blackmail for what?"

"Isabelle's murder. That's what all of this is about."

"He wouldn't have killed Isabelle. He loved her too much."

"That's what he says now. Who knows what he felt back then?"

"He wouldn't do that," she said without much conviction.

"Why not? Isabelle rejected him for David Barney. What could be more satisfying than to kill her and have the blame fall on *David*?"

I left her sitting there with the pillow in her lap. She'd twisted one corner until it looked like a rabbit's ear.

On the way back to Colgate, I stopped at a gas station and filled my tank. This crosstown driving was the equivalent of a round-trip to Idaho and I was beginning to regret the fact that I wasn't charging Lonnie for the mileage. It was just after 6:00 and traffic was heavy, most of it inbound, heading in the opposite direction. Clouds lay across the mountains like a layer of bunting.

I headed for Voigt Motors, trying to calculate the odds of Kenneth Voigt telling me the truth. Whatever his relationship with Curtis, it was time for some straight talk. If I couldn't get it out of Kenneth, I was going to track Curtis down and have a chat with him. I parked in the

20

little strip lot in front of Voigt Motors, tucking my VW between a vintage Jaguar and a brand-new Porsche. I went in through the front door, ignoring the saleswoman who stepped forward to greet me. I went up the wide stairs to the loggia of offices that rimmed the second floor—Credit, Accounting. Apparently the salespeople were required to be on the floor until closing time at 8:00. Those working the business end were a little luckier, already in the process of going home for the day. Kenneth's office door carried his name in two-inch brass letters. His secretary was a woman in her early fifties who'd gone on being a bleached blonde way beyond the legal age for it. Time had marked the space between her eyes with a goalpost of worry. She was tidying her desk, putting files away, making sure the pens and pencils were placed neatly in a ceramic mug.

I said, "Hi. Is Mr. Voigt here? I'd like to talk to him."

"You didn't pass him on the stairs as you came up? He left two minutes ago, but he may have gone down the back way. Is there something I can help you with?"

"I don't think so. Can you tell me where he parks? Maybe I can catch him before he takes off."

Her expression had changed and she regarded me with caution. "What is this regarding?"

I didn't bother to reply.

I ducked out of the office and continued along the upper level, peering briefly into every room I passed, including the men's room. A startled-looking fellow in a business suit was just shaking himself off. God, that would be convenient. If there were any justice in the world, women would have the little hang-down things and men would get stuck with putting the paper down on the seats. I said, "Ooops. Wrong room," and shut the door again. I found the back stairs through a door marked "Fire Exit." I took the stairs two at a time going down, but when I reached the parking lot, there was no sign of Ken and there were no cars pulling out of the exit.

I went back to my VW and headed out of the lot, turning left onto Faith in the direction of upper State. Curtis McIntyre's motel was only a mile away. This section of town was devoted to fast-food restaurants, car washes, discount appliance stores, and assorted small retail establishments, with an occasional office building sandwiched into the mix. Once I was past the Cutter Road Mall, the northbound freeway entrance appeared on the right. State Street angled left, running parallel to the highway for another mile or two.

The Thrifty Motel was located near the junction of State Street and the two-lane highway that cut north toward the mountains. I hung a left into the gravel entrance to the motel parking lot. I pulled into the unoccupied slot in front of Curtis's room. The lights in most rooms along the L were blazing, the air richly perfumed with the scent of frying meats, a heady blend of bacon, hamburger, pork chops, and sausage. Television news shows and booming country music competed for airspace. Curtis's windows were dark and there was no response to my knock. I tried the room next door. The guy who answered must have been in his forties, with bright blue eyes, a bowl-shaped haircut, and a beard like a tangle of hair pulled out of a brush.

"I'm looking for the guy next door. Have you seen him?"

"Curtis went out."

"Do you have any idea where?"

The guy shook his head. "Not my day to keep track of him."

I took out a business card and a pen. I scribbled a note asking Curtis to call me as soon as possible. "Could you give him this?"

The guy said, "I will if I see him." He shut the door again.

I took out another card and jotted down a duplicate message, which I slid in behind the metal 9 tacked to his door. The neon motel sign blinked on as I crossed the parking lot to the manager's office. *Thrifty Motel* was spelled out in sputtering green, the sound of flies buzzing against a window

screen. The glass-paneled office door was open and a NO VA-
CANCY sign, red letters on a white ground, had been propped
against one of the jalousie windowpanes.

The registration counter was bare, the small area behind it
unoccupied. A door in the rear was standing ajar and there
were lights on in the apartment usually reserved for the manager on the premises. He was apparently watching the rerun
of a sitcom, laugh track pummeling the air with recurrent
surges of mirth. Every third laugh was a big one and it wasn't
difficult to visualize the sound engineer sitting at the board
pushing levers up and back, up and back, WAY up and back.

A small sign on the counter said "H. Stringfellow, mgr.
Ring bell for service" with an old-fashioned punch bell. I
dinged, which got a big laugh from the unseen audience. Mr.
Stringfellow shuffled through the door, closing it behind
him. He had snow-white hair and a gaunt clean-shaven face,
his complexion very pink, his chin jutting forward as if he'd
had it surgically augmented. He wore baggy brown pants
and a drab brown polyester shirt with a thin yellow tie. "Full
up," he said. "Try the place down the street."

"I'm not looking for a room. I'm looking for Curtis McIntyre. You have any idea what time he'll be back?"

"Nope. Some fellow came and picked him up. At least, I
think it was a man. Car pulled in out there and off he went."

"You didn't see the driver?"

"Nope. Didn't see the car either. I was working in the back
and I heard a honk. Few minutes later, I saw Curtis passing
by the window. I just happened to glance out the door or I
wouldn't have seen that. Pretty soon a door slammed and
then the car pulled away."

"What time was this?"

"Just a little while ago. Maybe five, ten minutes."

"Do his calls come through the switchboard?"

"Isn't any switchboard. He's got a telephone in his room.
That way his phone bill's his own business and I don't have
to fool with it. I don't pretend I'm dealing with a classy type

258

of tenant. Dirtbags, most of 'em, but it's nothing to me. Long as they pay the rent in advance as agreed."

"Is he pretty good about that?"

"He's better than most. You his parole officer?"

"Just a friend," I said. "If you see him, could you ask him to give me a call?" I took out another business card and circled my number.

I unlocked the car door, just about to let myself in, when my bad angel piped up, giving me a little nudge. Right there in front of me was Curtis McIntyre's door. The lock looked respectable, but the window right next to it was open. The gap was only three inches, but the wooden frame on the window screen was warped along the bottom and actually bulged out just about far enough for me to tuck my tiny fingers in. Pop the screen out and all I'd have to do is push the sash up, reach around on the inside, and turn the thumb-lock. There was no one in the parking lot and the noise from all the television sets would cover any sound. I'd been a model citizen all week and where had it gotten me? The case was never going to get as far as court anyway, so what differ-ence would it make if I broke the law? Breaking and entering isn't *that* big a deal. I wasn't going to steal anything. I was just going to have a teeny, tiny, little peek. This is the kind of reasoning my bad angel gets into. Trashy thinking, but it's just so persuasive. I was ashamed of myself, but before I could even reconsider I was easing the screen out, slipping the naughty old digits through the opening. Next thing I knew I was in his room. I turned the light on. I just had to hope Curtis wouldn't walk in. I wasn't sure he'd care if I tossed his place. I was more worried that if he caught me there, he'd think I was hustling him.

His mother would have been embarrassed to see his per-sonal habits. "Pick up your clothes" was not in his vocabu-lary. The room wasn't very big to begin with, maybe twelve feet by twelve, with a galley-size kitchen—combination refrig-erator, sink, and hot plate, all filthy. The bed was unmade, no big surprise there. A small black-and-white TV sat on one of the bed tables, pulled away from the wall for better viewing in bed. Cords trailed across the floor, fairly begging to be tripped over. The bathroom was small, draped with damp towels that smelled of mildew. He seemed to favor the kind of soap with pubic hairs embedded in it.

Actually, I didn't care how he kept his place. It was the rickety wooden desk that interested me. I began to search. Curtis didn't believe in banks. He kept his cash loose in the top drawer, quite a lot of it. He probably figured that roving bands of big-time thieves weren't going to target room 9 of the Thrifty. A few bills were tossed in helter-skelter with the cash: gas, telephone, Sears, where he'd charged some clothes. Under the windowed envelopes was a heavyweight self-sealing envelope meant for mailing checks. The address was handwritten, with no return address visible in the upper left-hand corner. I flipped it over. The personalized name and address of the sender had been printed on the back flap: Mr. and Mrs. Peter Weidmann. Well, that was interesting. I tilted the shade on the little table lamp, holding the envelope so close to the bulb I nearly scorched the paper. The envelope was lined with obnoxious stars, obscuring the field so I couldn't see the contents. Happily the heat from the bulb seemed to soften the gum seal, and by picking patiently at the flap I managed to peel it open.

Inside was a check for four hundred dollars, made out to Curtis and signed by Yolanda Weidmann. There was no explanation on the check in the space marked "Memo" and no personal note tucked into the envelope. How did she know Curtis and why was she paying him? How many more people was the guy collecting from? Between Kenneth and Yolanda, he was raking in five hundred dollars a month. Add a few more contributors and it was better than a paying job. I slid the check back and resealed the envelope. The rest of the desk drawers contained nothing of interest. I did another quick visual survey and then flipped the light out. I peered around the edge of the curtain. The parking lot was deserted. I turned the thumb-lock and eased out, pulling the door shut behind me.

I bypassed the freeway and took surface roads back into Horton Ravine. Lower Road was dark, the few streetlamps too widely spaced to offer adequate illumination. The lights that had been turned on at the Weidmanns' house were the sort you offer up to burglars in hopes they'll go elsewhere. The porch light was on and there was no car in the drive. I left my engine idling while I rang the bell. Once I was convinced there was no one home, I backed down the driveway and parked around the corner on Esmeralda. The Horton Ravine Patrol would swing by at intervals, but I thought I'd escape notice temporarily. I opened the glove compartment and took out the big flashlight. To the best of my recollection, the Weidmanns didn't have electronic fences or a big slobbering Doberman. I grabbed my jacket from a jumble in the backseat. I shrugged myself into it and zipped it up the front. Time to go walking in the woods on a little toadstool hunt.

I approached the house on foot, my flashlight raking back and forth across the path in front of me. The porch light contributed a soft wash of yellow that blended with the shadows at the edge of the yard. I moved around the side of the house to the patio in the rear, where two harsh spotlights made the property inhospitable to prowlers. I crossed the concrete slab and went down four shallow steps to the formal garden. The cushion on Peter's chaise had been folded in half, possibly to spare it further weathering. Over the years, the sun had bleached the canvas to a tired and cracking gray. I could see that snails were currently using the surface as a playground.

The grass had been cut. I could see parallel paths through the back lawn, swaths overlapping where the mower had doubled back. Where I'd seen toadstools, there was nothing. I crossed the yard, trying to remember the placement of the fairy rings. Some toadstools had grown singly and some in clumps. Now everything had been obliterated by the passing mower blades. I hunkered, touching minced vegetable matter, whitish against the dark grass. Out of the corner of my eye, I caught movement . . . a shadow passing through the light. Yolanda was home, tramping through the wet grass to the place where I was crouched. She was wearing another two-piece velour running suit, this one magenta. Her walking shoes seemed to flash with short strips of reflecting tape, the pristine leather uppers sprinkled with clippings from the mown grass.

"What are you doing out here?" Her voice was low, and in the half light her face was gray with fatigue. Her platinum-blond hair was as stiff as a wig.

"I was looking for the toadstools that were here the first time I came."

"The gardener came yesterday. I had him mow all of this."

"What'd he do with the clippings?"

"Why do you ask?"

"Morley Shine was murdered."

"I'm sorry to hear that." Her tone was perfunctory.

"Really?" I said. "You didn't seem to like him much."

"I didn't like him at all. He smelled like someone who drank and smoked, which I don't approve of. You still haven't explained what you're doing on my property."

"Have you ever heard of *Amanita phalloides?*"

"A type of toadstool, I presume."

"A poisonous mushroom of the type that killed Morley."

"The gardener puts the clippings in a big heap over there. When the pile gets big enough, he loads up his truck and takes it all to the dump. If you like, you can have the crime lab come haul it away for analysis."

"Morley was a good investigator."

"I'm sure he was. What's that got to do with it?"

"I suspect he was murdered because he knew the truth."

"About Isabelle's murder?"

"Among other things. You want to tell me why you sent a four-hundred-dollar check to Curtis McIntyre?"

That seemed to stump her. "Who told you that?"

"I saw the check."

She was silent for a full thirty seconds, a very long time in ordinary conversation. Reluctantly she said, "He's my grandson. Not that it's any of your business."

"Curtis?" I said with such incredulity that she seemed to take offense.

"You don't need to say it like that. I know the boy's faults perhaps better than you."

"I'm sorry, but I never in this world would have linked you with him," I said.

"Our only daughter died when he was ten. We promised her we'd raise him as well as we could. Curtis's father was unbearably common, I'm afraid. A criminal and a misfit. He disappeared when Curt was eight and we haven't heard a word from him since. When it comes to nature versus nurture, it's plain that nature prevails. Or perhaps we failed in some vital way. . . ." Her voice trailed off.

"Is that how he got involved in all this?"

"This what?"

"He was set to testify in the civil suit against David Barney. Did you talk to him about the murder?"

She rubbed her forehead. "I suppose."

"Do you remember if he was staying with you at the time?"

"I don't see what that has to do with anything."

"Do you happen to know where he is at the moment?"

"I haven't any idea."

"Somebody picked him up at his motel a little while ago."

She continued to stare at me. "Please. Just tell me what you want and then leave me alone."

"Where's Peter? Is he here?"

"He was admitted to the hospital late this afternoon. He's had another heart attack. He's in the cardiac care unit. If it's not too much to ask, I'd like to go in now. I came home for a bite of supper. I have some phone calls to make and then I have to go back to the hospital. They're not sure he's going to make it this time."

"I'm sorry," I said. "I had no idea."

"It doesn't matter now. Nothing really matters much."

I watched with uneasiness as she tramped back across the grass, her wet shoes leaving partial prints on the concrete. She looked shrunken and old. I suspected she was a woman who would follow her mate into death within months. She unlocked the back door and let herself in. The kitchen light went on. As soon as she was out of sight, I began to cross the grass, my flashlight picking up occasional fragments of white. I hunkered, brushing aside a clump of grass clippings. Under it was a scant portion of mower-chopped toadstool—less than a tablespoon from the look of it. The chances of its being *A. phalloides* seemed remote, but in the interest of thoroughness I took a folded tissue from my jacket pocket and carefully wrapped the specimen.

I went back to my car, feeling somewhat unsettled. I was reasonably sure I understood now how Curtis had gotten involved in the case. Maybe he'd heard the jail talk among informants and had approached Kenneth Voigt after the acquittal came down. Or maybe Ken had heard from the Weidmanns that Curtis had been jailed with David Barney. He might well have approached Curtis with the suggestion about his trumped-up testimony. I wasn't sure Curtis was smart enough to generate the scheme himself.

I sat in my car on the darkened side road. I rolled the window down so I could listen to the crickets. The feel of damp air against my face was refreshing. The vegetation along the berm smelled quite peppery where I'd trampled it. I worked for the Y as a camp counselor (briefly) the summer before my sophomore year in high school. I must have been fifteen, full of hope, not yet into flunking, rebelling, and smoking dope. We'd gone on an "overnight," the whole batch of us from day camp, me with the nine-year-old girls in my charge. We did pretty well until we settled down for the night. Then it turned out the tree under which we'd arranged our sleeping bags was a vast leafy nest full of daddy longlegs spiders that commenced dropping down on us from above. Plop, plop. Plop, plop. You've never heard such shrieks. I scared the little girls half to death I'm sure. . . .

I glanced at my rearview mirror. Behind me, a car turned the corner, slowing as it reached me. The logo on the vehicle was the Horton Ravine Patrol. There were two men in the front seat, the one in the passenger seat directing a spotlight in my face. "You having a problem?"

"I'm fine," I said. "I'm just on my way." I turned the key and put the car in gear, easing forward on the shoulder until I could pull onto the pavement in front of them. I drove sedately out of Horton Ravine, the guys in the patrol car following conspicuously. I got back on the freeway, more from desperation than from any concrete plan. What was I supposed to do? Most of the leads I'd pursued had suddenly petered out, and until I talked to Curtis I couldn't be sure what was going on. I'd left word for him to call. My only choice seemed to be to head for home, where at least he could reach me if he got one of my messages.

It was 8:15 by the time I reached my place. I locked the door behind me and turned the downstairs lights on. I transferred the tissue-wrapped toadstool to a Baggie, pausing to search through a kitchen drawer until I found a marker pen. I labeled the Baggie with a crudely drawn skull and crossbones and tucked it in my refrigerator. I peeled my jacket off and perched on a stool. I studied the bulletin board with its road map of multicolored index cards.

It was aggravating to think there might be something right in front of me. If Morley had spotted something, it had probably cost him his life. What was it? I ran my gaze up one column of information and down the next, watching the sequence of events unfold. I got up and walked around the room, came back, and peered. I went over to the sofa bed and lay down on my back, staring at the ceiling. Thinking is hard work, which is why you don't see a lot of people doing it. I got up restlessly and returned to the counter, leaning on my elbows while I scanned the board.

"Come on, Morley, help me out here," I murmured.

Oh.

Well, there was a bit of a discrepancy that I hadn't paid much attention to. According to Regina Turner at the Gypsy Motel, Noah McKell was struck and killed at 1:11 A.M. But Tippy hadn't reached the intersection at San Vicente and 101 until approximately 1:40, a thirty-minute difference. Why had it had taken her so long to get there? It was probably only four or five miles from the Gypsy to the off-ramp. Had she stopped for a cup of coffee? Filled her tank with gas? She'd just killed a man, and according to David she was still visibly upset. It was difficult to picture what she'd done with that half hour. Maybe she'd spent the time driving aimlessly around. I couldn't think why it would matter, but the question seemed easy to clarify.

I reached for the phone and punched in the Parsons number, staring at the bulletin board while it continued to ring. Eight, nine. Oh, yeah. Friday night. I'd forgotten about Rhe's opening at the Axminster Gallery. I hauled out the telephone book and looked up the number for the gallery. This time somebody picked up on the second ring, but there was such a din in the background I could hardly hear. I pressed a hand to my free ear, focusing on the sounds from the gallery. I asked for Tippy and then had to make the same request only doubling the volume and pitch of my voice. The fellow on the other end said he'd go and get her. I sat and listened to people laughing, glasses clinking. Sounded like they were having a lot more fun than I was. . . .

"Hello?"

"Hello, Tippy? This is Kinsey. Listen, I know this is a bad time to try to talk to you, but I was just thinking about what happened the night your aunt was killed. Can I ask you a couple questions?"

"Right *now?*"

"If you don't mind. I'm just curious about what happened

between the time of the accident and the time you saw David Barney."

There was silence. "I don't know. I mean, I went up to my aunt's, but that's it."

"You went to Isabelle's house?"

"Yeah. I was like really upset and I couldn't think what else to do. I was going to tell her what happened and ask her for help. If she told me to go back, I would have done it, I swear."

"Could you speak up, please? What time was this?"

"Right after the accident. I knew I hit the guy so I just took off and headed right up to her place."

"Was she there?"

"I guess so. The lights were on. . . ."

"The porch light was on?"

"Sure. I knocked and knocked but she never came down."

"Was the eyepiece in the door?"

"I didn't really look at that. After I knocked, I walked around the outside, but the place was all locked up. So I just got in my truck and headed home from there."

"You went home on the freeway."

"Sure, I got on at Little Pony Road."

"And got off at San Vicente."

"Well, yeah," she said. "Why, what's wrong?"

"Nothing really. It narrows the time of death, but I can't see that it makes any difference. Anyway, I appreciate your help. If you think of anything else, would you give me a call?"

"Sure. Is that all you want?"

"For now," I said. "Did you talk to the cops?"

"No, but I talked to this lawyer and she's going in with me first thing tomorrow morning."

"Good. You'll have to let me know what happens. How's the opening?"

"Really neat," she said. "Everybody loves it. They're like freaking out. Mom's sold six pieces."

"That's wonderful. Good for her. I hope she sells tons."

"I gotta go. I'll call you tomorrow."

I said good-bye to an empty line.

The phone rang again before I could remove my hand. I snatched up the receiver, thinking maybe Tippy had remembered something. "Hello?"

There was an odd breathy silence, very brief, and then I heard a man's voice. "Hey, Kinsey?" Then the breathiness again.

"Yes." I found myself squinting at the sound. I pressed my fingers to my ear again, listening to the quiet as I'd listened to the party noises at Rhe's opening. The guy was crying. He wasn't sobbing. It was the kind of crying you do when you want to conceal the fact. The air was bypassing his vocal cords. "Kinsey?"

"Curtis?"

"Uh-hunh. Yeah."

"What's wrong? Is somebody there with you?"

"I'm fine. How are you?"

"Curtis, what's the matter? Is someone there with you?"

"That's right. Listen, why I called? I was wondering if you could meet me so we could talk about something."

"Who is it? Are you okay?"

"Can you meet me? I have some information."

"What's going on? Can you tell me who's with you?"

"Meet me at the bird refuge and I'll explain."

"When?"

"As soon as possible, okay?"

I had to make a quick decision. I couldn't keep him on the line much longer. Anybody monitoring the call would get cranky. "Okay. It might take me a while. I'm already in bed so I'll have to get dressed. I'll see you down there as soon as I can make it, but it might be twenty minutes."

The line went dead.

It wasn't nine o'clock yet, but there wasn't much traffic around the bird refuge at night. The preserve encompasses a freshwater lagoon on a little-used access road between the freeway and the beach. The twenty-car parking lot is usually used by tourists looking for a "photo opportunity." There was a tavern across the street, but the property was currently without a tenant. I wasn't going to go down there alone and unarmed. I picked up the phone again and called the police station, asking for Sergeant Cordero.

"I'm sorry, but she won't be in until seven A.M."

"Can you tell me who's working Homicide?"

"Is this an emergency?"

"Not yet," I said tartly.

"You can talk to the watch commander."

"Just skip it. Never mind. I can try someone else." I depressed the button and tucked the telephone in against my shoulder while I checked my personal address book. The "someone else" I called was Sergeant Jonah Robb, an STPD cop who worked the missing persons detail. He and I had had a sporadic relationship that fluctuated according to the whims of his wife. Theirs was a marriage of high drama and long duration, the two having met at age thirteen in the seventh grade. Personally, I didn't think they'd progressed much. At intervals, Camilla would leave him—usually without notice or explanation—taking their two daughters and any money they had in their joint bank account. Jonah always vowed each time was the last. It was during one of these periods of domestic upheaval that I entered, stage left. I was the understudy, a role I discovered I didn't like very much. I'd finally severed the connection. I hadn't spoken to Jonah now for nearly a year, but he was still someone I felt I could call in a pinch.

A woman answered the telephone in a bedroom tone of voice, Camilla perhaps, or her latest replacement. I asked for Jonah and I could hear the receiver being passed from hand to hand. His "Hello" was groggy. God, these people went to bed earlier than I did. I identified myself and that seemed to wake him up some.

"What's happening?" he said.

"I hate to bother you, babe, but a jailbird named Curtis McIntyre just phoned and asked me to meet him at the bird refuge as soon as I can get there. My guess is the guy had a gun to his head. I need backup."

"Who's with him? Do you know?"

"I don't have an answer to that yet and it's too complicated to go into on the phone."

"You got a gun?"

"It's in my office at Lonnie Kingman's. I'm just on my way over there to pick it up. Take me fifteen minutes max and then I'll head down to the beach. Can you help?"

"Yeah, I can probably do that."

"I wouldn't ask, but I don't have anyone else."

"I understand," he said. "I'll see you there in fifteen minutes. I'll drive past and then double back on foot. There's plenty of cover."

"That's what concerns me," I said. "Don't trip over the bad guys."

"Don't worry. I can smell them puppy dogs. See you down there."

"Thanks," I said and hung up.

I grabbed my shoulder bag and my jacket with the car keys in the pocket, congratulating myself that I'd had the presence of mind to get the VW gassed up. It would take all the time I'd allotted to get from my apartment to the office and back down to the bird refuge. Whomever Curtis had with him was going to be edgy about delays, suspicious if I didn't show up in the time I'd said I would. I drove faster than the law allows, but I kept an eye on the rearview mirror, watching for cunningly concealed black-and-whites. I hoped I wouldn't have trouble laying hands on the gun. I'd moved only five weeks ago, hauling my hastily packed cardboard boxes from California Fidelity to Lonnie Kingman's office. I hadn't actually seen the gun since I bought it in May. I'd resented the necessity for the purchase in the first place, but I'd heard that my name was at the top of somebody's hit list.

A private eye named Robert Dietz had stepped into the picture when I realized I needed help. Once I accepted the fact that my life was truly endangered, I gave up any passing interest in being politically correct. It was Dietz who'd insisted that I replace my .32-caliber Davis with the H&K. The damn gun had cost me an arm and a leg. Come to think of it, I wasn't all that sure where the Davis was either.

When I got to the office, I left my car out on the street with my shoulder bag tucked down against the driver's seat out of sight. There was little or no traffic and all the nearby office buildings were locked down for the night. I moved through the darkened arch along the driveway that led back to the little twelve-car parking lot. I didn't see Lonnie's Mercedes, but there was a section of pavement washed with the light from his offices above. Well, great. He was back. I couldn't stop and explain what was going on, but it probably wouldn't be hard to talk him into going with me. Despite his professional demeanor, Lonnie's a brawler at heart. He'd love the idea of sneaking through the bushes in the dark.

I used my keychain flashlight against the pitch-black stairwell. When I reached the third-floor corridor, I could see where Lonnie'd turned the lights on in the reception area. I bypassed the front entrance and used the unmarked door that opened closer to my office. I glanced to my right toward Lonnie's office, located one door down from mine.

"Hey, Lonnie? Don't disappear on me. I need some help. I'll be there in a second and tell you what's going on."

I didn't bother to wait for a reply. I opened my office door and flipped the light switch. My office space had once functioned as the employees' lounge/kitchen, with my current closet serving as a pantry of sorts. There were five cartons still stacked against the back wall, clearly stuff I hadn't needed in the new place so far. I couldn't even remember what was in those boxes. I've heard the theory that if you still haven't unpacked a carton two years after a move, you simply call the Salvation Army and have the damn thing hauled away. I'd cleverly marked each box "Office Stuff." I pulled one out and ripped off the wide brown sealing tape. I peeled the flaps back. This box contained all my income tax files. I tried the next box and hit pay dirt. Oh, yea. The Heckler & Koch was sitting right on top, still in the box, the Winchester Silvertips in two boxes just under it.

I sat down on the floor and took the gun out. I grabbed a box of ammo and opened it, pulling out the little white Styrofoam base. I began to push cartridges into the magazine. Once we'd arrived at the gun shop, Dietz and I had had yet another fractious argument about which model I should buy: the P7, which held nine rounds, or the P9S, which held ten. Guess which one cost more? I was in a bitchy mood anyway, feeling stubborn and uncooperative. The P7 was already priced at more than eleven hundred bucks. I'd also griped about the P9S, which I felt was too much gun for me. What I meant, of course, was expensive, which Dietz guessed right away.

I'd said, "Goddamn it. I get to win sometimes."

"You win more often than you should," he'd said. I wished now he'd won a lot more arguments, especially the one about my going off to Germany with him. . . .

The lights in my office went out abruptly and I was left in the pitch-black dark. I had no exterior windows so I couldn't see a thing. Had Lonnie left without saying a word? Maybe he hadn't heard me come in, I thought. I slid the magazine into the gun and slapped it home with my palm. Navigating in the dark is like escaping from a burning building—you stay low. I tucked the gun in my waistband and crawled to the doorway with no dignity whatsoever. It beat bumping into the furniture, but it wasn't going to look good if the lights popped back on. My office door was standing open and I peered out into the hallway. All the lights in the office were out. What the hell had he done, stuck a fork in the outlet? The whole place had been plunged into blackness. I said, "Lonnie?"

Silence. How could he have disappeared so fast?

I could have sworn I heard a faint sound from the vicinity of Lonnie's office. I didn't think I was alone. I listened. The office was so quiet the silence seemed dense, thick with sub-sounds. Even in the dark, I found myself closing my eyes, hoping somehow to hear better with my visual sense shut down. I sat back on my haunches, crouched in my doorway across from the point where Ida Ruth and a secretary named Jill had their desks.

Who was in the office with me? And where? Having called out twice now in clear bell-like tones, we all knew where I was. I eased back down on all fours and started belly-crawling the ten feet across the corridor toward the space between the two secretaries' desks.

Somebody fired at me. The report was so loud I levitated like a cat, in one of those miraculous moves where all four limbs seem to leave the ground at once. Adrenaline blew through me in a sudden spurt. I wasn't aware that I had shrieked until the sound was out. My heart banged in my throat and my hands tingled from the rush. I must have leaped the distance because I found myself exactly where I wanted to be, in a crouch, my right shoulder resting against Ida Ruth's desk drawers. I put a hand across my mouth to still my breathing. I listened. The shooter seemed to be firing from the vantage point of Lonnie's office, effectively cutting me off from the reception area, where the front entrance was located. The obvious maneuver here was to back my way down the wide corridor, which was now to my left. The un-marked door, leading to the main hall, was about fifteen feet away. Once there, I could crouch beside it, try the knob to make sure the door was still open, count to three, and then voom . . . go right through. Good plan. Okay. All I had to do was get there. The problem was that I was afraid to risk the distance without cover of some kind. Where was Ida Ruth's rolling chair? That might do. . . .

I put a tentative hand out, groping my way along the floor

in search of the chair. I found myself touching a face. I jerked my hand back, emitting a sound at the back of my throat as I sucked in my breath. Someone was lying on the floor next to me. I half expected a hand to shoot out and grab me, but there was no move in my direction. I reached out again and made contact. Flesh. Slack mouth. I felt the features. Smooth skin, strong chin. Male. The guy was too thin to be Lonnie and I didn't believe it was John Ives or the other attorney, Martin Cheltenham. It almost had to be Curtis, but what the hell was he doing here? He was still warm, but his cheek was sticky with blood. I put my hand on his throat. No pulse. I placed a hand on his chest, which was dead still. His shirt was wet in front. He must have made the call from the office. He was probably shot shortly afterward in preparation for my arrival. Somebody knew me better than I thought . . . well enough to know where I kept my gun, at any rate . . . well enough to know I'd never show up at a meeting without coming down here first.

I felt behind me in the dark again, encountering one of the sturdy casters on Ida Ruth's rolling chair. I blinked in the dark as another possibility occurred to me. If I could find an open phone line, I could dial 911 and let it ring through to the dispatcher. Even if I never said a word, the address would come up on the police station computer and they'd send someone to investigate. I hoped.

I came up on my knees, peering over the top of the nearest desk. Now that my eyes were adjusting, I could distinguish greater and lesser degrees of dark: the charcoal upright of a doorway, the block form of a file cabinet. I moved my hand across the surface of the desk with incredible care, not wanting to bump into anything or knock anything over. I found the telephone. I lifted the entire instrument. I cleared the edge of the desk and lowered it to the floor. I angled the receiver upward slightly, slipping an index finger onto the cutoff button. I put the receiver against my ear and let the button come up. Nothing. No dial tone. No light coming on.

I peered up over the desk again and scanned the dark. There was no movement, no shadowy silhouette framed in Lonnie's doorway.

I eased the gun from my waistband. I'd never fired the H&K in a tight spot. I'd gone up to the range a few times with Dietz before he left. He'd put me through numerous firing drills until I refused to take any more orders from him. Usually I'm pretty good about keeping in practice, but not lately. It was the first time I'd tuned in to the fact I was depressed about his leaving. Shit, Kinsey, get a clue. The gun was reassuring. At least I wouldn't be totally at the mercy of my assailant. I squeezed the cocking lever on the grip.

I could hear breathing now, but it might have been mine.

I wished I hadn't left the relative safety of my office. My phone had a separate line and it might still be functioning. If I could cross the hall and get back to my office, I could at least lock the door and shove the desk up against it. All I'd have to do then was hold out until morning. Surely the cleaning crew would be in. I might be rescued sooner if anybody figured it out. I thought about Jonah. He'd be waiting at the bird refuge, wondering what had happened. What would he do when I didn't show up? Probably assume he got the location wrong. To my mind, the term *bird refuge* didn't contain any ambiguity. There was only one parking area. I had told him I was coming here first to pick up my gun, but he'd sounded half asleep. Who knew what he'd remember or if it would ever dawn on him to check it out.

I pulled Ida Ruth's chair closer and crouched behind it, keeping it between me and my assailant as I crept toward the unmarked door. Another shot was fired. The bullet tore through the upholstery with such force that the plastic chair back banged me right in the face. It was all I could do to keep from screaming as the blood gushed from my nose. I scooted backward, pulling the chair along in front of me as I scrambled toward the door. I eased a hand up along the doorframe until I touched the knob. Locked. Another shot was fired. A splinter of wood sailed past my face. I dove toward the wall, using the baseboard like a lane marker as I swam my way along the floor, praying the carpet would part for me and let me sink beneath the pile. The next shot ripped along my right hip as if someone were trying to strike a giant match. I jumped again, making a short exclamation of pain and astonishment. The stinging sensation told me I'd been hit. I fired back.

I rolled toward the far side of the corridor. The only protection I had at this point was the dark. If my eyes were adjusting, then so were my assailant's. I fired at Lonnie's doorway again. I heard a bark of surprise. I fired again, crawling backward down the hallway toward the kitchen in haste. My right buttock was on fire, sparks shooting down my right leg and up into my right side. I wasn't even crawling as efficiently as a six-month-old baby. I hugged the wall, feeling tears well, not from sorrow, but from pain.

I don't presume to understand how the human brain works. I do know that the left brain is verbal, linear, and analytical, solving life's little problems by virtue of sound reasoning. The right brain on the other hand tends to be intuitive, imaginative, whimsical, and spontaneous, coming up with the inexplicable Ah-ha! answer to some question you may have asked yourself three days before. There's no accounting for this. As I huddled in the blackness, gun in hand, with my lips pressed together to keep from shrieking like a girl, I knew with perfect certainty who was shooting at me. And to tell you the truth, it really pissed me off. When the next shot was fired, I flattened myself, braced the gun in both hands, and fired back. Maybe it was time to declare myself. "Hey, David?"

Silence.

"I know it's you," I said.

He laughed. "I was wondering if you'd figure it out."

"It took me a while, but I got it," I said. It was weird talking to him in the dark like this. I could barely visualize his face and that bothered me.

"How'd you guess?"

"I realized there was a gap between the time Tippy hit the pedestrian and the time she bumped into you."

"So?"

"So I called her and asked where she was for that thirty minutes. Turns out she went up to Isabelle's."

There was a silence.

I went on, "You must have just killed Isabelle when you saw Tippy coming up the drive. While she was knocking at the door, you hopped in the truck bed. She drove you away from the house when she left. All you had to do then was wait till she slowed down. Out you hop on the driver's side, giving the truck a thump with your fist as you jump. Tippy turns left and you're sprawled on the pavement in plain view of the work crew across the street."

"Yeah, with Mr. Average Citizen ready to testify in my behalf," he chimed in at last.

"What about Morley? Why'd you have to kill him?"

"Are you kidding? That old buzzard was really breathing down my neck. When I talked to him on Wednesday, he'd just about made the leap. I knew if I didn't take him down quick, I'd be in the soup. Raiding his files was a snap after that. He's kind of a slob when it came down to his paperwork."

"Where'd you get the death caps?"

"The Weidmanns' backyard. That's what inspired the notion in the first place. I went over there one night and plucked up a dozen and then paid my cook a little extra to make the pastry. She didn't know *Amanita* from her ass. She's lucky she didn't taste for seasonings as she went along."

"I gotta hand it to you. You are one clever chap," I said, thinking hard. Behind me, the corridor made a left-hand turn into a cul-de-sac with the copy room on one side and the new kitchenette on the other. If I rounded the corner, I'd be out of the line of fire, but I'd have a couple of problems I wasn't sure I could solve. One, I'd no longer have a straight line of fire myself. And two, I'd be trapped. On the other hand, I was trapped where I was. The kitchen had a small window. With luck, if I got there, I could bust out the glass and holler real loud for help. Like maybe nobody'd heard the gunfight at the O.K. Corral in here. If I could persuade him to keep talking, he might not hear me shift locations. "I'm surprised you didn't slip up somewhere along the line," I said. As long as I was stuck, I might as well fish for information.

Reluctantly, he said, "I did slip once."

"Really? When was that?"

"I got drunk one night with Curtis and flapped my big mouth. I still can't believe I did that. The minute it was out I knew I'd have to get rid of him one day."

"God," I said. "You mean to tell me he was telling the *truth* for once?"

Barney laughed in the dark. "Oh, sure. He figured it was worth some money to someone so he went straight to Ken Voigt and tattled. Sure enough, Voigt started paying Curtis to ensure his testimony. Fool."

I closed my eyes. Voigt *was* a fool. So eager to win he'd risked his own credibility. "What about me? Is there some scheme in the works or you just doing this for yucks?"

"Actually, I'd like to run you out of ammunition so I can finish you off. I killed Curtis with an H&K, like the one you've got. I'm going to shoot you with the thirty-eight I used on Isabelle and put that gun in his hand. That way, it'll look like he killed her—"

"And I killed him," I said, completing the sentence. "You ever hear about ballistics? They're going to know the gun wasn't mine."

"I'll be gone by then."

"Smart."

"Very smart," he said, "which is more than you can say of most people. Human beings are like ants. So busy, so involved in their little world. Watch an anthill sometime. Such activity. You can tell everything looks so important from the ant's point of view. But it's not. In reality, it doesn't amount to anything. Haven't you ever stepped on an ant? Rubbed one out with your thumb? You don't suffer any great pangs of conscience. You think, There. I gotcha. Same thing here."

"Jesus. This is really profound. I'm taking notes over here."

That made him mad and he fired twice, slugs plowing into the carpet to my right. I matched him shot for shot just for the hell of it.

"You're so innocent," he said. "You think you're such a cynic, but you were easy to fool—"

"Let's not jump to conclusions," I said. I thought I saw his head appear in Lonnie's doorway. I fired two more times.

He disappeared. "You missed."

"Sorry to hear that." I slipped out the magazine and counted cartridges by feel. All that nice ammo in the other room.

"You have a problem over there?"

"I broke a fingernail."

He was silent for a moment. "Be careful with your ammo. You only have one shot left."

"Bullshit. I have two."

He laughed in the dark. "Oh, right. Uh-hunh."

I was quiet and then I said, "What makes you so sure?"

"I can count."

I put my head down briefly, gathering my strength. Time to move along, I thought. I slipped my left shoe off and placed it on the floor in front of me. I slipped my right shoe off, my eyes crossing at the heat in my right hip. I could feel a numbness spreading and I couldn't quite compute how pain and nothing could share the same nerve path. "That was only seven," I said.

"It was *eight*."

"I have a ten-shot," I said piously. I began to ease back toward the point at which the corridor made a left.

"A ten-shot. What crap. You're such a liar," he said.

"Oh, really? What kind of gun do you have?"

"A Walther. An eight-shot. I have two shots left."

"No, you don't. You have one. I can count, too, bird-breath." I was moving by degrees, nearing the corner, feeling backward with my foot. David Barney didn't seem to notice the change in my location.

"You can't fool me. I did my homework on you."

"Like what?" I said. I reached the corner and angled myself around until only the upper portion of my body was in the corridor. David Barney was now about twenty-five feet away. I was resting on my right side, my blue jeans wet with blood. I looked down at myself. My hip had started to glow. I lifted myself on one elbow. I'd put my weight on my key-chain, activating the little plastic flashlight that was shaped like a flattened oval and turned on when you pinched it. I eased the keys out of my jeans pocket and took the flash off the key ring. I pushed the keys to one side, uneasy about their jangling.

"Like this business about your lying. You take a lot of pride in the fact."

"Who'd you hear that from?"

"I get around. It's amazing how much information you can pick up in jail."

"I bet you tell a lot of lies yourself," I said. "You probably have a nine-shot."

He actually sounded flattered. "You never know," he said.

"What made you so sure I'd come down here tonight?" I pulled myself up onto my hands and knees.

"You didn't figure that out? You told Curtis you kept your gun here. That's why I set up the meeting at the bird refuge. I knew you'd never go down there without your gun."

Let's get this over with, I thought. I came up to a half crouch, like a runner at a starting post, painfully aware of the throbbing in my butt.

Behind me, I heard him say, "You still there?"

I didn't answer.

"Where'd you go?"

I limped in my sock feet as quickly as I could toward the kitchen door. The room glowed a faint gray from the outside light. I realized at a glance there was no place to hide. I veered out of the room and across the hall. I tiptoed to the far corner and I crouched down beside the Xerox machine with my back to the wall. Bending my right leg hurt so bad I had to grit my teeth. I made it to a sitting position, my gun in my right hand, the little flash in my left. My hands felt greasy with sweat and my fingers were cold.

"Kinsey?" From the hallway. Any minute he'd figure out I was gone and come barreling after me.

I was squeezed in beside the Xerox machine with my knees drawn up. I was hoping to keep the target area as small as possible, though crammed in a corner was probably not such a hot idea. Guy fires one bullet, he hits everything you got.

"Hey!" he said. "I'm talking to you." I could tell from his voice he was still down around Lonnie's office. The man was annoyed.

I tried to still my breathing.

He fired.

Even down the hall and around the corner, I jumped. That was eight. If the man had an eight-shot, I was doing okay. A nine-shot, I was screwed. Once he figured out where I was, I was fair game. It was really too late to go anywhere else. I was feeling clammy, that cold, sick sensation that overwhelms you when you're about to pass out. I wiped my cheek against my shirtsleeve. Fear had settled over me like an icy vapor, rippling against my spine.

The notion of dying is, at the same time, trivial and terrifying, absurd and full of anguish. Ego clings to life. Self lets it go, willing to free-fall, willing to soar. If I regretted anything, it was simply not knowing how all the stories would turn out. Would William and Rosie fall in love sure enough? Would

Henry reach the age of ninety? With all the blood oozing out, would Lonnie ever get his carpet clean?

So many things I hadn't done. So many things I wouldn't get to do now. Dumb to die like this, but then again, why not?

I took two deep breaths, trying to keep my head clear.

In the hallway, quite close, I heard David Barney's voice. "Kinsey?" He was checking the kitchen as I had, realizing there was no place of concealment. He'd probably scouted the place while he was waiting for me to show up. He had to know the copy room was the only place left. I could hear his shallow breathing.

"Hello. You in there? Now we can have a little liar's contest. Do I have one bullet or no bullets?"

I said nothing.

"And what about the lady? She claims she has two left. Does she lie or tell the truth?"

My hands were shaking so hard I couldn't steady the gun. I pointed in the general direction of the door and fired.

His "Oh" was full of pain. He made a humming sound that told me I had hit him and he was hurting. Well, good. It made two of us. He shuffled into the room. "That makes nine," he said. His voice turned grim and silly and theatrical. He was clowning. "Are you prepared to die?"

"I wouldn't say prepared exactly, but I wouldn't be surprised." I held the small flashlight in my left hand and pinched the center. It gave off a scant tablespoon of light, but it was enough to see him with. "How about you?" I said. "Surprised?" I fired at him point-blank and then studied the effect.

This was instructional. In the movies, you shoot someone and they're either blown back a foot or they keep coming at you, up from the bathtub, up from the floor, sometimes so full of bullet holes their shirts form red polka dots. The truth is, you hit someone and it hurts like hell. I could testify to that. David Barney had to sit down with his back to the wall and think about life. A wet red stain was forming on his left side, fairly ruining his shirt and causing his expression to shift from smug superiority to consternation.

I studied him for a moment and then said, "I told you I had a ten-shot."

He didn't seem interested in that. I pulled myself into a standing position, leaving a sticky handprint on the Xerox machine. I crossed the room to the wall he was propped against. I leaned down and took his gun, which he offered up without resistance. I checked the magazine. There was one bullet left. His eyes had gone empty and his fingers opened slowly as he released his own life. Something like a moth fluttered off into the dark. I limped into the hall, raking my little flashlight across the wall until I found the fire alarm box. I busted the glass door and pulled the lever.

Epilogue

Now that I've learned how to sit down again, I suppose I should fill in the few remaining gaps in my paperwork. The new year has rolled over and the torrid romance between Rosie and William continues unabated. Henry has threatened everything from a hunger strike to fisticuffs to no avail. I can understand his concern—William would be a trial in any event—but there's still something wonderful about love at close range.

The police referred Tippy Parsons to the district attorney's office, where she had a lengthy and candid conversation with one of the deputy DAs. I'd thought her age might be a mitigating factor in the hit-and-run death, but what it came down to in the end was the simple fact that the statute of limitations on the vehicular manslaughter had already run out. When Hartford McKell heard the driver had been found, he insisted on writing me a check for the twenty-five thousand bucks despite the fact that Tippy was neither arrested nor convicted. I took the money. I did the work so why not get paid? Now all I have to decide is what to do with it. In the meantime, spring is just around the corner and life is very good.

Respectfully submitted,

Kinsey Millhone

About the Author

Sue Grafton lives in Santa Barbara, California.